NORTHERN FRIGHTS 3

© VAN DER LINDE 95

Edited by
DON HUTCHISON

Mosaic Press
Oakville, ON - Buffalo, N.Y.

Canadian Cataloguing in Publication Data

Main entry under title:

Norhtern frights 3

ISBN 0-88962-589-1

1. Fantastic fiction, Canadian (English).* 2. Fantastic fiction, American.
3. Canadian fiction (English) - 20th century.* 4. American fiction - 20th century.
I. Hutchison, Don.

PS8323.S3N66 1995   C813'.540876608054
PR9197.35.S33N66 1995   C95-932068-7

Published by MOSAIC PRESS, P.O. Box 1032, Oakville, Ontario, L6J 5E9, Canada. Offices and warehouse at 1252 Speers Road, Units #1&2, Oakville, Ontario, L6L 5N9, Canada and Mosaic Press, 85 River Rock Drive, Suite 202, Buffalo, N.Y., 14207, USA.

Mosaic Press acknowledges the assistance of the Canada Council, the Ontario Arts Council, the Ontario Ministry of Culture, Tourism and Recreation and the Dept. of Canadian Heritage, Government of Canada, for their support of our publishing programme.

Cover Illustration by Henry Van Der Linde
Book design by Susan Parker
Typeset by Jackie Ernst
Copy editing by John Wen

FIRST EDITION
Printed and bound in Canada
ISBN 0-88962-589-1

In Canada:
MOSAIC PRESS, 1252 Speers Road, Units #1&2, Oakville, Ontario, L6L 5N9, Canada. P.O. Box 1032, Oakville, Ontario, L6J 5E9
In the United States:
MOSAIC PRESS, 85 River Rock Drive, Suite 202, Buffalo, N.Y., 14207
In the UK and Western Europe:
DRAKE INTERNATIONAL SERVICES, Market House, Market Place, Deddington, Oxford. OX15 OSF

NORTHERN FRIGHTS 3

Contents

Introduction
DON HUTCHISON

There are seventeen stories in this book. They are branded "horror" by nature of our title and cover. But it's not all fear and loathing. Many of these works *are* genuinely terrifying, but some are darkly humorous, some intriguingly atmospheric, and one, at least, imbued with a sense of cosmological mystery.

In the initial *Northern Frights* I promised readers as much variety of mood and subject matter as possible in a theme anthology. We must have hit on something because that volume was a finalist for Canada's Aurora Award as well as the prestigious World Fantasy Award.

Frankly, when I dreamed up this title I wasn't certain that there *was* such a thing as Canadian horror outside of Ottawa. Fortunately, the writers were there, just waiting for something like this to come along. Since then, many previously unpublished authors have gone on to sell work elsewhere and a number of our short story professionals have graduated to successful first novels.

A full five of the stories in our second outing were chosen by editors Ellen Datlow and the late Karl Edward Wagner to be reprinted in their "Year's Best" horror anthologies. (Charles Grant's contemporary ghost story, "Sometimes, in the Rain," not only made it into the Datlow book but will also appear in the British *Best New Horror* anthology edited by Stephen Jones and Ramsey Campbell). I would like to honor the titles picked by Wagner because DAW Books cancelled their long-running series before our stories could be reprinted, They are: Nancy Kilpatrick's "Punkins," Garfield Reeves-Stevens's "The Eddies," and Dale L. Sproule's "Fourth Person Singular." Among his may attributes, Karl Wagner was an astute judge of talent. If you haven't read these stories, I urge you to seek them out. We are immensely proud of them and of the authors -- *all* the authors -- who honor us with the product of their imaginations.

So, yes, Virginia, there is such a thing as Canadian dark fantasy. But it didn't really begin -- and hopefully won't end -- with *Northern Frights*. In a way , this series was inspired by *Borderland*, the excellent Toronto-based magazine published in the 1980s by Raymond Alexander and edited by our respected friend and advisor Robert Hadji.

A further inspiration was Canada's ubiquitous "Master Gatherer" John Robert Colombo, whose 1981 reprint book *Not to be Taken at Night* (co-edited by Michael Richardson) was arguably the first major anthology of classic Canadian horror. Authors researching background ideas for *Northern Frights* are advised to seek out *Mysterious Canada* (Doubleday, 1988), Colombo's mammoth documentation of paranormal mysteries.

And while we're at it, (hope this doesn't sound like an Oscar speech) I'd like to acknowledge my ongoing indebtedness to Howard Aster and the staff at Mosaic Press. Thanks also to Lorna Toolis of the Toronto Public Library's Merril Collection of Science Fiction, Speculation and Fantasy, and to my dear wife Jean, who has to put up with me *and* all the phone calls and scary manuscripts that go bump in our mail box.

Now go read. Enjoy.

Wild Things Live There
MICHAEL ROWE

Award-winning journalist Michael Rowe was born in Ottawa, Ontario, and raised in Beirut, Havana, and Geneva. While abroad, his mother imported British books by the crate, among them numerous volumes of horror and dark fantasy. The books must have made an impression because, as Toronto correspondent for Fangoria *magazine, Michael has produced articles and essays on the horror genre that have been translated into several languages and read throughout the world.*

Michael wrote the first draft of "Wild Things Live There" at Harvard University in a creative writing class taught by editor Kathryn Cramer. Publication of the story in Northern Frights *marks his promising debut in the horror fiction field.*

Last night, I woke to the sound of fingernails scratching on the glass of my bedroom window eight floors above the ground, and for a moment I was eleven years old and back in Milton, and Mrs. Winfield had found me like she said she would.

Just before I opened my eyes, I heard a low, muddy chuckle, but the sound tattered away into the darkness. The room was silent, except for the pounding of my own heart and my wife's soft breathing. I reached across the bed and felt for her. The sheets were drenched in sweat, and Claudia had moved as far to the other side of the bed as she could. I saw the soft skin of her shoulder and her long blonde hair, both touched by moonlight. Claudia knows about my nightmares. She tried to wake me once during one of them, before we were married. When she laid her cool fingers on my chest, my dream shifted and I felt claws moving like a murderous caress towards my throat. I saw yellow eyes before I woke, and smelled sulphur. When she touched me, I began to scream. I think Claudia was as frightened as I was. When she had calmed me, Claudia gave me some Xanax from her private pharmacy of pills, and I fell into a sleep so deep that I woke the next afternoon feeling like there were ice picks methodically tearing my brain apart, strip by strip.

"How's your head?" she asked me sympathetically when I came into the living room. Through the haze of my pain, I caught a glimpse of myself in the bathroom mirror. "Do you want a Tylenol, Randy?"

"What are you, Claudia?" I said irritably. "My pusher? Drugs to make me sleep, drugs to keep me awake. Drugs for headaches..."

"I wish I had something to alter your mood," she said crisply. I must have winced, because her eyes darkened with concern. "Poor baby." She reached over and brushed my hair out of my eyes. "Do you want to talk about your dream?"

"I can't remember it," I lied, and I dropped the memory of my nightmare into the dark green waters of my subconscious. Years later, Claudia told me that she decided then and there to marry me, if only to protect from the monsters that visited me in the hours before dawn.

I pushed back the damp sheets and walked naked to the window of the bedroom. The bloated October moon hung low and orange over English Bay, and the West End was bathed in amber light. From our eighth floor apartment on Pendrell Street, I saw the Sylvia Hotel to the left, and the dark mass of Bowen Island and the mountains in the distance. We were one block from Stanley Park, but the park, with it's caves and ravines, disturbed me. It reminded me of the escarpment behind Auburn. Claudia was born in West Vancouver, and everything about the city was a joy to her. We skied at Whistler, and we took her father's boat out on weekends. But I never came to love Stanley Park. Wild things lived there: raccoons, foxes, and lately, worse. Stanley Park has become a dangerous place to walk after dark, when creatures crueller and more hostile than animals stalked and waited with lethal patience behind trees and boulders. I've always associated muggings and murders with the East, with Toronto. But nothing is immune, not even a paradise like Vancouver.

I peered out the window and looked down the wall of our building. There was nothing to see except the worn brick. The glass of the bedroom window was grimy at its base. There were vertical smudges near the latch.

They could have been caused by anything at all, I told myself. Shivering, I reached for my robe on the chair by the bed. I would call the management of our building in the morning. Christ knows, we pay enough for clean glass. I didn't like the smudges. In the moonlight, they look too much like fingerprints.

Although I traded the muted brick-reds and greys of southern Ontario for the vivid blues and greens of Vancouver nearly fifteen years ago, I was born in Milton, and I will always carry the flinty soil of southern Ontario within me, however long I live in British Columbia. I grew up in a small town called Auburn, nestled between Milton and Campbellville, at the foot of the Halton Hills, near the forests and gorges of the Niagara escarpment. My father died when I was five, and I was raised by my mother and my Aunt Etna. Both Mum and Aunt Etna were from Milton, but my grandfather gave my mother a farmhouse in Auburn when my father died, and I grew up there surrounded by women. There wasn't much to Auburn except a general store and a United Church, so I attended the J.M. Denies School on Thomas Street in Milton. After school, I would bike down Main Street to Tremaine Road, then west down the number 5 Sideroad towards home.

Every town has at least one house that children don't want to pass in the dark, especially on nights when the moon is out and riding. In Milton, it was Mrs. Winfield's house on Martin Street. Everyone in town knew that it was bad news. Nobody said "haunted," because they knew that Mrs. Winfield lived there, and a house couldn't be haunted by something living, could it? Mrs. Winfield had been a widow since God wore short pants. In a small Ontario town, removed by many miles from a major city, the fabric of life is shot through with legend. In a town like Milton, where gossip was mother's milk, the legend of Mrs. Winfield was nearly an epic.

Rumor had it that one night, back in the 1920's, she'd killed Mr. Winfield with an axe. Just cut him up into small pieces and stored him, cured and salted, in her icebox. Rumor further had it that she'd fed off him for months, one chunk at a time, and that she'd made mincemeat tarts and headcheese with what was left. But this was just ugly gossip, as my mother pointed out. The town constable called on Mrs. Winfield, and she was as nice and sweet as she could be. My mother and Aunt Etna told me that she'd wrung her hands and sobbed that he'd never been a reliable man, always away on business, and that one day he left and told her he wasn't coming home.

A local Catholic priest, formerly of Holy Rosary Church and dead these many years, claimed that he'd had tea at her home in an attempt to convince her to attend church now that she was alone. She'd invited him into her parlor, given him tea and tarts, after which he was violently ill. He refused to speak about Mrs. Winfield until the day he died.

But Mrs. Winfield wasn't from Milton. She was an outsider who'd moved there with her husband in 1914. When Mr. Winfield vanished she kept to herself, which was almost impossible to do in a small town. But she paid her taxes and hired a man to keep the outside of her house looking nice. Her shutters were always closed, and she never came to the door for her milk or her newspaper. What could the town do? No one ever saw Mrs. Winfield in church, and that bothered the town worthies, but there was no law against being godless.

One afternoon in early September, the second day of school, I was sitting at the kitchen table with my best friend, Patrick Cross. We were eating warm ginger cookies, and we each had a glass of milk. We heard Aunt Etna's old brown Buick on the gravel outside.

"It's your aunt," said Patrick.

"Duh," I answered him. "Of *course* it's my aunt, Einstein." Patrick was my best friend, but he was a little slow sometimes. We heard Aunt Etna open the door, and moments later she walked into the kitchen and put two bags of groceries on the counter.

"Hi, Aunt Etna!" I called out.

Usually she ruffled my hair and gave me a wet kiss, but this time she just looked at me and said, "Randy, don't you have homework?"

I looked up at Aunt Etna, and saw that her face was pale. Her hair seemed damp around the edges, and she looked sick.

"It's only four o'clock Aunt Etna. Patrick and I are going outside to play."

"Don't you sass me, boy!" Aunt Etna snapped. "You just go upstairs and do your homework right away!" I almost fell out of my chair. I'd never heard Aunt Etna raise her voice to me in my life. She must have noticed, because her voice softened a little. "Patrick can go up with you if he wants, and stay for dinner if he'd like."

"Thank you ma'am. I would," said Patrick winsomely. Everybody's parents loved Patrick.

"Randy, where's your mother?" Aunt Etna asked me. She sat down heavily in her chair beside the stove.

"She's in the garden," I replied. "Aunt Etna, what's wrong?"

"Nothing, dear," she said. "You two run upstairs now and let me talk to your mother."

In my room, I said told Patrick to keep it down.

"Ssshhh!" I whispered.

"Why?" Patrick asked. I crossed my room on tiptoes, Patrick following, also on tiptoes, and I opened the latch to my bedroom window. My mother's flower garden was directly beneath the window, and I leaned out to hear what Aunt Etna was saying.

"...right outside of Ledwith's," Aunt Etna gasped. "I was just standing there with the groceries, and she walks right toward me!"

"Etna!" Mother said in a shocked voice.

"As God is my witness," said Aunt Etna, crossing her heart. "What could I do? I said hello! I *had* to. It was the only polite thing to do."

"What happened then?"

"She looks right at me," Aunt Etna went on.

"Mrs. *Winfield?*" My mother sounded like she didn't believe Aunt Etna.

"As surely as I see you standing there."

"Jesus Christ," said my mother, who never took the Saviour's name in her life.

"And for a minute there, everything got a little dark." Aunt Etna shivered, though the September light was still warm. "Her eyes," Aunt Etna marvelled. "She had the strangest eyes. For a minute there, I could have sworn they were yellow, then they were just green. But...different."

"What do you mean different?"

"Nothing a body could put a finger on," Aunt Etna said nervously, "but different. About as human as an animal's eyes."

They were silent for a moment, then I heard my mother's voice again.

"You tell Randy about this?" my mother said.

"No," Aunt Etna replied. "I sent him upstairs with Patrick."

"Don't say a word about this to him, Etna, I swear. I don't want him going near that old woman, and you know how he gets with his questions."

"I won't," Aunt Etna said. She and my mother embraced, and held each other for a long time.   When they drew apart, I heard my mother say, "God, I wish Phil were still alive." She rarely spoke of my father, and something in her voice made me feel as though I were intruding on some grief that I wasn't a part of. I drew away from the window.

"That was *so* weird," Patrick said.

"It sure was," I agreed. I went over and turned my record player on. I put a Rolling Stones 45 on the turntable and cranked the volume until my mother called up and told me to *turn that gosh darned racket down, Randy!* and we went down to dinner, pausing to wash our hands in the upstairs bathroom because we knew she'd ask, and my mother always seemed to know when we hadn't.

As I drifted off to sleep that night, I heard my mother and Aunt Etna sitting in front of the fireplace, talking in hushed whispers about what Aunt Etna had seen outside of Ledwith's grocery store that afternoon.

The following Friday, quite by accident, I met Mrs. Winfield myself. I passed her on my bicycle as she shuffled down Martin Street, moving in that sludgy way that old people have, as though they had forgotten how to move. A twig caught in my spoke, and I nearly lost control of my bike. When I brought it to a wobbling halt, I almost fell on the sidewalk in front of her. She was looking down, so I didn't see her face.

"Good afternoon ma'am," I said, doing a fair imitation of Patrick's brilliant politeness. I still couldn't see her face, and I was curious too. I wanted to see if what Aunt Etna had said about her eyes was true or not.

She stopped then, and slowly raised her head to look at me. Her eyes were milky green, caught in a web of wrinkles around heavily hooded lids. She looked about a hundred years old. Her eyes widened slightly, and for a moment I thought I felt the air about me chill. Mrs. Winfield smiled, but somehow it wasn't the happy, senile smile of an old woman. Her teeth were yellow and twisted, and they seemed sharp, crueller somehow than the teeth of an old woman ought to be.

"Hello, Randy Murphy," she said, her voice like dry sand at noon. "You certainly are growing up to be a big boy." She said it in the same way that she might discuss a cut of lamb at a butcher's shop, and I again felt the cold and darkness that Aunt Etna had mentioned that night in the garden.

"How do you know my name?" I whispered. "I've never met you before."

"I know all the children's names," Mrs. Winfield said. "I've watched you all grow up, you know. I take an interest."

She smiled again, as though we both knew that there was a double meaning behind the perfectly innocuous old-lady words she'd selected. I mumbled something about having to get home for dinner, and took off on my bike as though wolves were snapping at my pedals. I rode away in the opposite direction from Auburn, because I remember thinking that she might follow me, I didn't want her to know where I lived.

That night, I dreamed I was walking through Mrs. Winfield's yard, with the full moon floating above me like the angry yellow eye of God. I dreamed that it was following me as I moved. I dreamed that I looked up at one of the windows and saw things slithering in the shadows behind filthy glass. I heard sighs and soft giggling, but it didn't sound happy or good in the dream, just cruel and unspeakably malevolent. When I tried to move away from the glass, I couldn't. You know how dreams are.

Then I saw Mrs. Winfield's face at the window. She glared at me with her red eyes and her mouth full of ripping teeth, her face covered with bristling brown hair, and she said, "Welcome, Randy Murphy. You're a *big* boy now, aren't you? Come inside."

When she reached up with her yellow-clawed hand and scratched on the glass, I woke up screaming. Yes--Christ, peal after peal until my mother came running in and grabbed me. She shook me and shouted at me to wake up. *Etna, he's hysterical!* she shouted at my aunt, not because she was angry but because I was screaming to wake the dead.

I slept in my mother's bed that night, but I stayed awake for hours afterwards, watching the door. I knew, deep inside, that the thing in the window of Mrs. Winfield's house on Martin Street wouldn't be bothered by my mother one bit.

That fall, we had a scare in Auburn. A little red-haired girl named Audrey Greystone was found about three miles out of town. She'd been murdered and...played with.

Aunt Etna said it was a pervert, probably from Toronto. A week later, they caught some tramp in Warner's field whacking off in broad daylight, and you can bet your ass they slapped that one in handcuffs and hauled him off for safe-keeping. We had our transients in Auburn and Milton, and our town drunks, but this one was a stranger and the only thing worse than a stranger in a small town is an old stranger amusing himself in public a week after a child-murder. There was no comfort for the Greystone family, but the town wanted to believe that the monster from the world outside Milton who had invaded their lives was locked up and awaiting justice. There was talk of lynching, talk of cutting off the old party's hands, and his thing, too. So the town constable did right by taking him away. But mostly, there was relief that the killer had been caught, and the kids could have a safe Halloween after all.

Patrick and I were a little old for Halloween, but it was my favorite time of year, Patrick's too. I loved the spicy air, the smell of leaves dying, apples and woodsmoke. In those days, you were still allowed to burn your leaves, and that smell was my favorite of all. I loved the way pumpkins looked in the windows, winking fire through their slashed eyes.

I was a pirate, and Patrick was a white rabbit. My mother made my costume out of a pair of old red bloomers and an old dinner jacket of my Dad's. She had to convince me that it was O.K. to wear her earrings. I'd seen pictures of pirates with earrings, but it still felt weird.

After we'd done our trick-or-treating, we hiked across the fields that separated Auburn and Milton. We'd taken in quite a haul, and we couldn't resist dipping into our stash on the way home, even though Mum would've taken a strip off us if she'd known we were eating our stuff before she checked it. She always worried about razor blades in apples.

There were scrubs of trees here and there at the foot of the escarpment, and small hills and caves. We called them Indian caves. Patrick and I had built tree forts there every summer since we'd been old enough to lift a hammer. The moon was brilliant that night, like a fire in the sky. The stars sparkled like diamonds against black velvet. It wasn't as if we couldn't see, because we saw *everything*.

We ran across the fields, laughing and talking about nothing at all, the way best friends do. Patrick jumped up and down like a rabbit, which made his white satin ears flop, and we both laughed harder.

People asked me afterwards why I didn't hear the man behind us, but I don't think he wanted us to hear him. And I think he knew how to keep that from happening. I remember I was looking over Patrick's shoulder when I saw something like a hulking black shadow separate itself from the copse of trees behind us. It grabbed Patrick and pulled him backwards into the trees. I might have run at this point, but when I heard Patrick screaming, all I could think about was how everyone picked on him at school for being slow. For some crazy reason I had this idea that it was Billy Macadoo or Dave Carruthers waiting for the perfect chance to beat holy hell out of Patrick. I was a big kid at eleven, and I always stuck up for him.

So I charged into the trees, fists swinging, ready to settle this bullying shit for all time. Patrick was struggling and screaming. By the time it registered that whatever had Patrick was taller than either Butch or Billy, I was deep into the darkness of the trees. I caught a powerful whiff of sweat and stale body waste. Something reached out a hand and smashed me hard across the head. I saw a shower of stars explode in front of my eyes, and I was falling, falling, with no ground beneath my feet.

I woke in pain. I could barely open my eyes, but I realized that I was naked, and my wrists and ankles were tied. The ropes cut into my flesh. Patrick was lying a few feet away, also naked and tied. He was unconscious.

''This is where I come to play,'' said a harsh voice to my left. I tried to turn, but the blinding pain in my head which surged forward with the effort made the bile rise in my throat. The man came around and stood in front of me. He was compact and well-muscled, and covered with tattoos. His hair was close-cropped, like they do it in a prison or an asylum. He was rubbing the front of his trousers.

I looked up at his face. He had cold little eyes and dark eyebrows. He grinned at me, and a long stream of drool hung from his bottom lip like a silver web. I felt my bowels empty themselves under me, and the stink of it drifted up to me. I gagged. I think that's when my last shred of hope that this was a dream disappeared. He reached down and flicked my nipple with his fingernail.

"*Bad* boy!" he hissed. "*Baaaad* boy made a mess!" He grinned even wider as he said it, showing a mouthful of decayed teeth, and I knew I was going to die.

"Please don't hurt me," I whispered. Patrick wasn't moving.

"I'm going to play with you, not hurt you," he giggled. "I like you very, very much!" He squealed with laughter.

As the pain in my head subsided to a rhythmic throbbing, I became aware of the subterranean coldness of the room. I saw that the light came from torches on the wall, and that the ceilings were oddly high, and vaulted. I saw a stone staircase winding upwards and disappearing into the gloom. I had seen cellars before, but never one like this.

"Is this a church?" I whispered, as much to myself as to the madman looming in front of me. "Where are we?"

"I come here," he sing-songed. "Through the hole in the hill nobody ever sees. Through the tunnel I found in the caves. Sometimes I bring friends to play with." He giggled again, and covered his mouth with his filthy fingers, like a sour child eager to tattle. "Friends like the little girl with the pretty carrot hair. Friends like you."

He fumbled in the dirty grey canvas rucksack at his feet. I hear the sound of metal scraping on stone. He turned slowly, and I saw that he held a carving knife. The blade was clotted with gore, and what looked like matted red hair.

"I like to cut," he whispered. "I cut, and cut, and cut. But first I like to play and have fun. Watch."

He stuck out his tongue, and ran the blade across it's tip. Blood spurted from the wound, and he rolled his eyes in ecstasy. He was smiling. I screamed, then, pain be damned. I shrieked and shrieked, and he shrieked right along with me, except his shrieks were interrupted by wild fits of giggling. He did a little dance, slapping his knees.

Then suddenly, he stopped. He cocked his head to the side, towards the stairs.

"Shut up," he whispered fiercely, but I was long past being able to shut up. He turned towards me and swung his fist in my face. "Shut the fuck *up*!"

The shock of the blow made me stop screaming, and I tasted copper in my mouth. He dropped the knife beside me and scuttled off towards the stairway. "Who's there?" he screamed. "Who's that?"

And then I heard it too. Slow, measured footsteps coming down the staircase towards us. The click of shoes on worn stone.

The man backed up with a look of stupid surprise on his coarse features. He fumbled for the knife on the floor beside me. He found it, and grasped it's handle, holding it out in front of him as though it were a sword. He was blocking my view of the staircase, but I heard the footsteps stop. The torches flared.

I heard the man babble something, but I couldn't make it out. Then he began to levitate. That's what I saw. His feet just left the floor, and he drifted up towards the vaulted ceiling. I heard him squeal again, and this time he sounded terrified. I blinked, and I knew that I was seeing something that couldn't be happening. People didn't float in the air, even mad giants with knives, who held the power of life and death over small children.

I heard another voice then, old and dry, and cold as ice. *Corrupt* is a word I'd use today, but at eleven I just remember thinking that I'd rather take my chances with the man hanging suspended in front of me. At least he was human. Whatever owned that voice was not.

"Callers," chortled the voice appreciatively. "Surprise visitors. How very nice."

The heels of the man's boots still obscured most of my vision, but I could see the hem of a black skirt, and black stockinged legs in black shoes walking towards me. I heard that slow, measured click, and saw sparks fly where the heels of the shoes struck the stone floor.

"Somebody found my trap door," scolded the ancient voice. "Nobody's ever found that trap door. Not for, oh, hundreds and hundreds of years." And then, a ghastly underground laugh that made me think of creatures squatting by open graves, devouring corpses. The man above me began to spin lazily in circles, and his knife arm hung limply at his side. He began to scream.

"I like to cut sometimes too," said the voice, addressing the whirling madman in the air above me. "Show me how *you* do it."

And then I saw the man's knife hand jerk upwards, as though it were attached to a string. He plunged the knife into his belly. The shrieks that came from him as the knife reared and plunged into him, and cut upwards, will be with me to my dying day.

The thing screamed with laughter, rocking back and forth. The man spun madly in the air and his blood sprayed across the walls like a geyser.

Then, suddenly, the spinning stopped and the man crumpled to the floor. The knife clattered against the flagstones. What was left of him lay on the ground, quivered once, then stopped.

I looked up then, and what I saw was a hundred million times worse than anything I'd seen.

"Hello, little Randy Murphy," said Mrs. Winfield. Her face was streaked with the dead man's blood. As I watched, she licked some of it off her lips. She brought her face close to mine, and I smelled sulphur on her breath. Her eyes weren't milky green anymore. They were incandescent yellow. Her glance flickered across Patrick, unconscious beside me. She licked her lips again, smearing the blood.

"Rude to invite yourselves," she scolded. "Rude to come to an old lady's house at night and scare her half to death."

And then she began to change.

She...shrivelled. That's the only way I can describe it. I saw a snake shed its skin once by rubbing against a rock. Mrs. Winfield's skin just...fell off. Her face turned brown, and the wrinkles deepened until they looked like craters in her face. She opened her mouth, and as I watched, her teeth grew long and sharp. She licked them with a tongue that was now easily a foot long, and purple. She shrugged out of her black dress, and stepped out of her shoes.

She stared at me with her blazing yellow eyes. Her hideous breasts sagged to her belly, and her misshapen arms, roped with sinew, ended in long-fingered claws. Her mouth stretched into a nightmare rictus, and I realized she was smiling.

"I usually have to go out to eat," she said. She shambled over to Patrick, and traced a razor-sharp nail down his naked back. At that moment, I prayed to God that Patrick was dead, and wouldn't wake up to see this nightmare thing standing over him. Blood spurted from the cut on his back. The creature smiled. And to my horror, I saw Patrick stir, and heard him moan.

"I like the animals better alive," it croaked. And then it began to eat.

Patrick's screams of pain and terror blended into one scarlet blood-drenched sheet of sound. That's what I hear in my nightmares. Patrick screaming, and the awful wet ripping sounds of that...thing...killing him, bite by bite.

I think I was screaming then, too, but I don't think I was terrified anymore. I don't think I felt anything except the pressure of my sanity straining to break. The world turned red, then black. Then I felt nothing, saw nothing.

I woke up in Milton District Hospital, a white world inhabited by angels dressed in white robes, holding silver instruments and whispering sweet words to me about shock, and trauma, and sleep. My mother was there, and Aunt Etna, and I knew that Mrs. Winfield had killed and eaten me, and that I was in heaven.

I felt a cold sting in my upper arm, then I slept again, deeply and without any dreams.

I was in the hospital for six weeks. I missed a lot of school, and a psychiatrist from Hamilton worked with me every day so that I could understand what had happened.

The town constable explained to me that Mrs. Winfield had called him in hysterics. Apparently, she had gone downstairs to her basement to look for her kitty-cat, and discovered three bodies. She was quite upset. No one expects to make a discovery like that on Halloween night after coming home from a walk.

The constable explained to me that Mrs. Winfield's storm-cellar door had been forced open. Apparently, he said, the R.C.M.P. had spent two months hunting the killer. He had escaped from an institution for the criminally insane in Alberta, cutting a murderous swath eastward, killing five children between Edmonton and Toronto. What drew him to Milton on Halloween night was anybody's guess.

"Milton," the constable said, shaking his head. "Who would have ever expected? I always knew it couldn't have been a local man." He asked me to brace myself, then told me that Patrick was dead. The madman had mutilated Patrick's body almost beyond recognition before he turned his knife on himself. Aunt Etna told me that she'd read in the papers that pieces of Patrick were missing. Apparently he'd had two final child murders on his mind before he committed suicide. And what a suicide. He cut himself to ribbons.

The constable said that the man's body had been covered with dirt, so he must have been hiding over in the meadow up by the caves. It was only through God's good graces that he hadn't done to me the things he'd done to poor Patrick. They released the old man they'd caught in Warner's field, clearly a nutcase, but the wrong man. The other one was obviously the murderer of Audrey Greystone. They'd found bits of her scalp and hair in his rucksack.

Mrs. Winfield had been very upset, but she was away visiting a cousin right now, before she returned home to her own house on Martin Street. She was all right, though.

A few days after I had been found, my mother and Aunt Etna went to visit Mrs. Winfield, to offer her some comfort, poor thing. My mother said that Aunt Etna regretted all the awful things she'd said, and it was only because poor Mrs. Winfield found me in time that I was even alive. Mrs. Winfield had served them tea, and delicate meat pies, in her lovely sitting room. The pies were delicious. Mrs. Winfield must have special spices. Imagine cooking like that at her age? The sitting room was a little dusty, said Aunt Etna, but quite normal for an old lady.

No, the constable explained again, patiently, the basement was an ordinary one, nothing like the one I described in my delirium, No torches, no vaulted ceilings. Nothing like that, just dusty cans of old peaches and preserves. An old lady's basement: lawn furniture, old Mr. Winfield's tools, and a filthy old icebox, stained and covered with cobwebs.

On the night before I was to be discharged, my favorite nurse, Tasia, poked her head through the doorway.

"You have a visitor Randy," Tasia beamed. "A surprise. An old friend of yours." She wagged her finger at me and smiled. "I've told her you can't stay up too late. You're going home tomorrow." I remember smiling as I heard Tasia pad off down the corridor.

And then I heard the click of old-lady lace-up shoes on hospital tile. The darkness swam toward me, and I felt my throat constrict. I couldn't reach for the call button to tell Tasia that if she didn't come back to room 7008 right away, I would never leave the hospital alive.

The footsteps paused outside my door. It swung slowly inward, as I had known it would. Mrs. Winfield walked in slowly, dressed from head to toe in black, her face wreathed in the hungry shadows of my hospital room.

"I'm so glad you're better, little Randy Murphy," she growled, and I saw a flicker of yellow fire in her milky green eyes. "The doctors tell me that in time you'll forget about the awful things that happened in my cellar." She chuckled mirthlessly.

I couldn't speak. Couldn't say a word. Couldn't move at all. Whatever was going to happen would happen.

Mrs. Winfield opened her jaws then, very wide.

Her sharp teeth were dripping with saliva, and she licked them. I wet the bed in a warm gush, part of my mind feeling guilty about the piss, the other part knowing that I was going to die, and she would make it seem like an accident. The fire in her eyes blazed so brightly that I could see the bed's shadow reflected on the wall.

Then, suddenly, she closed her mouth and her eyes. She shivered. When she opened her eyes to smile coldly at me, she was just an old lady again. No one would ever believe me. I knew it, and so did she.

"I'm going away for a little while, Randy," she whispered in a voice like darkest winter. "You and your friends have made it a little crowded for me here." I heard the thwarted fury in her voice, and I was afraid. "I've sealed the tunnel between the hills and my house on Martin Street. No one will ever find it, so never mind your stories.

"I've lived here for a long time," she said, adjusting the flesh of her index finger as though it were a glove. "In one form or another. Longer than you can imagine. I was already old when the English and the French came across the ocean with their religions, and tried to claim this country as their own." She narrowed her eyes. "We've *always* been here. We are *everywhere*. Wherever there are rocks, or caves, we make our homes."

She patted my leg on the bed, and I felt the ice of her fingers through the wool blankets.

"You just get better. Get over your...trauma." Here she gave another clotted laugh. "Don't tell any silly stories," she whispered, "or I'll have to visit you some night and talk some sense into you." She gathered up her black purse and shuffled to the door. She looked fragile, like somebody ought to get the door for her or something.

"Stay away from the caves, boy," she growled. "It's dangerous. Wild things live there." And she hobbled off without turning back. Click. Click. Click.

I stood in front of the window of our apartment for an hour, until the moon went down and the sky began to lighten in the east. Claudia breathed softly. No nightmares for her, just healing sleep. The fog drifting in from English Bay would run down into the smudges at the base of the glass, and in the morning light, they wouldn't look anything like fingerprints. I wrestle with my memories by myself, in my nightmares. I've never told anyone about Mrs. Winfield, not ever.

She'd find out somehow. I've always known that she would.

When the psychiatrists told me that I had suffered a concussion and imagined everything, I told them I believed them. I mourned Patrick's death in a way that I'd never been able to mourn my father's, and I grew closer to my mother because of the shared experience of grief and loss. When I graduated from Milton District Highschool, I moved across the country, and I've never been back to Auburn. I won't go back. I won't. There are more than memories waiting for me there.

And yet, I can't stop thinking about things. Last week, the daughter of a friend found the mutilated body of a racoon in Stanley Park.

"It was awful," she said. "It was all mangled. Other animals must have gotten to it. It's awful what they do to their own kind."

I think about dead squirrels and cats that seem to line the paths of the park more often than they used to. I think about the missing children whose innocent, trusting faces adorn the *Have You Seen This Child?* posters which have lately blossomed along the streets that line the West End. I think about the snowy nights at our cabin in Whistler, when the crack of a frozen branch can be heard for miles, when the winter cold is so cutting that wild things come down from the mountains to feed. I think about tracks in the snow in the mornings, tracks that we can't identify and which Claudia always jokes are made by trolls.

We've always been here, she'd said. *We are everywhere. Wherever there are rocks or caves, we make our homes.*

I think about the old couple beside the seawall yesterday evening, who looked at Claudia and I with their milky blue eyes, and smiled approvingly at our ten-year romance as we strolled past. I looked back and smiled at them. For a minute, the dying sunlight glanced off the old man's glasses and reflected a glitter of yellow fire. Then he turned his head and looked at the ground before shuffling off towards the Sylvia Hotel with his wife. I shivered.

Wild things, I thought as the sun sank behind the mountains, and I hurried home with Claudia through the chilled blue dusk towards Pendrell Street. Wild things live here, too.

Silver Rings

RICK HAUTALA

Rick Hautala is the author of fourteen novels of horror and psychological suspense, with more than two-and-a-half million copies of his books currently in print, including the national best sellers Night Stone, Little Brothers, Cold Whisper, Ghost Light, Twilight Time *and the forthcoming* The Mountain King *and* Shades of Night. *In August, 1994, his novel* Cold Whisper *was published as* Haamu *in Finland and immediately hit the Finnish national best seller lists. He has written five screenplays, including one based on his novel* Cold Whisper, *which is now in development with Aurora Productions.*

Hautala lives in Southern Maine with his wife and three sons. He reports that when he isn't writing, he generally can be found either reading or sleeping.

Her hands felt small and cold in mine as we walked the rain-slick streets of Quebec. We were going back to her apartment, and I remember thinking as we walked about the time I had caught a barn swallow up in my uncle's hayloft. Trying desperately to escape, the bird had fluttered frantically against the cobweb-draped window. The instant I had closed my hands around it, its fragility had terrified me. Small and warm, it lay trembling in my cupped hands, its heart beating so fast I couldn't possibly count the rate. I was afraid that even the slightest pressure would crush the life out of it.

But her hands had none of the heat and pulsing life of a bird. Her hands were cold, and she shivered as she leaned against me and gripped my hand almost desperately with both of hers, lacing her fingers between mine and cupping my hand just as I had cupped that frightened bird.

I also remember the cold sting of the silver rings she wore, found on each hand. I'll never forget that she wore so many silver rings. It is significant, I think.

We followed a winding pathway through back alleys and along uneven cobblestone streets that seemed strangely deserted. The bright lights of downtown fell behind us, oddly distant, like a dim memory of another city, another world. The night's chilled dampness drifted in off the St. Lawrence and closed around us, seeming to bond us, making my flesh hers, and hers mine.

You have to understand that right from the start--that's what I had been looking for all evening--someone who wanted to bond her flesh to mine, so to speak--to make the "beast with two backs," as Shakespeare so elegantly phrased it. It was spring break, and rather than spending two straight days of driving to get to Fort Lauderdale, a few of my friends and I had decided to head up to Quebec for a week of hell-raising. I'd left my buddies back at some strip joint and had ended up--I'm not even sure how-- in the small cafe where I met her. I can't recall that the place even had a name. I never noticed a sign, either when I was going in or later, when we walked out together.

She spoke very little English, never even told me her name, but I remember how her voice had a odd lilt to it. When I try to recall it now, I can only approximate it in my memory. It remains tantalizingly distant, but the teasing memory of it fills me with a deep, dull yearning. Even when she spoke in French, her worlds were strangely accented as though she were speaking a form of French from a different era.

But it wasn't just her touch or her voice; her eyes, too, enchanted me. Moist and dark, they glistened in the candlelight like rain-slick streets, glistening rivers of shifting light and darkness. They were eyes you could get lost in--eyes that I *did* get lost in even though I kept reminding myself not to feel too much. I certainly wasn't looking to fall in love that night.

Far from it.

I was looking for one thing, and although we never mentioned it directly, I assumed she knew what I wanted, and that she was looking for the same thing.

We first touched hands there at the table in the cafe. I commented on her rings then and boldly reached across the table to grasp her hands and inspect each finger. Her fingers were long and slim, delicately tapered like white church candles. I can't honestly say that first touch was electric. It was somehow more than that, deeper. It was like tentatively holding a high-power electric cable and knowing that a charge of energy strong enough to kill you was rippling dangerously just below the surface. Even then in the cafe, I noticed that her hands were cold.

Turning her hands over in mine, I made a show of studying each of her rings although, in fact, none of them were anything more than plain, silver bands. But they flashed in the orange glow of candlelight, reflecting bright spikes of light that dazzled my eyes. I jokingly asked if the ring on her left ring finger was her wedding band. She replied that they all were, and that if she accumulated any more husbands, she would soon be wearing rings on her toes. I'm fairly certain the word she used meant *husbands*. My French wasn't even as good as her English. She might have meant *lovers*.

Of course, that's what I wanted to be--her lover, at least for the night. One of the friends I was with had taught me what he said was the only sentence in French I needed to know: *Voulez-vous coucher avec mois?* but I never had to say it because simply touching her hand, I experienced a level of unspoken communication between us. I was certain she felt it, too.

After sharing a bottle of red wine, I paid the tab, and we got up and left. As we walked out the door, I remember how the other patrons in the cafe--mostly elderly men, sitting in small groups around dark tables-- watched us, shifting their eyes and barely moving their heads. I could feel their envy, their barely disguised desire that they were young enough and handsome enough to be the one who was walking out of there that night with her. I experienced a thrill of pride and grew almost dizzy with elation as we walked outside. The cafe door swung softly shut behind us.

She directed me along dark, narrow backstreets, and by the time we found her room, I was disoriented enough to have no idea what part of the city we were in. Smiling and squeezing my hand, and still leaning her head against my shoulder, she led me up the narrow, darkened stairway to the second floor landing. After fishing a key from her purse, she unlocked the door and opened it to allow me to enter the apartment first.

Her place was small and dark, and what I could see of it in the dim light looked quaint, charming. I remember, as soon as I entered, that I was almost overwhelmed by a curious aroma--a exotic mixture of scented soap, cloves and other spices, and something else--something much older that stirred deep memories within me.

I stood there in the doorway, waiting for her to turn on a light; but without a word, she walked into the dark kitchen. Suddenly a sputtering tongue of flame flared out of the darkness as she struck a wooden match and touched it to a candle on the small table. The blossoming orange glow of candlelight filled the small room like the sunrise.

She indicated for me to take a seat at the table. Without saying a single word, she took down from the cupboard a bottle of red wine and two cut crystal glasses. I remember noticing how the wine looked thick, almost black as she poured it. Taking my glass, I held it aloft, waited a moment, and then said, ''To the night's beauty'' as we clinked glasses and then drank.

She smiled before she drank, although I wasn't even sure she had understood what I had said.

Taking the candle from the kitchen table in one hand and my hand with the other, she led me into the living room. Distorted shadows shifted at odd angles across the walls. Side by side, we sat down on the small couch, our knees occasionally touching as we drank and talked. The wind seemed to go quickly to my head. I can remember almost nothing of our conversation because I was so caught up simply in listening to her voice. The small living room window overlooking the city was dimpled with rain that refracted and distorted the light into dizzying patterns.

She smiled and laughed at our attempts to communicate. For some reason, her laughter--light and airy--reminded me again of the bird I had caught back when I was a boy. I wanted to tell her about this but knew that I didn't know enough French to explain the significance, if there was any. I'm not even sure I know the significance now, much less then; but before long, we had no need to talk. She laughed at something I said and then reached out to touch my face. Her hand was warm, now, as she caressed my cheek and then ran her fingertips lightly down my neck and inside my collar. We embraced and kissed tenderly. There was none of the passionate, almost desperate groping I usually felt with women. When she took my hand and led me into her bedroom, I remember wondering if it might be a cultural thing--that French girls know more subtle ways of making love.

Judging by that night, I'd have to say that is so. The wind was still buzzing in my brain like a soft breeze blowing through a field, pressing down the grass like a huge, invisible hand. Her touch and the feel of her skin sent shivers of ecstasy racing through me. Lulled by the soft patter of rain on the window, we folded together and were transported to places I, at least, had never been before.

I awoke as dawn was streaking the sky with pale fingers of gray. It was Sunday morning. The rain had stopped, and I could sense even without going outside the bracing freshness of the day. I rolled over in bed to look at her, to admire her, to kiss and touch her again, but was surprised to see that she was gone. Thinking she had gotten up early, possibly to go to church, I swung out of bed and, wrapping the bed sheet around me like a toga, walked out into the kitchen. *"Hello . . . bonjour,"* I called out softly, but there was no reply. I realized I was alone in the apartment. I had no idea why she had left and where she might have gone. Even if she had left me a note, it would no doubt have been in French, so I wouldn't have understood it.

Shivering, I went to the bedroom, hurriedly dressed, and then walked back into the kitchen and sat at the table. For several minutes, as the apartment steadily brightened with the strengthening daylight, I wondered what to do next. I considered helping myself to her refrigerator, maybe preparing breakfast for the both of us in case she returned soon, but I gave up that idea. It struck me as something a crass American would do, and I wanted to preserve the other-worldly delicacy of her place.

I got up and walked into the living room, looked around and then sat down on the couch. In the gray light of dawn, the apartment looked much older than it had appeared by candlelight the night before. I sniffed the air but could catch no lingering trace of the spicy, scented aromas of last night. All I could smell was an antique mustiness that reminded me of how my grandmother's house used to smell. I noticed a thin patina of dust coating everything like gray shadows. The candle we had lit the night before was still on the coffee table. It had burned itself out, but even the glass candle holder and stub of melted wax were coated with a fine layer of dust.

I sat there on the couch and watch the sun rise over the shimmering river, all the while wondering when she would return and if I should wait. I was certain my friends wouldn't be worried about me. They no doubt would assume I had "gotten lucky" and would show up back at the hotel sometime before noon, which was when we were planning to head back to the States.

I waited for more than an hour and then finally, feeling increasingly impatient, left. I was careful to lock the door behind me before descending the narrow steps.

I wandered around the sleepily stirring streets for more than two hours before I finally found a landmark I recognized. The air was filled with the pealing of church bells and the muffled sound of traffic. I got back to the hotel sometime around ten o'clock.

I say I got back to the hotel, but a part of me wasn't there at all. I still felt as though I--or at least some vital part of me--was still back at her apartment, still sitting on the couch in the dusty, predawn silence of her small apartment, still waiting for her to return.

I never even knew her name.

It was Sunday morning, and my friends and I wanted to get back to Orono campus by evening so we wouldn't be too burned out when classes started again on Monday, but I told my friends that I didn't want to leave just yet. Since it was my car we had come in, they couldn't very well argue. When they asked why I didn't want to leave yet, I didn't answer them.

How could I?

What would I say?

They tried to guess, and before long started teasing me about having fallen in love. I denied it, of course, and as God is my witness, it was true. I wasn't in love, at least not the kind of love I had experienced up to that point in my life.

It was something else, something deeper than that--something more involving and more consuming and, I knew, more dangerous. After lunch, I told my friends that I was going for a walk. They wanted to come with me, but I refused, saying that I had to meet someone.

The streets I wandered didn't look at all the same in the harsh glare of the midday sun. I wandered around in circles, searching for a familiar landmark, but the rain-swept streets I had walked with her last night now seemed like an illusion, the traces of a dream that was rapidly dissolving into airy nothingness.

But somehow, toward evening, I found the cafe. Just as I remembered, there was no sign above the door, but I knew this was the right place. I entered the shallow darkness of the room,. pausing a moment to let my eyes adjust before seating myself at one of the tables. A few patrons sat in the cafe. I couldn't help but cringe when I sensed them watching me askance with slitted eyes.

The waitress came over and took my order for a cup of tea. I sat in silence, staring across the room at the table where she and I had sat the night before. But the table--the cafe itself seemed altered, somehow, much smaller and danker than I remembered. The only words that come close to expressing it are that it looked somehow more solid, more *real* in the daytime than it had the night before.

I shivered, and when my tea came I took a sip; the warmth did nothing to dispel the feelings I had of loneliness and of being caught up in something that I wasn't supposed to understand. Once I'd finished my tea, I considered simply paying my tab and leaving, but I had noticed one particular group of men seated at a table in the far corner. I was sure these were the same men who had been here the night before, so I walked over to them.

They looked at me with thinly veiled mistrust when I smiled and said, *"Bonjour."* Obviously, they had pegged me an American, and it was just as obvious they didn't like me simply on principle.

But I had to try, so in English sprinkled with stammered French, I asked if they knew the girl with silver rings. I didn't know the French for *rings* but kept circling my fingers. I was sure they understood, but none of them said much except for what I knew was French for *Sorry, I do not speak English.*

"The girl," I kept saying. "*La femme* with . . . with *rings*. Silver rings."

They all smiled tightly and shook their heads.

"I was with her. Here. Last night. I know you saw me with mer."

I was starting to get mad, now, and couldn't help but let it show; but they continued simply to stare at me, murmur, and shake their heads. Finally one of them nodded and said, *"Oui."* He made it clear that he recognized me and had seen me here the night before, but when I pressed him, asking if he knew *la femme*, he merely shook his head and said something that ended with what sounded like *solo*.

"What do you mean, *solo?*" I practically shouted. "I wasn't here alone! Yes, I came here alone, but I left with her. Last night. Sometime around midnight. I know you saw me. So please. Tell me. Who is she?"

They exchanged meaningful glances again and shook their heads all the more. Several of them seemed to shift their gaze away from me, not wanting to look at me except from the corners of their eyes.

"I wasn't here alone! I went home with her! The girl! The *femme* with silver rings!"

But either they didn't know or they didn't want to understand me.

Finally, in frustration, I paid my tab and walked out into the purple evening. I considered trying to retrace our steps from the night before and find her apartment again, but I knew I couldn't. I had no idea even in which direction to start. I began to wonder if she had purposely doubled back and taken a roundabout way to her place in order to confuse me.

What I couldn't figure out was, why?

She had wanted me. Perhaps not as much as I had wanted her, but she had been willing, and she had made passionate yet tender love to me in the warm and inviting darkness of her bedroom.

This all happened more than twenty years ago. I'm married now, have a nice home, a job I can tolerate, a wife I love and two wonderful children; but still, once or twice a year, I drive up to Quebec. Alone. I walk the streets after dark and am particularly happy if it happens to be raining, but I can no longer even find the cafe. I watch the rivers of light reflecting off the rain-slick streets, and I fill my mind with memories of how her hands had held mine. And I think often of that barn swallow I had caught when I was a boy.

I can almost accept the idea that the men in the cafe may have been right--that I had never left there with her. It was all so long ago, I have myself half-convinced that it never even happened, that it had all been a dream, and that she was--I'm not sure what--a figment of my imagination . . . or something else.

But one thing I do know is that she still holds something of mine in her hands. I can feel the cold sting of her silver rings as she cradles my heart like a trembling bird in her cupped hands. I know that, with the slightest amount of pressure, she could squeeze the life out of it, stilling the warm, steady pulse that throbs inside my body. And I know that someday she will, and that maybe then I'll see her again.

❋

A Debt Unpaid

TANYA HUFF

Although she has published a number of fantasy novels, Tanya Huff's main contribution to dark fantasy is her quartet of "Blood" novels (Blood Price, Blood Trail, Blood Lines, Blood Pact), *all published by DAW Books, and all featuring Toronto-based private investigator Victoria Nelson and her vampire sidekick, Henry Fitzroy.*

In this, the latest example of her infrequent short fiction, Tanya spins a ghostly tale set in the hard rock mining country of her native Nova Scotia. The title comes from The Cremation of Sam McGee *by Robert W. Service. "A promise made is a debt unpaid..." Incidental Canadiana.*

"*Don't... bzzzt... too deep. Over.*"

Noting the continuing absence of a methane level, Stuart Bell slipped the methnometer into the front pocket of his heavy jacket and unclipped the walkie talkie from his belt. "Say again, surface. We're getting breakup down here. Over."

"*I... bzzt... don't go too deep. The last... bzzt... we need is another incident. Over.*"

Incident. Stuart curled his lip at the euphemism. Eight months before, eleven men had died when a methane explosion had flattened the lower two drifts of the Imap Mine. Only five bodies had been found. Rescue efforts for the other six had been called off after four days when, as the official statement had it, conditions determined no one could have survived and further attempts would put the rescue workers at risk. *Although for a change*, Stuart mused grimly, *the official statement was bang on.* He'd led the crew in and they'd damned near lost one of the younger brothers of the men they were searching for when a ceiling collapsed. *"...bzzt... hear me, Bell?! Over!"*

"No need to panic, surface. I'm barely down a hundred meters and I'm going to work my way out to the end of this drift before I go deeper. Try to remember gas rises. Out.

"You ought to know that, you asshole," he added, clipping the walkie talkie back onto his belt. Alex Brekenfield fit the profile of a company mouthpiece completely; a clean-cut, articulate chameleon, capable of projecting sincerity regardless of the bullshit he spouted. No one at Imap liked him, a few actively hated him, and Stuart Bell hated him most of all.

"Look, Stuart, we've got the powdered limestone you wanted, six hundred and sixty bags of it." Brekenfield flashed a capped smile and spread his hands. *Clean hands. Hands that had never had coal dust ground into the creases. "The problem has been taken care of."*

"The problem has not been taken care of until the limestone's been applied. You've got highly combustible coal dust building up down there..."

"And a tight economic situation up here," Brekenfield interrupted. *"Production is way behind where it should be and head office is chewing on my butt. We'll shut down operations and give that mine a thorough rock dusting the moment we can afford it."*

"Mr. Brekenfield, as the safety engineer on site..."

"You want to keep the mine open don't you? If we fall too far behind in production, head office'll close us down. You know Toronto only cares about the bottom line. And what would happen to this area if the jobs provided by the mine are lost?"

Bottom line, eleven men were dead and eight months later they were trying to open the mine up again because the chance of ending up dead and abandoned, three hundred and fifty meters underground meant little against the systemic unemployment that was the norm in Atlantic Canada. Financially, between private donations and compensation packages, the families of the dead were better off than the miners beginning to wonder how they were going to feed their kids.

"Financially better off," Stuart snarled, kicking at a chunks of gob with the steel toes of his hip waders. "So let's ask any one of those families if they'd rather have the money or their men back? And here I am, helping to open this fucking tomb up again!"

Breathing heavily, helmet light rising and falling in the dark, he pulled out the methanometer and took another reading. Still zero. Hand half way back to his pocket, a sound froze him in place.

Picks?

Imap might use considerably less than state of the art equipment but, even here, power cutters and blasting separated the coal from the face. Not picks.

Head cocked, he moved carefully forward, towards the sound. Ten meters along the drift, he knelt and laid his bare hand against the damp rock. Faintly, very faintly, he could feel a regular vibration.

"But there's nothing down there," he muttered sitting awkwardly back on his heels. "It's solid goddamned rock for almost fifty meters."

The impact of the pick grew louder, a distinct and unmistakable rhythm.

Frowning, Stuart took off his helmet and propped it up so that the light shone on the rock in front of him. Then he laid his ear against the stone.

It was damp. And cold.

The sound stopped.

He was almost positive he could hear voices.

The next impact nearly deafened him.

"God damn it!" He jerked up, cupping his left ear and noticed that the angle of the light threw a tiny line of shadow across the stone. "There wasn't a crack there..." Then his gaze happened to fall on the methanometer still in his right hand. He had just enough time to see the needle flip up into the red before, with a tortured roar, the floor of the tunnel dropped out from underneath him and the world fell on his head.

Someone was singing a Rita MacNeil song. Badly. Stuart groaned, opened his eyes and realized it made no difference to the darkness.

"Shut your gob, McIsaac, he's awake." The voice, for all its genial good humor held an unmistakable note of command.

The singing stopped. "Is he alive?" asked a third voice.

"Heart's beating," replied the first, "so I guess he is."

Stuart wasn't so sure but a quick inventory seemed to indicate that all parts were working. He tried to sit up and fell back gasping for breath as the edges of a broken rib ground together.

"Bet that hurt."

It took him a moment to find his voice and a moment after that to manage a coherent word. "Wh... wh... who?"

"Christ, you sound like an asthmatic owl. Don't you know who we are, Stuart?"

"I was... supposed to be... alone."

"What do mean, you want to reopen the mine?" Alex Brekenfield looked sincerely concerned. "It's 275 jobs, Stuart. Jobs this county could desperately use. But in order to start the ball rolling, we need a safety check and you are our safety engineer."

Two hundred and seventy-five jobs. Two hundred and seventy-four, plus his. Somehow, Stuart managed to unlock his jaw. "All right. You'll get your safety check. But the first time I go down, I go down by myself."

"Are you sure that's wise?"

"There's eleven dead already. Let's try not to go over an even dozen." He ground his heel into the thick carpet as he turned but the hinging mechanism on the office door defeated his best effort to slam it hard enough to bring the ceiling down on Brekenfield's head.

"You were alone. Technically speaking, you're still the only living man in this mine."

"...and feel the wind beneath my wing!"

"Shut your gob, McIsaac. Isn't it enough you slaughter the tune without screwing up the words as well?"

Waiting for the rest of his shift to come up out of the new cross-piece, Robert McIsaac leaned back against the mantrip and crossed his arms. "You know what your problem is, Harry? You don't appreciate music."

"How the hell would you know?" Harry asked mildly, folding his six foot four inches onto the seat beside Stuart. "You wouldn't know music if it bit you on the ass."

Stuart's sudden struggle to breath had nothing to do with broken ribs. "You're... dead."

"You're right." Harry's chuckle was as unmistakable as McIsaac's singing.

He couldn't stop the scream. The calloused hand gripping his chin was not the hand of a living man. "Please..." Terror dropped his voice to a suppliant whisper. "...let me go."

Lifeless fingers gently shook his head back and forth. "Well now, that's the question isn't it? See, me and the boys, when we heard you come down, we decided that we needed to have a little talk, you and us." The hand fell away and a sudden clattering rattled around in the darkness. "Is that your teeth Stuart?"

Stuart clenched his jaw so tightly his temple throbbed and a warm line of blood dribbled into his ear.

"Have we frightened you, Mr. Safety Engineer?" McIsaac's voice was closer than it had been. "That's good. 'Cause you killed us."

"There should never have been a mine here." The new voice belonged to Eugene Short. Stuart didn't know much about him except that his death had left two little girls without a daddy. "The whole damned area's too unstable, the seam itself has too many fault lines, and there's too damned much gas. We all knew it. But the company said the technology could handle it and we believed the company."

"Silly us," said Harry. "We worked up quite a hate list once we realized what had happened. It went right up to the right honorable asshole who approved the government loans that got this mine working; but it started with you."

"You were supposed to be looking out for our safety, Stu." Eugene's wife had begged the rescue crews to go back down just one time. One more time. Once more. "You did a piss poor job."

"I did my job the best I could!" The words jerked out before Stuart could stop them. "The company never listened to me!"

"Uhhhh. Uhhhh. Uh." The sound was pure inarticulate rage.

"That's Phil Lighthouse. You remember Phil don't you? Rock landed on Phil's face, smashed it all to hell and gone. Phil doesn't talk much now." Clothing rustled as Harry settled back. "Most of us are in better shape although I had to splint a knee to keep it from bending both ways and Bobby's ribs kinda grind together when he moves."

They were dead. They'd been dead for eight months. "H, h, how?"

"Well, we've thought about that too. You remember that explosion at Albion? About eight years ago? It was eleven days before they got the last three bodies out and all that time, even though logic said the men had to be dead, people kept believing in the possibility of a miracle. You see, Stuart, when something like this happens and there's no body to prove that death's won, a lot of folk'll keep believing their men are alive and waiting for help. I figure that me and McIsaac and Phil and Eugene here, well, we had folks topside believing in us long enough that we just kinda were forced to hang around."

Stuart wet lips gone dry in spite of the damp. "We didn't... find Al Harris or Peter... Talbot."

"Proves my point." He could feel the darkness thicken as Harry leaned towards him. "Harris has no family around here and Talbot's old lady would believe the worst if you told her she'd won a lottery."

"She's sure gonna look hot in black though," McIsaac observed with a sigh. There was an answering murmur of agreement from the other three men.

Stuart, who had a sudden vision of the widow at the funeral service where she seemed barely confined by her clothing, wondered how the hell he could think of a thing like that at a time like this.

"Anyway," Harry continued, "we spent the first few months bitchin' and bellyachin' about being stuck haunting this shit hole and then we thought, hey, we're miners, we've got plenty of time, why not dig our way out. Eugene remembered where someone had left a couple of picks -- technology often responds to a good kick in the ass -- and we headed for the surface."

"It's been eight months. You should've..."

"Decomposed?"

With the condition of his ribs, puking would probably kill him. Stuart swallowed bile and tried not to think of rotting faces appearing out of the darkness.

"Haven't. Aren't. But..." Harry's hand clamped around his arm. Even through his jacket, a sweater, and a flannel shirt, Stuart could feel the cold. "...we can't leave either. We broke out at the bottom of ventilation shaft three and couldn't go any further. That pissed us off some, you bet. Then Eugene had his brilliant idea. Tell him, Eugene."

"I wanted to see how my daughters were doing so I figured if even we couldn't leave the mine, there wasn't anything stopping us from taking the mine with us."

Eugene lived in Ridgeway, in one of the seven houses clustered up tight to the Imap fence. It was plausible they could get that far but... "How could you find them?"

"I'm their father," Eugene said as though it should be obvious. "They're a part of me."

"Had to stop the stupid son-of-a-bitch from breaking right through into the rec room," muttered McIsaac.

"Who're you calling a stupid son-of-a-bitch! That room's underground. It would've counted as part of the mine!"

"And I'm sure the girls would've loved a visit from their dead daddy."

"Asshole!"

"Butthead!"

"Can you imagine an eternity of that crap?" Harry gave Stuart's arm a little squeeze. "Anyway, it seems we can find our families and dig our way close enough to hear what's going on in their lives but we can't find the bastards who put us down here. Which was why we were so glad to hear you were coming for a visit."

"It was an accident!" The beginnings of hysteria ripped a ragged edge off the protest.

"An accident waiting to happen," McIsaac snarled.

Somewhere in the dark, Phil Lighthouse grunted an emphatic agreement.

"I wasn't my fault!" He could hear his own terror bouncing back at him off the rock. "I did everything I could!"

"Stuart. Stuart. Stuart." With each repetition of his name, Harry gave his arm a shake sending hot needles of pain into his right side. "You were the safety engineer. If you'd done everything you could, we'd still be alive. We're not, so you didn't. So now, you're going to die too. Maybe you'll join us. Maybe you won't. Frankly, we don't give a flying fuck, as long as you die.''

"Someone has to pay," McIsaac growled. "And you're the only someone we've got."

He was going to die. He could almost deal with that. But they'd never find his body, and maybe, just maybe Kathy and the kids wouldn't be able to let go. Maybe they'd believe he was still alive, waiting for help and maybe they'd believe long enough and hard enough that he'd be trapped forever in the darkness with four men who hated him. Maybe they'd trap him for eternity in his own personal hell. "Noooo..."

"Fraid so, bud."

Then he had an idea. It fought its way up through the fear and he spat it out before he could change his mind. "I could bring you the others."

For a long moment, he could hear nothing beyond his own tortured breathing then Harry muttered, "Go on."

"You said I was at the bottom of the list. There's got to be guys you want more than me. But you can only find your families so you can't get to those guys. I could bring them to the mine."

"You'd throw another seven..."

Phil Lighthouse grunted.

"Sorry, Phil, I forgot. You'd throw another eight guys to our vengeance in order to save your own miserable life?"

No. He couldn't. He wouldn't. But he heard himself say, "Yes."

"Tempting. But how do we know you'll keep your end of the deal?"

"I'll swear."

"On what? We've got a distinct shortage of bibles down here, Stuart."

"On, uh, on..." On what? He rocked his head, back and forth, trying to think and another warm trickle ran into his ear. "On blood."

"Blood, eh?" Harry sat back, releasing his arm. "What do you think, boys?"

"There's power in blood," Eugene admitted. "It took us to my girls."

"There are guys I'd rather have down here than him," McIsaac pointed out. "As murdering assholes go, Stu here's small change."

"Uhhhh. Uh."

"Sorry Phil, you're out-voted. Three to one we let our boy buy his way out. Okay Stuart, put your thinking cap on 'cause you've got eight names to remember."

The pain kept distracting him.

"One more time, Stuart. You're not leaving until you get it right."

He had to get out. Nothing else mattered.

"About fucking time," McIsaac grumbled when he finally got all eight right.

The unmistakable sound of a knife blade snapping open almost stopped Stuart's heart. "This is definitely going to hurt you more than it hurts us," Harry told him cheerfully.

The pain of the knife slicing his palm was only a smaller pain buried in the greater. He bit his lip and endured. Anything to get out. Anything. Then dead flesh pressed against the cut, not once but four times. By the end, he couldn't stop gibbering as his whole body shook, protesting the contact.

"Okay boys, lets get him to where they can find him before he dies on us anyway."

"He's pissed himself, Harry."

"What do you care? You're dead."

When they picked him up, merciful darkness claimed him.

"Stuart? Stuart, honey? Can you hear me?"

He felt a warm hand gripping his and his fingers tightened around it. "Kathy?"

"Yeah, baby, it's me. Everything's going be all right."

"Kathy, they're dead." He forced his eyes open in time to catch her exchanging a worried glance with the white-coated doctor standing at the foot of his bed. "Kath?"

Her smile held comfort and concern in spite of the exhaustion that painted grey shadows on her face. "Everything's going to be all right," she repeated, but there was more hope than certainty in her voice.

"What's wrong?" The doctor stepped forward. "You broke a rib, Mr. Bell," she said. "Cracked the two on either side and got a nasty bump on the head."

"No." His throat felt as if he'd been swallowing chunks of coal. "There's something else." Dragging his free hand up onto his chest, he stared at the bandage wrapped around his palm. "Something else."

Something dead.

"Stuart! Stuart stop it! You're out! You're safe!"

His wife's fear reached him in the darkness and he stopped trying to dig his way back through the hospital bed. Slowly, his vision cleared and his heartbeat calmed. "They're down there, Kath. Harry Frazer, Robert McIsaac, Eugene Short, Phil Lighthouse. Down in the mine. Trapped. Dead. Not dead." Another eight names echoed in the confines of his head. He tried to tell her about the promise he made, but he couldn't get the words past the shame.

He saw her swallow. It looked as though she was searching for words of comfort she couldn't find. "You're not surprised," he said slowly.

"You've been repeating their names since they brought you up." Tears spilled over the curve of her cheeks and her nose started to run. "And when they tried to work on your hand you screamed it wasn't your fault. They had to sedate you to put the stitches in."

The doctor perched on the edge of an orange vinyl chair and scooted it up close to the bed. "Mr. Bell, are you familiar with the phrase, survivor guilt?"

He stared at her suspiciously. "Doesn't it have something to do with the holocaust?"

"It is a condition that has been linked with holocaust survivors, yes, but it can occur any time some people die and some people don't."

"Like in the mine?"

"Exactly."

"And you think that's what I've got? Survivor guilt?"

She smiled professionally at him. "It would help explain why you seem to be haunted by those four men."

Haunted. Four dead men, trapped by the hope of their families. Under the harsh hospital fluorescent lights it seemed like a crazy idea. The kind of an idea a guilty mind could come up with while lying in the dark. But he could still feel Harry's cold fingers grasping his jaw and with the memory of the dead man's touch, he could smell his own fear. "What about the cut on my hand?"

"What about it, Mr. Bell?"

"I didn't cut it on a rock, did I?"

"No. You didn't." The doctor exchanged her smile for slight frown, equally meaningless. "You cut your hand on a sharp piece of metal. I'm sure there's plenty of that down where you were."

There was. The explosion had twisted the roof supports out of place and blown shrapnel all over the tunnels. Stuart stared at the bandage. "Survivor guilt," he murmured at last. "They aren't trapped down in the mine. I made it up to punish myself for letting them down."

"That's right." The doctor stood. "We'll be setting up some counselling sessions for you while you're here with us but I think you'll be fine." She nodded at them both and strode purposefully from the room.

Still clutching his unbandaged hand, Kathy whispered, "Everything's going to be all right."

"Daddy's coming home today!"

"I know, stupid." Tod Bell shoved his little sister with a six year old's finely tuned instinct for just how much violence he could inflict on a sibling half his age.

Looking harassed, Kathy dragged them apart. "Stop it you two, or Daddy'll wish I'd left you at home."

"Daddy wants *me* here." Lindsey leaned up against her father's legs. "Doncha Daddy?"

"Of course, I want you here, Lindsey-lee." Stuart smiled down at his daughter then swept the smile over wife and son as well. "I want you all here." He was feeling pretty good. The physical injuries were healing and the hospital therapist assured him that the nightmares would stop in time. Zipping shut his overnight bag, he slung it over his shoulder and held out a hand to each child. "Come on, lets go home."

"No." Shaking her head, Lindsey backed away, wide eyes locked on the bandage wrapped around her father's palm.

"It's okay, sweetheart, you won't hurt me." He stretched just a little and gently caught her hand in his.

She screamed.

"The bandage is gone, the stitches are out, and she still won't let me touch her with my left hand." He worked his palm, working flexibility into the scar. "What am I supposed to do?"

"Give her time," the therapist advised. "Your daughter sees that injury as a symbol of how close she came to losing you. This kind of accident can be very traumatic for a child but once she believes you're not going to leave her, she'll be fine."

"You think?"

"I'm positive. How are the nightmares?"

Stuart shrugged. "I've pretty much stopped dreaming about being trapped in the mine."

"Good, good."

Now my head repeats eight names at me, over and over all night. I wake up shouting, go back to sleep, and it happens all over again. Kathy's spent the last two nights on the couch. But he couldn't tell the therapist that because he'd have to explain whose eight names they were and what he'd promised to do in order to get out of the mine alive. What difference that he'd made the promise to phantoms created out of guilt; he couldn't bear that anyone would know how low he'd been willing to crawl.

"Kath, have you seen Lindsey?"

"I think she's in the rec room watching TV." His wife's eyes were shadowed. Obviously she hadn't been sleeping well either. "Why?"

"The therapist suggested I spend some quiet time with her." He started down the basement stairs. "God, I hope it's not time for Barney."

The television was off and the room was empty.

"Lindsey?"

Sometimes she liked to play under the laundry tubs in a space too small for her brother to invade.

"Lindsey?"

Down on one knee, he scooped up a plastic pony and wondered where she could've got to.

Then he heard the unmistakable sound of a pick striking stone.

"Stuart? Stuart, what is it?" Kathy ran into the laundry room, hands covered in dish soap.

He stared at her, back pressed up against the far wall. He couldn't remember moving.

"Stuart?" She took a cautious step towards him. "You shrieked..."

He couldn't remember shrieking but when he swallowed, it felt as though the inside of his throat had been flayed. "Can't you hear it?" The sound of the pick was a distant tick, tick. Like a clock. Like a clock he'd set in motion and time was running out.

"Hear what?"

If he told her what, he'd have to tell her why. "Nothing. It's nothing." Grabbing her arm, he dragged her towards the stairs. "Don't you have things to finish in the kitchen?" The kitchen could, in no way, be considered part of the mine.

"Stuart!"

She struggled, but he got her up the stairs and slammed the basement door. He could hear Lindsey out playing in the yard and Tod was still at school. Everyone was safe. "I don't want anyone going downstairs."

"Are you out of your mind?"

He'd frightened her and, as he watched, the fear turned to anger.

"What is going on, Stuart?"

If he told her, she'd despise him and that wouldn't stop the dead. He couldn't explain so there was only one thing he could do.

"Thank you for meeting me out here, Mr. Brekenfield."

"The company appreciates your discretion, Stuart." Alex Brekenfield flashed him a we're-all-in-this-together smile. "The last thing Imap Mines needs right now is bad publicity."

"So no one knows you're here?" Stuart's head jerked from side to side as he scanned the area around the headframe. "'Cause I'd hate for the press to get wind of this."

"No one knows. What did you want to tell me?"

"I think you'll understand the problem better if I show you." He took hold of the other man's elbow, the scar on his palm throbbing against the tweed jacket. "It's over by number three ventilation shaft."

"Wasn't that near where they dug you out?"

"Yes."

"So how're you feeling, Stuart?"

"Fine."

"I uh, meant to visit you in the hospital, but you know how things come up. As I'm sure you've heard, we're still intending to reopen the mine. I've got an incredible workload right now."

"It's okay."

"Isn't this a long way around to number three?"

"A little, but this way the ground's solid." He twisted enough to see they were leaving no tracks.

Brekenfield misunderstood. "Good thinking. I'd hate to have an accident out here."

The housing had been taken off the shaft when the rescue crew had pulled Stuart out. It had never been replaced. Dropping to one knee, Stuart pointed down into the darkness. "There."

Grunting, Brekenfield knelt beside him. "I don't see anything."

"Wait a minute. Your vision has to adjust to the lack of light."

"I still don't see anything." Stuart closed his eyes. He could hear the picks approaching. "You will." The scar felt hot and cold and, pressed against Brekenfield's back, it pulsed in time to Brekenfield's heart. One-two. One-two. One.

He forced himself to listen to the impact. It was softer than he thought it would be. And wetter.

After a moment, the sound of the picks stopped and the screaming started. Stuart scrambled to his feet and ran for the fence. Retching. Crying. Afraid of what he'd hear if he stayed.

Afraid they might thank him.

"Lindsey! How many times have I told you not to play under there!" He grabbed her arm, his hand wrapped all the way around the soft child flesh, and dragged her out from under the laundry tubs.

She stared at him for a moment, too frightened to react, then the moment passed and she started to sob.

"Oh sweetheart." Stuart dropped to his knees on the concrete floor and gathered the terrified three year old into his arms. "I'm sorry, sweetheart. I didn't mean to scare you. Daddy's just...

"Daddy's just..."

He could hear the picks. He could hear McIsaac singing. Still holding his daughter, he twisted and stared under the tubs. The naked bulb that hung from the laundry room ceiling painted the shadow of a tiny crack.

"NO!" Stuart dove, rolled, and clawed his way over the crumbling floor to the basement stairs, Lindsey's arms clutched desperately around his neck. Darkness yawned suddenly under the bottom step but he raced it to the kitchen finding strength in the precious life he had to save. Three steps from the door, the stairs dropped out from under his feet.

He threw Lindsey onto the linoleum and flung himself after her but too much of his body remained over the pit.

"NO!"

He began to fall back. Caught the doorframe and fought for life. Then Kathy was there. And Tod. They grabbed his arms and pulled, panic lending strength.

His torso was in the kitchen. His legs; his legs were in the mine.

Then his knees cleared the threshold. He kicked up, caught the edge of the door with one foot, and slammed it shut.

It was surprisingly quiet in the kitchen.

Breathing heavily, Kathy sank down onto the floor beside him. "Jesus God, Stuart. What happened?"

They'd had him memorize eight names.

There were seven still to go.

"We're moving," he said.

Stuart got a job in Halifax, working for the provincial Industry Minister. Her predecessor was one of the seven but as she'd only just taken over the portfolio her name wasn't on the list. They lived in a flat on the second floor of an old frame house in what was once the monied section of the city. Tod settled into a new school and Lindsey adopted the elderly couple who lived on the first floor as surrogate grandparents. Kathy was sharing his bed again.

The worst thing that happened over the winter was Lindsey's inexplicable delight in Don Cherry's Coach's Corner. Fortunately, it faded with the end of the hockey season.

He wasn't sure what woke him. Bare feet whispering against the carpet, he padded first into Lindsey's room and then Tod's. Both kids were sound asleep.

Frowning, he slid back under the sheet. Then he grinned. Faintly, through the hot air duct beside the bed, he could hear old Mr. Verge bellowing out a Rita MacNeil tune.

Probably serenading the missus before a bit of the old in and out. Still smiling he settled back against the pillow and closed his eyes.

And opened his eyes.

It wasn't old Mr. Verge's voice coming up through the furnace ducts.

The furnace was in the basement.

When they moved to Toronto, they stayed for a few months with Kathy's brother and his family in Don Mills before renting a ninth floor apartment at York Mills and Leslie. Kathy found a part-time job at a day care center and Stuart tried to line up consulting contracts. Unfortunately, there weren't a lot of jobs for mining engineers in this part of the country. Tod hated his new school and Lindsey started wetting the bed.

It took just over a year for things to improve but Kathy finally found a full time job with great pay and better benefits. Stuart threw himself into being a full-time house husband. Tod started little league. Lindsey got her first permanent tooth.

He was down in the building's laundry room, folding the laundry, when he heard the picks.

He moved to Thunder Bay by himself. He would've gone further but the car died just outside the old Port Arthur city limits and he couldn't afford to either fix or replace it.

He got a job with a maintenance firm and lost it because he wouldn't go into basements.

He got a job with the parks department and lost it when he ran screaming from a co-worker who'd intended to take a pick to a hardhead on a park road.

It took them three years to find him.

He went over the seven names and returned to Nova Scotia, stood on the sidewalk outside a pretty white frame house as the sun was setting, watched the ex-Industry Minister pull the living room curtains, and couldn't do it.

He bought the rope with the last of his money, tied one end of it very carefully to a safety railing on the Angus L. MacDonald bridge and put a slip knot in the other. The Halifax/Dartmouth authorities made it as difficult as they could for jumpers but short of closing the bridge between the cities to pedestrian traffic they couldn't do quite enough.

Someone yelled as he jumped. A car horn honked. Tires squealed. He could see the harbor ferry down below. As the knot jerked tight, he smiled. Just let them try to find him here.

Someone was singing a Rita MacNeil song. Badly. Stuart groaned and opened his eyes. It took a moment's concentration but he managed to focus on the people standing around him although there wasn't much light and he couldn't seem to straighten his head.

"Where's Brekenfield?" he asked, when the singing stopped and the mine was quiet. Eugene shrugged.

"I guess no one believed in him."

"No one believes in me..."

"That's where you're wrong, Stuart." Harry smiled and patted his cheek so that his head flopped onto his other shoulder. "*We* believe in you. Welcome to hell."

Imposter

PETER SELLERS

Peter Sellers' short stories have appeared in Ellery Queen Mystery Magazine, Mike Shayne Mystery Magazine, Alfred Hitchock Mystery Magazine, Hardboiled *and in anthologies such as* Criminal Shorts and Northern
Frights. *He has edited five volumes in the Mosaic Press* Cold Blood *series,
and was awarded the Derrick Murdock Award by the Crime Wrtiters of
Canada for his contribution to the mystery genre.*

The vampires next door were having a party. It didn't happen often.
Generally they were pretty quiet neighbours. Nathan hardly knew they
were there half the time. But once every two or three months they'd have
friends in and things would get a little livelier.

From the beginning, Nathan wondered what the parties were like. Did
vampires dance? If so, what kind of music did they play? Were the
conversations intricate and philosophical discussions or shallow and transitory chit chat? Were charades popular? Nathan even tried to envision what
they served as canapés. He already knew how the bar was stocked.

The morning after the second of the vampires' parties, Nathan found
an empty plasma bag lying in the hall between the vampires' front door and
the incinerator room. It was then around ten in the morning and the empty
bag must have been lying there since before dawn, making Nathan wonder
how many people had seen it on their way to the elevators and the office but
had simply pretended it wasn't there.

Nathan went back into his apartment, put on the rubber gloves he
used for washing dishes, and picked up the empty bag. He took it into the

incinerator room and dropped it and the gloves down the chute. Then he washed his hands for a long time under very hot water.

The night of the vampires' first party, Nathan had been very nervous. He knew the fear was irrational. After all, the vampires had told him all the things he needed to do in order to stay safe. Still, there he was, living next door to a couple of undead things that survived by drinking human blood. And they were having company. He was terrified.

He tried telling himself it was no different than living next to a couple with any other dietary quirk. Vegetarians perhaps, or Catholics who ignored Vatican II and still ate fish on Friday. Or people who always ate the middle of the Oreo first, or who ate the red Smarties last. He tried thinking that way, but it didn't really help.

The vampires had been very good about preparing Nathan for their first party. Three days before, they came to Nathan's apartment for a visit. They brought a bottle of Bordeaux dated 1837 and they sat on the sofa holding hands. Every once in a while one or the other would laugh at something that was said and their fangs would peek briefly from behind their burgundy lips causing Nathan to suppress a shudder.

"We're going to have a party," Bianca told him.

Nathan's jaw dropped. "A party? Like an open house? For the neighbors?" He couldn't help wondering if anyone else in the building knew.

"No, silly," Bianca said. Laughter. Fangs. "For our old friends."

"Friends?"

"Yes," Mikhail told him. "Some friends from uptown. Some friends from other parts of the country. And some friends who just flew in from overseas."

Nathan smiled weakly. "And boy are their arms ever tired," he said.

Mikhail looked confused. "Yes," he said in his rumbling tones, "the strain it puts on the muscles here..." He started to indicate areas of the upper arm and shoulder when Bianca laid her hand on Mikhail's wrist and stopped him.

"It's an old joke," she said.

"Oh," Mikhail said, looking embarrassed. Nathan figured he came as close to blushing as a vampire ever could.

"The party will be Friday night," Bianca said.

The thirteenth, Nathan thought. Figures.

"We're expecting a large number of guests. We'll try and be as quiet as possible, the parties seldom become rowdy unless an infiltrator is found. Then things can get out of hand. If you're planning to be home that night, we advise you to take several precautions." Then she described in detail how Nathan could use crosses and garlands of fresh garlic to keep any overly enthusiastic partygoers at bay.

"But I don't take these precautions with you."

"That's because of our arrangement. Unfortunately, our friends aren't all as," she paused, hunting for the right word, "*avant garde* as we are. If you're careful, the worst that should happen will be the odd annoying phone call. You'd perhaps be best not to answer the phone at all that night."

The next day, Nathan bought several crosses in a variety of sizes from a Christian supply store he found in the Yellow Pages. Then he went to his local grocer and bought all the garlic buds they had. The grocer looked at him oddly as Nathan piled up the fragrant vegetables on the counter.

"I'm making soup," Nathan said.

The grocer nodded. "Thought maybe you were worried about vampires or something," he said. "Course, you make a soup with this much garlic, you'll keep more'n them suckers away." He laughed, showing wide, uneven teeth.

Nathan smiled back unhappily and walked home with his packages.

As it turned out, the party was one of the most subdued Nathan had ever lived beside. There were some peculiar noises, what he thought was the flapping of leathery wings outside his window, and what sounded like a large dog sniffing loudly at the base of his front door, but for the most part he was not bothered.

At two in the morning his phone did ring, as Bianca had told him it might, and a cold, hypnotic voice said, "Come next door and be the life of the party." But the call was abruptly cut off and Nathan unplugged the phone and sat up on the sofa for the rest of the night.

Nathan hadn't realized at first that his new neighbors were vampires, although it was unusual to have people moving in after midnight. He'd heard them thumping and banging in the halls and he recognized the universal cries of the do-it-yourself mover. "A little to the left." "Hangonhangonhangonhangon!" "Just let me get a better grip."

He went out into the hall to have a look and that's when he got his first glimpse of Bianca.

Her back was to him, clad entirely in black, with lustrous hair, the blackest Nathan had ever seen, falling almost to her slender waist. She wore snug black designer jeans, Nathan spent a long time trying to read the label, and black leather boots reached up almost to her knee. She was moving backwards toward the open door of the apartment next to Nathan's, and she was struggling with an awkward-looking box. As she moved she was giving directions to two men who followed her carrying a large dark wooden chest, like a long low sideboard, with ornate brass handles.

They were big, fierce looking men and Nathan hoped they hadn't noticed him looking so longingly at the woman's behind. He stepped forward. "Let me help," he said, grabbing the other end of the awkward box in the woman's arms.

She shot him a look of consternation. Sensing that perhaps she was new to the big city and uneasy about strange men offering assistance in the middle of the night, Nathan said, "I live next door". He pointed to his apartment and smiled at her with such bland innocence that she let him take some of the weight of the box. Nathan's knees buckled and the smile left his face. He'd expected linens or something, but it felt like there was an anvil in there. He struggled forward, expecting any second to feel something in his stomach tear apart.

They brought the box into the living room and set it down, Nathan dropping his end with a grunt and a crash the neighbors below must have loved. The woman set her end down as gently as a mother laying a newborn's head on a pillow. Nathan wondered how many hours she'd spent on a Nautilus machine to be able to do that.

The two men followed them into the apartment and set the sideboard against the dining room wall. "That's it," the woman said. "That's everything." She turned her gaze to Nathan and his heart swelled. He'd never seen eyes so black and he instantly fell in love. "Thank you, Mr..."

Nathan held out a hand. "Nathan," he said. "Since we're going to be neighbors, just call me Nathan."

"My name is Bianca." She took Nathan's hand. The night outside was edging down toward freezing, and she'd been working without gloves so her hands were cold. Releasing Nathan's grip, she indicated the two men with her.

"This," she said, pointing to a tall man with heavy shoulders, a handsome face deeply lined by the elements and eyes nearly as dark as her own, "is my husband Mikhail." Mikhail looked at Nathan with penetrating intensity and bowed slightly and briskly. "And this is our friend, Raoul." She drew the second syllable out so that the name sounded like an abbreviated howl. Raoul was, Nathan thought, the hairiest man he'd ever seen, his eyes sandwiched between a thick beard and heavy overhanging eyebrows.

Raoul immediately turned to Mikhail and grunted something, and then stalked out of the apartment.

"You must excuse Raoul," Bianca said. "He's a little lacking in the social graces. He's something of a lone wolf."

Nathan nodded. "Well," he said, "I better be going too. If there's anything else you need, I'm right next door."

"Must you go?" Bianca edged closer to him, her tongue moistening her upper lip.

"Won't you stay for a little nightcap?" Mikhail's voice was rich and textured, like a Slavic Richard Burton. "After all we're your new neighbors and you can give us a little taste of life in the building." There was something about the way Mikhail said it, and the way Bianca was rubbing her cold hands over Nathan's chest, that made him nervous.

"That's awfully nice of you," Nathan said, "but I have to work tomorrow, and it's so late..." He began backing toward the door.

"Oh? And what work do you do?" Bianca asked, although it sounded to Nathan like a polite cocktail party question.

"This makes a lot of people uncomfortable, but I work at a blood bank," Nathan said. "Testing blood."

Bianca pulled back from Nathan as if she'd been stung. He'd had that reaction before from women who thought his job was disgusting. He couldn't understand it, really. What he was doing was very important. What with all the horrible bacteria swimming around in the world's blood streams he, and those like him, were all that stood between national health and pandemia. So he wasn't surprised when Bianca drew away. He *was* surprised when he looked at her face, and then at Mikhail's, and saw a level of interest he'd never witnessed before.

"What exactly do you do," Bianca purred, "with the blood?"

"Well," Nathan confessed, "I don't actually do the testing. But they look for HIV, Tay-Sachs, sickle cell, syphilis, you name it, before they store it or ship it out for operations, transfusions, whatever. Naturally, they don't want to keep the bad stuff. That's my job. I'm in charge of disposal. There's a joke around the lab, there's always bad blood between me and everyone else."

Bianca laughed and Mikhail smiled ever so slightly. Then Bianca placed a hand on Nathan's elbow and steered him to the door with a strength that made him increase his estimate of how much time she'd spent in the gym. "But we must let you get some sleep. You have important work. And Mikhail and I have much to discuss about arrangements here in our new home."

The arrangements were made plain to Nathan two days later. Mikhail and Bianca invited him over for a drink and, they said, a chance to get better acquainted. Nathan wasn't entirely comfortable after their peculiar behaviour of the other night, but he found himself curiously unable to refuse.

Nathan sat in a very comfortable arm chair and looked at Mikhail and Bianca on the sofa. "So," he said with a smile, "now it's my turn." He took a sip of the wine they offered him. It had turned, but he tried not to show it. After all, unless the label was a gag, the bottle was over 150 years old. "What do you guys do for a living?"

Mikhail and Bianca looked at one another for quite some time. It was obvious to Nathan that they were trying to figure out how to answer, or even if they should. Maybe I shouldn't have asked, he thought. Maybe they do something really weird or gross. Maybe they're worm pickers and that's why you never see them during the day. Maybe they run a phone sex business. He mentally kicked himself. But just as he was about to try and steer the conversation in a new direction, Bianca turned her eyes from Mikhail to him.

"We're vampires," she said simply. Just like that. Flat out and straight faced. Like she was telling the guy at the deli how much smoked meat she wanted.

Nathan stared at her. "Pardon me?"

"We're vampires."

"You know, the undead," Mikhail added, by way of helpful explanation.

Nathan started to laugh. "You guys," he said, slapping his knee with a loud flat sound. "The clothes, the crazy hours. Look, if you don't want to tell me what you do, I understand. Everybody has secrets. It's okay with me."

Bianca shook her head. "We're not kidding, Nathan. We're really vampires."

There was something in her tone that made Nathan stop laughing. He'd heard of people who called themselves vampires. Little groups of fringe dwellers, the kind of wingnuts you found clinging like barnacles to the underside of any big city. People who drank the blood of animals or licked it from small wounds opened in one another's chests and fingertips, late at night, in the glow of dripping candles, often for sexual reasons.

Nathan looked at the thick crimson richness of the wine in his glass and felt queasy. Maybe they were being serious. Maybe they did consider themselves vampires. Maybe they were the kind of lunatics he'd really rather not have living next door, the kind he certainly didn't want to spend the evening with in idle chatter while they sized up which of his veins to open first. He started calculating how far it was to the front door.

Mikhail leaned forward suddenly. "We'll prove it to you," he said brightly.

"That's okay!" Nathan threw up his hands and shrank back. "If you say you're vampires, hey, who am I to argue?" He looked at his watch. "Whoa, where does the time go? I really...I gotta...I...."

Mikhail waved off his objections. "No, no," he said. "We must prove it to you. We sense, very strongly, that you are not sure in here." He touched the middle of his chest. "We will not rest easily if we feel there is any doubt."

Nathan was frantic. "I don't doubt! I don't doubt! Please don't feel you have anything to prove on my account."

"But we will," Mikhail barked. "Look!" Then he and Bianca pulled their lips back in exaggerated wedding photo grimaces and their fangs gleamed.

Nathan stared at the teeth. He had expected something more dramatic. He didn't say anything for the longest time, and Mikhail and Bianca's eyes darted uncertainly back and forth. As the silence lengthened, their upper lips began to tremble from the strain and a tear squeezed out of the corner of one of Mikhail's eyes.

"So what?" Nathan asked finally. "Those teeth you can probably pick up for ten bucks at a costume shop. I've got a pair at home that look every bit as good as that." It was true. Nathan's teeth had been provided by the cousin of a friend of his brother, who worked in the movie make-up and special effects business. Nathan had worn them to a Hallowe'en party and knew they looked every bit as real, if not more so, than what he was looking at now.

Bianca and Mikhail lowered their lips back over their fangs and Mikhail rubbed his jaw. "You want more proof?" Bianca couldn't entirely hide her displeasure at Nathan's disbelief. It showed in her eyes, but not in her voice. "Very well. Then we need you to do one small thing for us. With your hands."

Involuntarily, Nathan's fingers curled up as he imagined her sucking beads of crimson from their trembling tips. He started to shake, but neither Mikhail nor Bianca moved towards him. Instead she kept talking in her soft, hypnotic way. "Just take your hands," she said, "and place the index finger of one hand over the index finger of the other, at right angles, to make the shape of the...you know...the..." She waved a hand in the air to fill in the word.

"Shape of the cross, you mean," Nathan said. He had never in his life hit a woman, unless you counted Melissa Levinson when he was seven, but simply saying that word made him understand the feeling. Bianca's head snapped back and she grunted as if he had driven a vicious blow to her abdomen.

"Ahh!" Nathan cried. He felt like a heel. "I'm so sorry. I didn't think..."

"It's alright," Bianca said weakly. "Please, when I say ready, make the sign."

She reached over and took Mikhail's hand. They looked at one another again, this time with more sadness than Nathan thought he had ever seen, and then Bianca turned to him and nodded. "Ready." Nathan lifted his hands, index fingers extended, and he made the sign of the cross in the air in front of him.

It was as if a bolt of lightning had blasted from his fingers and hammered the two vampires back into the sofa cushions. They arched their backs and howled, trying desperately to avert eyes that were held riveted to

Nathan's fingers. Their faces flushed red and the veins in their necks stood out, pulsing as if they would burst. Nathan stared in awe at the two writhing, groaning wild eyed figures who squirmed and convulsed before him. He was so mesmerized by what was happening that he forgot for a moment that he was causing it. Then his gaze fell for an instant to his hands and with a cry he yanked his fingers apart as if they were burned. Mikhail and Bianca slumped onto the sofa, leaning panting against one another, tears rolling down their faces as the brilliant red faded gradually returning them to their usual pallor.

"Wow," Nathan said. "That was something." The question remained, what? It was an impressive display, true. But it could have been acting. It could have been autosuggestion. If these people believed so deeply that they were vampires, they could have this kind of reaction automatically. He figured they probably had the idea so firmly fixed in their minds that if they went outside during the daytime, they'd break out in hives in about five seconds. But there was no way they'd crumble to dust.

As if he read Nathan's thoughts, Mikhail rose and walked toward him. Normally, Mikhail stood very tall and erect. But now he stooped and lumbered forward unsteadily and when he held out his hand it shook as if he were a thousand years old. "I sense you still don't believe. Take my hand."

Nathan reached out unsurely and took hold. If Mikhail was acting, he was awfully good. His grip was still strong and he half pulled Nathan to his feet, then he put his hand around Nathan's shoulder and walked him to a large cloth covered object hanging on the wall. Nathan had figured it was a painting they wanted protected from the sunlight, but Mikhail pulled a cord at the side and the cloth fell away, revealing a large gilt framed mirror.

Nathan stared into it. He felt Mikhail's hand clamped on his shoulder. He felt Mikhail's cool and trembling body next to his own. He heard Mikhail's rasping breath at his ear. But when he looked in the mirror he was quite alone.

Nathan glanced sideways. Mikhail. He looked in the mirror. No Mikhail. He shut his eyes and opened them again. Still no Mikhail in the mirror. "Oh my God," he said. And that's when he broke for the door.

Somehow, Mikhail got there first and Nathan hit him on the dead run. It was like running into a moose. Nathan wound up sitting on the floor, shaking his head in an effort to clear it, and looking up at the imposing vampire who reached a hand down to him. "We will not hurt you," Mikhail said. And he bent down and jerked Nathan to his feet. "We have a deal for you. A proposition."

"What kind of proposition?"

"We want you to supply us with blood," Bianca said in a voice that made Nathan's testicles contract.

Involuntarily, Nathan's hand flew to his neck. Bianca and Mikhail both laughed. "Not from your body, you foolish man," she said. "From where you work. Instead of throwing all that rejected blood away, bring some of it home to us."

"What?" Nathan asked in disgust. "You can't drink that blood."

"Whyever not?" Bianca asked, looking at him in puzzlement.

"Because it's bad. Diseased. It'll make you sick. It'll kill you."

Bianca laughed. "But, Nathan, we're already dead. More or less. What would hurt you can sustain us."

Nathan shook his head. "I don't like it."

"You'll get used to the idea."

"Well," he sighed, "I used to deliver pizzas. I guess it's not really that much different. But why are you doing this?"

"The old way is no good anymore," Bianca said with a wistful smile. "It lacks dignity. And besides, nowadays people aren't as superstitious as they were in the old days. And they all know what they're doing. With the books, and the movies, and on television even, everyone knows about vampires. Do you think if people started showing up with holes in their necks and bloodless veins they wouldn't come after us right away? We'd die horrible, helpless deaths."

"Writhing around with big sticks through our chests," Mikhail added, leaning forward in his seat and jabbing his finger at Nathan's chest for emphasis. "Pinned like butterflies to a cork board. Spewing blood, our eyes bursting." He sat back again, content to let Nathan dwell on the images.

"And don't believe what they say about vampires, either. We don't hate our half-lives, really. We don't have to worry about getting older, about sagging or wrinkles. I haven't colored my hair in over 260 years. And we never have to use aerobics or stair climbers to stay trim. True, we don't tan, but that's no longer good for you anyway. And the diet really isn't bad."

"Oh," Mikhail said, "the diet is wonderful. The variables of blood varietal, vintage and geographic region make for an astounding array of taste sensations. And every so often you hit upon a truly rare specimen and it's an experience any gourmet would sell his soul to sample."

Nathan struggled to control his nausea, the bile pressing frantically against the back of his clenched teeth.

"We just believe in changing with the times," Mikhail said.

"Even vampires have to evolve," added Bianca. "Will you help us?" She looked longingly at him. "If not..." She reached out and ran a cold, soft hand along the side of his neck.

Nathan started supplying blood to the vampires next door the following Monday. Smuggling the tainted samples out was easier than he expected, although with his liquid cargo hidden under his trench coat he felt like it was Prohibition and he was on his way home from the speakeasy.

And, as Bianca had predicted, he did get used to it. That was, in part, because he realized he had no choice. If he didn't supply them with blood, they'd take it. From him. Also, they were being very civilized about the whole thing. Preferring a life of middle class domesticity to one of terrorizing the city and condemning others to their fate.

For well over a year, everything went without a hitch. Nathan delivered every day. The vampires even created a card system. They'd leave one under his door every night, shortly before dawn. It would indicate the order for the day and Nathan would fill it as best he could, noting which particular requests he'd been unable to meet and making it up the following day. He wondered what Mr. O'Sullivan, the milkman he remembered from his youth, clanking from house to house in his white trousers and black bow tie, would think of Nathan and the hideous red pop he delivered now. Lord, how times have changed, Nathan thought to himself as he passed another day's supply into Mikhail and Bianca's eager hands.

Delivering blood got to be as routine as shaving or having lunch. And, after the first half dozen, the parties got to be that way too. But as Nathan's fear diminished, his curiosity increased. And so it was that when the vampires next door announced their latest gathering, Nathan decided he simply had to go, invitation or not.

He knew it would work. For over a year he'd studied two vampires up close. He knew how they talked and acted. He had teeth every bit as good looking as theirs. He knew Mikhail and Bianca would not be happy to see him, but he also knew they wouldn't expose him as an imposter to their friends and risk losing their safe source of supply. He knew the power he had in his fingers, how that simple sign of the cross could immobilize any vampire long enough to let him get away should things go wrong. And he also knew he wouldn't stay long in any event. Pop in, check it out, then head home. A daring commando strike on the vampire bash.

He prepared his apartment as usual with crosses and garlic, for protection when he returned home. He left the door unlocked for quick entry. Then he got himself ready. He wore black Levi's and black western boots, and a grey T-shirt beneath a dusty rose sport shirt. Then, of course, the teeth. He combed his hair and checked the fangs in the mirror, gave himself the thumbs up, and went out into the hallway.

He was about to knock on the vampires' door when a sudden thought occurred to him. Suppose no one arrived this way. Suppose they just materialized from under the door in a puff of smoke, or fluttered through the bedroom window on leathery bat wings. Oh well, he reasoned, those options weren't open to him. So he raised his hand and knocked, hoping no one inside would notice that he hadn't buzzed up from the lobby.

The door opened almost immediately by a young woman with short orange hair and large gold earrings. "Hi," she said, her kewpie doll eyes studying him and her lips forming a tentative smile. "I only just got here," she said. "It looks like quite a party. I've never been to one of these before."

"Neither have I. Can I come in?"

"Oh, sorry." She stepped back and Nathan entered, jumping in his skin at the sound of the door closing behind him.

"My name's Lucy." Nathan turned to se the orange-haired girl holding out a hand to him. He didn't want to touch her, knowing his hands would be too warm, but he wasn't sure how to avoid it without being rude. Finally he reached out quickly and gave her hand a light swift shake. Her hand felt clammy but she didn't react to the warmth he had feared would give him away.

"Do you know Bianca and Mikhail well?"

Nathan almost blurted out that he'd supplied the blood for the party, but caught himself in time. "Not really. But I better find them and say hello. Excuse me."

He made his way into the apartment. It was full of vampires. For an instant, Nathan had a dread thought that they would know automatically that he was not one of them. In the way he'd heard that gays could tell about each other. But there were only the usual casual glances one partygoer gives to another, unfamiliar face. There were vampires on the sofa, leaning against the walls, sitting on the seats and arms of the chairs. It seemed like any normal, casual gathering although everyone was drinking something that looked vaguely like cranberry cocktail and there were no chips and dip in sight.

Nathan headed for the kitchen. As with most of the parties he'd ever been to that was the liveliest room. It was solid vampires, many of them making their way to the two Coleman coolers filled with plasma bags, others pushing their way back through the crowd, drinks held aloft, calling, "Excuse me. Pardon me, please." That was where Nathan abruptly came face to face with Bianca.

At first it was as if she didn't know who he was. He was undoubtedly the last person she ever anticipated seeing at her party so placing him took a while. Then her face drained a shade paler. "What are you doing here?" she hissed.

Nathan smiled, proudly displaying his fangs. "Just checking it out. It's actually pretty dull, just a bunch of half-dead people sitting around talking."

"Many of them haven't seen each other in a hundred years and more. They're catching up. But if you don't leave this might get more exciting than you'd like."

"I'll be fine," he said, smiling and holding up his two index fingers like six guns.

Bianca shook her head and said simply, "I can't protect you here. No one can. Please, leave now. Before it's too late."

Nathan felt a hand on the small of his back and the chill of it shot through his shirts. "Oooh," a voice murmured, "who's this Bianca? He's dishy."

Nathan looked around and saw a vampire of about his own age, plunging neckline, short skirt, and dangerously sharp heels. "I'm Ruby," she said. "What's your name?"

"Nathan," he said, reflexively smiling wide enough to show her his fangs.

"You're new," she said.

He nodded. "This is my first party."

"No. New to this, uh, life," she said. "I can always tell."

Suddenly Nathan was overcome by panic. What had he hoped to accomplish? How close was he to being caught? Did Ruby know? Even Bianca couldn't protect him. He turned to her, trying to sound calm. "It was a lovely party. Thanks, but I have to go." Bianca looked at him very sadly. "Excuse me."

His impulse was to just shove his way through the crowd, bulldoze to the door. But he knew he'd never make it. He swallowed hard and eased past the revelers as inconspicuously as possible. God, if only he could turn himself into a wisp of smoke and vanish that way. He felt beads of sweat stand out on his forehead and he realized it had never occurred to him before, do vampires sweat? Thinking about it made it worse.

Somehow, Nathan managed to stay calm as he inched forward. The door, though, seemed to have been moved much further away than it was when he came in. It got closer and closer with agonizing slowness as Nathan waded through the blood drinking throng. He was almost there when he suddenly felt a hand clutch his arm and someone whisper in his ear, with a feral excitement that chilled him, "We've got an imposter."

Nathan froze. If he hadn't been so frightened he would have screamed. He felt tears beginning to build behind his eyes and felt the hand on his arm begin to turn him back until he faced into the apartment. "Come on, Nathan," Ruby said. "Come back. We've got ourselves an imposter."

It took a few seconds for the meaning of the words to sink in. They had an imposter and it wasn't him. There was another one at the party. Nathan almost wept now, but with relief. Unthinkingly, he let Ruby propel him towards the kitchen and it was only after a few steps that he began to wonder who the other imposter was.

Then, outside the kitchen door, at the centre of a seething knot of vampires, was the orange-haired girl who'd opened the door for him. She was held fast, arms and legs, by at least half a dozen different eager guests, where their fingers pressed her flesh it showed true vampire white. But her eyes were wide with panic, her mouth open and a terrified keening was all that came out. It made Nathan's knees go weak.

Nathan looked at Ruby whose eyes glittered. "How do you know she's an imposter?" he asked in a whisper.

Ruby didn't take her eyes off the struggling girl. "Someone spilled a glass of blood on her and she used the name of the deity."

It took Nathan some time before he understood this further, and he only just stopped himself from repeating the error by muttering aloud, "Oh, she said Jesus Christ." Lucy managed to turn her head in his direction and their eyes met. He tried to give her a look of sympathy but her keening rose in intensity and Nathan understood right away. She recognized him as like her. Perhaps she thought he could help her. Perhaps she thought she could expose him in return for her freedom. He had no idea which.

"How did she get in here?" he asked.

"Doesn't matter. But she's here. And she's ours now. It's always so much better when this happens. And I think she likes you." Then Ruby was moving forward, dragging Nathan with her. "Look out," she said. "Let me through." She drew Nathan up to within three feet of the captive. He could smell the fear of her.

Then Ruby was talking again, this time to the hungering crowd. "This is Nathan. It's his first party. And he's new. He gets the first bite."

This sent Lucy into a new frenzy of anguished struggle. More hands reached in to hold her fast, two of them gripping her head and wrenching it to the side exposing the vein on her neck. Her face was flushed red with her terror and her struggling.

Nathan was frozen. Oh God, why didn't he stay home? He extended the index fingers of his hands and looked down at them but knew they were as useless as a water pistol against the horde. They'd simply bring him down from the rear. The door was unreachable, the crowd pressed in around him and from somewhere a chant went up that built and built as Lucy struggled in vain. ''Bite! Bite! Bite! Bite!''

Ruby leaned forward and whispered in Nathan's ear. ''Go ahead, Nathan. Bite.''

Nathan took one last look around for an avenue of escape but there was none. Then he looked into Lucy's stricken eyes, tried to tell her with his gaze how sorry he was. He stared at the fat vein bulging in the side of her neck. He listened to the ravenous chanting. Bite! Bite! Bite! He said a short and silent prayer. Then Nathan shut his eyes and opened his mouth very wide.

Exodus 22:18

NANCY BAKER

Nancy Baker's short story, "Cold Sleep", appeared in our initial North-ern Frights *volume. It introduced her 500-year-old-vampire, Dimitri Rozokov, to the world. Rozokov was a leading player in Nancy's first novel,* The Night Inside, *which was published in 1993 to international acclaim. Following the success of that book, as well as a sequel,* Blood and Chrysanthemums, *Nancy left her job as Direct Marketing Manager for* Canadian Living Magazine *in order to write full time.*

About Exodus 22:18, *she confides, "I wrote the song first, back when I was in a basement band, trying hard to be the next Siouxsie and the Banshees. When it became apparent that such a thing was highly unlikely, I switched to writing fiction."*

The posters led him to her. They grew along the axis of the city's main streets, planted there by her acolytes. Festooning the walls of construction sites, circling lamp posts, tacked onto trees, they were the signs he used to trace her paths throughout the city.

At first, he had barely noticed them. He had been too intent on hunting down another of the sinners he had vowed to eradicate. But when she, too, had played him false, proving, despite extensive examination, to be no more than any other wicked daughter of Eve, the posters had been waiting.

He stood before a wall of them now, while the October wind chased leaves in circles at his feet. How could he have missed the signs? She flaunted them like twisted badges of honor; the shock of midnight hair, the eyes black-lined and hellishly bright against the corpse-like pallor of her skin. Even her name--Lilith. The rejected first wife of Adam, cast out of Eden for witchcraft, she had thrown in her lot with the Arch-Deceiver. What woman who was not a witch would choose such a name?

They had thought themselves safe, the Daughters of Evil. Thought that in a world of televised carnage and sensual corruption, they could hide. Who would believe in such ancient evil, when modern ones abounded like mushroom clouds?

But he had not forgotten. He remember his Lord's injunction. It was written down for all to see, even if none would heed it. "THOU SHALT NOT SUFFER A WITCH TO LIVE."

The command was very clear and, clear of mind and conscience, he obeyed it. It was not hard to find the offenders; they advertised their presence freely. Fortune-tellers, dancers, whores, writers of occult pornography, what were they all but manifestations of that one great whore, the first witch?

So he had obediently tracked them down and submitted them to the ancient tests: the needles to search out the devil's mark that did not bleed; the racks; the water that would purify them in death. That not all confessed to their crimes had disturbed him at first, as did the incontrovertible evidence of innocence the drowned corpses represented. Then he realized that they were mere dupes of the greater evil, bound to it by their sex, if not by their conscious will. They had been set in his path to distract him from his true quarry. After that, the confessions did not matter.

The world, of course, did not understand. The papers, the television, were full of news of his exploits, of how he'd completely baffled the police. What did they expect? He was about his Lord's business; his Lord would protect him. But the words hurt sometimes. *Psychopath, maniac, sadist.* If they only knew the trust, he knew they'd praise him for his actions, acknowledge the righteousness of his lonely crusade.

Rapist was the word that hurt the most. True, he had fallen, once or twice, tempted beyond resistance by the naked, bruised body spread out before him. But that was their wickedness, not his. How could any man resist for long the wiles of a witch? He had scourged that weakness from himself now, and that printed lie at least had stopped.

Yes, the sin was gone, so he had thought. But now, standing before the wall emblazoned with her image, he felt the traitorous stirring in his groin. There could be no doubt now. The weak humanity in him knew the lure of her evil, was rising to point it out, for all to see. There could be no clearer sign.

He began to track her then, through the cavernous temples where she held her rites. Their very names were infamy to him. . .The Cave, The Pariah Club, Zone Zero. It cost him to pass through those hell-holes untainted,. The darkness, the sleek bodies in black and silver, even the thunderous, seductive rumble of her music, all had an allure that drew him, even though he could see the corrupt, rotting features of the damned beneath the painted faces and hear the laughter of demons in her soaring voice.

As the nights passed, he learned where she lived, what she looked like under her mask. It had surprised him at first, that the Queen of Darkness would look so. . .ordinary. Without the erotic allure of her paint, she was no more than a passably pretty young woman. Then he saw the subtlety of that trap and marvelled once again at the infinite, deceptive power of evil. No one, unmasking the witch Lilith, would see the danger in those pale features. And so would turn away, forgetting that they had ever suspected her.

Night after night, he watched her whirl about the stage, a lean black dervish. He listened to her voice wail out over the screaming crowds. Her songs were blasphemy, as wickedly seductive as her lithe body, her black-lipped mouth. She sang of shadows, and demon lovers, and the power of darkness. Night after night, he followed her home and crouched on the fire escape outside her window, watching the seemingly innocent rituals of her life.

He could have taken her a thousand times, but some voice inside told him the time was not right. This was no simple task he had set himself, this destruction of the greatest of Evil's whores. When the time came, he would know it.

The posters told him, just as they had led him to her. "Special Halloween Midnight Show."

The day of All Hallow's Eve dawned cold and gray. He barely noticed; the anticipation that surged through him made the world a flame in his eyes. All the weeks of waiting and watching would come to an end tonight. And so would his increasing nervousness, the itchy twitch between his shoulder blades that made him feel watched, and kept him away from her fire escape. Tonight, his great duty would be done. What would come after that, he did not know, but he distantly imagined a rapture that would trumpet him to heaven.

He was in the club early, pushing his way closer to the front than he had ever dared to go. Tonight he was stronger than all her rituals. Tonight, he was omnipotent.

The announcer took the stage at midnight, seizing the microphone and staring down at the costumed crowd. "Good evening," he drawled. "It's Halloween. Do you know where your soul is?"

The crowd around him surged and howled like the demons whose garb they affected. He knew where his soul was. He could feel it, bright and hungry, filling him. "Well, we're going to take it. . .we're going to shake it. . .and we're going to steal it. Because tonight, Zone Zero is proud to present our own Queen of Darkness. . .LILITH AND THE NIGHTWALKERS!"

The lights plunged out and around him he heard the crowd screaming her name. He was screaming too, he realized, in challenge.

The bass rumble began, then the heavy heartbeat of the drums, the wail of the guitar. Finally, as the music built to an ominous crescendo, came her voice, caressing the darkness.

"I'm on the night shift
Oh, tonight I'm waiting. . ."

He had not imagined she could be more wicked than before--but she was. Her eyes burned like amber flames and her body coiled and uncoiled on stage with savage grace. Her voice was incandescent. It burned along his nerves, sapping his strength. He found himself swaying and jumping with the tightly-packed crowd and when he tried to fight it, they seemed to laugh and push him closer to the stage.

He clung to his resolution, to the memory of the great responsibility with which he had been charged. He chanted the sacred instructions under his breath, a charm to ward off the pull of her voice, her eyes, her body.

"This song," she said, in a lull in the cacophony of sound, "is for someone out there. I know who you are. I know what you want." She

stared out over the crowd for a moment, then bent her dark head and began
to sing.

"You hear her singing, with a voice like temptation
Like the one you hear in your guignol dreams
Painting demons over throbbing drums
She's stealing souls in the steely hum
And you know, you know what she really means. . ."

She *knew*, he realized with shock. She knew. Knew he was there,
knew his mission, knew his very soul. The thought horrified and revolted
him. How could she know? Had she been toying with him all along,
sending out her decoys to tempt him, then the posters to draw him to her?

"You see her moving like a serpent in the garden
Like the one that leaves the fire in your veins
Just like all the good books say
Everyone's gonna thank you someday
Cause you know, you know they're all the same. . ."

He tried to turn, to flee that mocking, knowing voice, but he could
not move, hemmed in by the surging crowd. Fists pounded the air around
him, driving him forward. Desperately, he fumbled in his pocket for his
knife, anointed now with holy water and blessed in preparation for the
night's work. He clung to it like a talisman.

"As you're pulling down the shade
You can hear her calling
As you're reaching for the blade
You can see her falling
Just one touch and she'll be falling, falling, falling
Falling for you. . ."

She repeated the last line over and over, beckoning, cajoling. She
was on her knees, calling to him, her voice a promise. He felt his body
respond again, felt the rush of fire along his limbs and the heavy heat
centering in his groin.

"No!" he screamed, above the thunder of the music. "No!" She
could not do this to him. He had to make her stop. Had to end her evil now,
no matter what the cost.

The thin row of people between himself and the stage melted away,
then he was alone, scrambling up into the light. In its glare, time seemed to
stop. He saw her eyes widen in terror, her mouth open to scream. There

were shouts from his right and he half turned to stare into the black barrels of the guns. Distantly, he heard the policemen ordering him to freeze.

Why had she called them? he wondered. This had been between the two of them. Didn't she know that the battle between good and evil must always be fought alone? Betrayed, he turned back to face her.

The first bullet shattered his shoulder, spun him back to take the second through his chest. The din in his ears faded to a buzz of sound and the lights wavered over his head. Dimly, he realized he was lying down and couldn't remember how he'd gotten there. Where was she? He turned his head, his vision narrowing, and found her crouched in the arms of one of the policemen.

As the light went out, he thought he saw her smile.

Lilith sat on her bed and stared at the red-wrapped bundle in her lap. The candles, melted to mere stubs after their long duty the night before, cast flickering shadows across her face.

There was a sound from the street. Out of habit, she avoided glancing at the fire escape outside the shrouded window, where the dark figure had crouched so many nights. She let a long breath sigh out. Living out the routine of her life beneath the heavy weight of that mad gaze had been more draining than she thought, especially after the police had finally admitted the suspected identity of the voyeur.

They had managed, even in their self-congratulatory triumph, to remember to reprimand her for not telling them about the song, about her plan to lure the killer into their sights. How long could you have protected me? she had countered. All he had to do was wait. I wanted to end it once and for all.

Lilith shifted in her cross-legged stance on the tumbled sheets. She had not made the bed that morning, and the faint scent of sex hung in the air. It was a good thing he hadn't been outside her window last night, she thought, narrow lips quirking a little. Bedding Lieutenant Davis had been necessary, but that did not mean she had to find it unpleasant. What had followed had been equally necessary and, she reluctantly admitted, strangely more exciting.

Slowly, she unwrapped the red silk, one corner at a time. She began to hum, faint, lullaby-like tones that seemed the antithesis of the wild violence she conjured up on stage. She drew out, one by one, the objects the red flower in her lap unfurled to reveal.

Six bullets, the ones she had taken from Davis's gun the night before and replaced, after proper ritual, with ones she had purchased earlier. One spent shell, marked with symbols in red and black.

She stared at the last object for a moment. The cotton doll was clumsily made, features stitched roughly across its face, course brown yarn for hair. It was hard to create one without a possession of the person it was to represent; that was why there had been no room for subtlety in either its appearance or its purpose. The method had been crude, but the outcome certain. When she put her finger to the bullet hole in its chest, bits of charred cotton flaked away and clung to her skin.

She wondered absently what his name had been. She'd find out, no doubt, when the papers came out the next day. Whoever he was, he'd been right. Righter than he would ever know.

Singing softly, Lilith rose and headed for the incinerator shaft.

The Suction Method
RUDY KREMBERG

Rudy Kremberg's short stories have appeared in Canadian, U.S. and British publications. His work ranges from dark fantasy/horror to so-called mainstream. A full-time writer, Rudy has also published numerous articles on such topics as food, medical research, business and marketing procedures. Once considered a leading cheese expert, he wrote on the subject for various magazines and co-authored The Great Canadian Cheese Directory.

So just where do horror authors get their ideas? Rudy confides: "I got the idea for The Suction Method *while vacuuming my living-room carpet."*

Max Hoover was on the Persian carpet in the living room when the phone rang. He didn't get up until the fourth ring. The carpet, which was made of the finest silk, was almost too cozy: it had an addictive feel to it that not even the water bed upstairs could match. Katie, the redhead from across the street, moaned in protest.

"Might be Joanna at the airport," he told her. "Better answer it."

He remembered the last time he'd neglected to do just that. Half an hour after the ringing had stopped, Joanna had arrived in a taxi, back early from her parents' and peeved he hadn't been at her disposal to chauffeur her from the airport. His guest on that occasion had rushed out the side door without finishing her drink, and he hadn't heard from her since.

He picked up the receiver.

"Mr. Hoover?" It was a female voice, much softer and younger than Joanna's.

"Speaking."

"Mr. Hoover, Lucille from Family Carpet Cleaners. Your wife asked me to make an appointment with you."

He hesitated, fascinated by the voice. It was as smooth and seductive as the hand-knotted silk at his feet. Which reminded him: Joanna *had* mentioned she wanted the carpet cleaned. She was disgusted, she'd said before leaving for her parents', by the filth it had accumulated over the years.

"Yes, that's right," he told the voice, visualizing the mouth that went with it. The image that formed in his mind made him want to prolong the conversation. "I'm sorry, but I don't know much about cleaning carpets. Would this involve shampooing or steaming?"

"Not in your case. We'd use our own exclusive method. It works on a suction principle."

"You mean, like vacuuming?"

"Sort of. Only our method gets rid of a lot more dirt. It's the most thorough cleaning process there is. Works for any kind of material, too."

He traced one of the carpet's patterns with his naked toe, saw how much the colors had faded. Still, the carpet wasn't as badly off as Joanna kept making out. Unlike their marriage, which she had a funny habit of linking to the carpet whenever they got into a fight. Take the last one. She was going back to her parents and staying there, she'd vowed, unless the carpet was properly cleaned--and he decided to honor the "family commitment" he was supposed to have made when they'd got engaged. His answer to that, he recalled with satisfaction, had sent her packing: *If what you mean by family commitment is knocking you up and changing diapers, I'm not ready for it. And until I am, you're not going to suck me into--*

"Mr. Hoover? You there?"

"I was just thinking. Do you make house calls?"

"Sure do. As a matter of fact, this week we're offering a special introductory discount in your neighborhood."

He asked what that discount was. She quoted him a price that she said was based on the information his wife had given her. He pretended to mull it over.

"When can you come?"

"Well, I've got another job on your street late tomorrow. Will you be free in the evening?"

"Let me check my schedule." He glanced at Katie, who by now was getting dressed and looked as if she missed her husband. He lowered his voice. "Tomorrow would be fine. My wife's out of town, but I'll be here."

"Why, that's perfect."

He let the words sink in, just to be sure he'd heard them right. Then she set a time and had him confirm his address.

"Looking forward to seeing you, Mr. Hoover."

"And I'm looking forward to seeing you, Lucille."

He smiled as he hung up, and pictured her mouth smiling back.

He smiled again when he greeted her on his front doorstep the next evening. Yes, she was every bit as young and enticing as her voice had led him to expect. And it was her mouth that enticed him most of all. Those strikingly wide, lush crimson lips drew his attention like a magnet, making him overlook everything else for the moment. They beckoned him, blatantly and unabashedly. The whole mouth seemed to be simmering with a quiet but potent energy, waiting to do something dramatic.

He managed to look away at her long raven hair, then into her dark, shining eyes. The eyes were scanning him, as if taking his measurements. As for the rest of her, all of it except the hands and feet was hidden by a coat. Her fingers, he noticed, had no rings on them.

"Couldn't be better," he said, and let her in.

He helped her off with the coat. And when he saw what was underneath, his mouth fell open.

She was wearing black tights that hugged her body from the neck down, revealing the shapeliest legs and hips and breasts he had ever seen. Her physique was, quite simply, breathtaking. And so was the outfit. It was like a second skin, stretching seamlessly with every muscle she moved, making her look like the world's most supple ballerina.

"It's my working uniform," the girl said matter-of-factly. "It's made of a special elastic material."

"Forgive me for staring. It's just that I've never seen a . . . uniform quite like that."

"I understand. Most of my customers react exactly the same way."
She stepped into the living room. "So this is it. Must have cost a fortune."

He followed her gaze to the carpet and nodded, but he could only guess at the actual price. The carpet, along with the house, had been a wedding present from Joanna's well-heeled parents.

"I'm afraid it's been a little neglected," he said. "It gets vacuumed every once in a while, but there's something wrong with our vacuum cleaner. The suction's weak."

"I can see that." She crossed to the spot where he and Katie had been, stooped to pick something up.

"Your wife's?"

Her lips stretched into a disarming smile. He looked at the long strand of red hair she was holding.

"Must be," he answered nonchalantly.

She picked up another hair, a blond one. He stiffened.

"Oh, don't feel uncomfortable," she said. "Hairs are common. This is my fifth carpet today that's had them." The disarming smile widened. "I'm just here to make sure--" she stooped again, came up with a brown hair and black one "--your wife doesn't see them. Right?"

He stared at her, astonished and relieved. Astonished as much by the hairs--it hadn't occurred to him to check the carpet that closely--as by her directness. And relieved because she'd spared him the tiresome ritual of making excuses, of pretending.

"I bet you learn a lot about your customers from their carpets," he said, and it struck him that most of the hairs must have been there before Joanna had left. Had Joanna learned anything from that? Surely, if she'd noticed the hairs she would have assumed the worst and done something to get even with him by now--she was that type of bitch. But she hadn't. She'd prompted him to get the carpet cleaned, that was all.

"Yes, you'd be surprised," the girl from Family Carpet Cleaners said. She was still studying the carpet.

"What are you learning now?"

She shrugged. "Nothing much, except you've picked up a few years' worth of dirt and dust. No problem stains like red wine or blood. If you've got anything to hide, it isn't showing on your carpet. Unless you count the hairs."

They both laughed.

"I hope you don't think too badly of me," he said.

"Oh, it's nothing I can't stomach."

The mysterious dark eyes continued their survey of the carpet. There was a look of understanding in them, as if they knew about everything that had ever taken place on the luxurious silk. The intimate evenings he'd shared with Joanna long, long ago. The parties, the board games. The good times despite her parents' view of him as a fortune-seeking lowlife. Eventually the arguments. First over things like coordinating the furniture and choosing a second car, then over having kids and loving each other. Then the stormy visits from her father, the I-told-you-so diatribes, the threats to cut off financial support. And through it all, the affairs, the countless one-night and one-afternoon stands.

"It's too bad," the girl said, and he blinked at her. "About the carpet, I mean. It must have been beautiful when it was new." She turned to him. Her eyes lit up. "But I can make it beautiful again. In fact, I'll make it cleaner than it's ever been since you've had it."

Those beckoning lips defied all scepticism.

"Should I move the furniture?" he asked.

"No, I'll take care of all that." She went around to the windows, drawing the curtains. "Just give me twenty minutes to myself and I'll surprise you. In the meantime maybe you could fix us a drink."

Her mouth stretched into another smile, a smile filled with promises. God, this was too good to be true.

"What about your equipment? Can I give you a hand bringing it in?"

She shook her head. "I'll look after everything, thanks."

That smile made it impossible to argue. "Twenty minutes, okay? And no peeking. That would spoil the surprise."

He left her alone in the living room and stood in the hall, trying to convince himself she was for real. The living-room door closed. He waited, listening for sounds, but all he heard were her words echoing in his head: *I'll surprise you . . . I'll make it cleaner than it's ever been since you've had it.*

Great. But with *what*?

His curiosity became tinged with uneasiness. And impatience. Why did he have the feeling she was trying to suck him into something? Why, for chrissakes, was he letting a total stranger shut him out of his own living room?

He marched back to the door, put his head against it, and heard what sounded like a rapid succession of deep breaths. He gripped the doorknob. The noise abruptly stopped.

"I'll be with you soon, I promise."

The soft voice made him pause. He thought of her mouth again, and before he knew it he'd let go of the doorknob.

"Hurry up," he said lamely. "What can I get you to drink?"

"Whatever you're having."

He started for the bar in the rec room. No sooner had he reached the basement stairs than his curiosity and impatience returned in full force. He was thinking of going back into the living room when he looked through the window at the top of the stairs and saw a van parked in the driveway. It was night by now, but the light from the house was bright enough for him to make out the words painted on the side of the van:

FAMILY CARPET CLEANERS
Guaranteed In-Home Service
The Solution to Your Dirty Problems

Below that, there was a phone number. And, in smaller letters, the words "A Division of Beta Laboratories, Inc."

Beta Laboratories and Family Carpet Cleaners . . . what kind of an affiliation was that? He slipped out the side door, peered through the van's rear window, and saw a row of what looked like heavy-duty garbage bags. Four of them were on the floor, stuffed and sealed; a fifth was fastened to a stand, wide open, as if waiting to be filled. A beam of light fell on a prominent bulge in the nearest stuffed sack, and for a second the bulge reminded him of Katie's smooth buttocks.

He tried all the van's doors, found them locked, and went to the rec room. There was a Yellow Pages under the extension phone by the bar, and he took a quick look under "Laboratories". He came across a tiny ad for Beta Laboratories, Inc. "Genetic Engineering and Research," it said above the phone number and address. He helped himself to a shot of scotch, then filled two glasses with Dubonnet and headed upstairs. He was going to see what the hell the girl from Family Carpet Cleaners was up to.

When he got to the living room he set the glasses down and opened the door without knocking.

She was standing in the middle of the room, waiting for him, surrounded by a carpet so clean it actually seemed to glow. Once again, her smile left him defenceless.

"You've done a fantastic job," he found himself saying.

"I try."

"Amazing. Where did all the dirt go?"

The smile widened, pulling him closer. Was it the scotch, or had her stomach . . . stretched a little?

"Let's just say it's in temporary storage," she said, patting her belly. "When I've collected the rest of it I'll throw it up into the garbage. Then it's off to the incinerator."

He tried to back away from her but couldn't. A vision flashed before him: she was in the van, bent over the open sack, vomiting her guts out. The vision made him bite his lip, and the pain brought him back to his senses.

"The rest of it? I don't see any more dirt."

"There's just one more piece of it left," she said, her smile widening even further. "It's the biggest piece."

Her mouth suddenly stretched to a width of three or four feet, and there was a deafening rush of air all around him. For a brief moment he was sure this, too, was a fantasy. Then the words "Genetic Engineering and Research" sprang to mind, and nothing seemed too fantastic. By the time he realized he was being sucked headfirst into the mouth, it had already enveloped him in pitch darkness. He shot through a warm, narrow passageway, bouncing off slippery walls and making them expand, brushing against debris that felt like hairs and globs of dust. The debris thickened. Finally he crashed into a deep pile of it and came to rest. Dust invaded his nose and mouth, accompanied by an odd mixture of stale smells. Smells of grime and sweat, of after-shave and vaguely familiar perfume. Smells that reminded him of gum-chewing kids and household pets. He gasped for air, but there wasn't enough--he was suffocating. He tried to scream. The effort only robbed him of more air. Just before he blacked out he heard the muffled sound of a phone being dialed, and then, straight above him, the girl's soft young voice.

"Mrs. Hoover?" the voice said. "Lucille from Family Carpet Cleaners. You can come home now. Your carpet's clean."

Sasquatch

MEL. D. AMES

According to Webster's International Dictionary, *the Sasquatch is "a hairy manlike creature reported to exist in the northwestern U.S. and western Canada and said to be a primate between six and fifteen feet tall." In the Hamalayas they call him the Yeti or Abominable Snowman (ABSM for short). In the U.S. he's better known as Bigfoot. Whatever his moniker, this ambling nightmare may be one of the last unexplained mysteries of our rapidly shrinking world.*

British Columbia author Mel Ames tell us that in his years of adventuring he covered all of B.C. from Whitehorse to Osoyoos and from the Peace River to Port Alice on Vancouver Island. He leaves to our imagination whether he ever experienced anything like the events described in his new story.

...a frigid Arctic high is reported moving down from the Beaufort Sea, bringing unprecedented low temperatures to populated areas in the Yukon, Northwest Territories, and northern British Columbia. Five deaths have already been attributed to the plummeting thermometer and meteorologists cannot foresee any relief in sight, nor any meaningful shift in the system's relentless trek to the south...

Professor Elliot Danforth Bliss-White reached out with a mittened hand to click off the small battery radio. He looked with concern at the huddled shape of his wife, only her eyes and nose visible in the shadowed depths of her parka. Still, the eyes were enough, he thought, to betray the chilling fear that lurked beneath the surface anger.

"We've got to get out of here," she said icily. Her voice was a frail echo from inside the fur-trimmed hood, barely escaping enough for him to hear.

"*Alive,*" he added with emphasis.

"Alive? Christ Almighty, Elliot, anything's better than this, this--" her eyes swiveled as though in search of an appropriate image

" -- fucking ice hole."

He knew she could not see him smile. He had never, ever, heard her swear; even so, he was not entirely certain whether she had blasphemed him or the environment.

He reached back for a log to replenish the fire that burned at the open flap of the tent. More than half the canvas floor was given over to the wood they had gathered when the weather had begun to move in on them; the remaining space was an exercise in togetherness for two people on friendly terms. It was a refuge born of necessity, conceived in panic; yet it gave him an hiatus, of sorts, a time to assess their plight without haste, to further plan his research, and, to contemplate their subsequent safe return to civilization.

"And all for a goddamn monkey. Flatfoot-- "

"*Bigfoot,*" he interjected patiently. "In Canada, we call it Sasquatch."

"Whatever. And if you find it -- then what?"

He stirred the fire without answering.

"What if it attacks us?" she persisted.

"I've got the Remington 30:06, as you know -- take out a bull moose at fifty yards."

"But you won't use it." Her words were laced with derision.

"Not if I can help it, Liz. You know that. I'd rather shoot it with the camera."

"Christ Almighty," she muttered helplessly.

They had been dropped off about a hundred and fifty miles south of the Yukon border, well into the Strikine Range of the Cassiar Mountains, in northern British Columbia. The three day hike on snowshoes, in from Cry Lake, could peg their base camp somewhere near the foot of Dark Mountain, a towering juggernaut of snowbound rock and timber. A beer-guzzling bush pilot had flown them in, landing with skis on the frozen surface of the lake, then leaving in reckless haste with a slurred promise to pick them up in ten days. Thinking back, Elliot began to doubt whether the man would be capable of remembering the day of rendezvous, much less the remote landing site.

The trek in from Cry Lake had not been easy, laden down with supplies and gear, but the weather had been good and their get-along even better. Give Liz credit, there; her sturdy underpinnings had proven to be almost as enduring as his own, an honest legacy of being country born and bred. *Continuing blue skies and seasonal temperatures,* the weather-man had predicted. That was before the cold high had begun to drift south over the God-forsaken tundra, dragging with it the frigidity of the Arctic winter. The snow had come first; they had seen it moving in on them, pushed from behind by the cold front like a great white swirling cloud, too heavy with snow to even get off the ground. It had scarcely given them time to set up camp and gather wood before it overwhelmed them.

"Just a short hike in from the lake, *you said.* A quick look around, *you said.* We'll be back out and home before you know it, *you said.* Shit--"

"Shut up, Liz."

Elliot's quiet reproof brought her bickering to an abrupt halt. He had never seen her like this. From the time he had first known her, she had never been anything but prudently reserved, almost taciturn; an innately shy person, even in their marriage bed, in spite of her barnyard beginnings. This was an entirely new Liz, a Liz he did not know; a mutant, of a kind, born of fear and frustration.

He got to his feet and ventured out into the fading twilight, cautiously skirting the open fire. The sky had cleared, sending the mercury hurtling down, well below the frosty 40s where Celsius and Fahrenheit had met briefly in cold accord. No sound, not even a cold-riven plaint of bird or beast disturbed the pervasive hush, nor could he detect a solitary rift in the veneer of total whiteness. Perfect. He could not have imagined a more promising arena. Even the bitter cold would now be to his advantage, forcing anything born of flesh and blood to forage down at lower, more accessible levels. But the light would be gone within the hour; he would have to delay his search until morning.

They slept apart, preferring not to add the chill of their own disaffection to that of the night. Elliot dozed fitfully, rising every hour to fuel the fire, his broken sleep troubled by real or imagined fancies; disembodied shadows creeping in with the encroaching cold as the fire darkened, only to recede in the fresh glare of a rekindled fire. At one time, during the night, a grim delirium had menaced his thoughts just prior to waking; a fleeting spate of sounds, the crunch and squeak of dry-cold snow beneath a heavy foot, heel then toe, *crunch squeak,* the tenuous echoes suspended in air as keen and sheer as glacial ice. Then, when he turned an ear -- silence.

Utter silence.

Elliot awoke at first light to a world suddenly gone mad. A bitter wind had come whipping in just before dawn, out of the northeast, scooping up a mountainside of dry surface snow along the way, then hurling it back down in stinging, blinding sheets at the beleaguered campsite. Visibility was reduced to the width of a grizzly's grin, and not a decibel of sound could prevail over the incessant shriek of driven snow beyond the fire. Never in his memory had Elliot seen a whiteout of such magnitude.

Liz had retreated as far back in the wind-tossed tent as the ever-depleting cache of wood would allow, her haunted stare bearing mute witness to the lingering depths of her wretchedness. To Elliot, the ugly turn of weather meant yet another frustrating delay in his search for the elusive man-beast he had come to find, and he hunkered down beside the fire to ponder his limited options.

The expedition, as such, had begun to take shape in Elliot's mind when first he heard of a 'sighting' by two American game hunters. Their story had an unique quality in the telling of it; a subtle ring of authenticity that he could not ignore. The fact that they were hunting out of season, without licences or game tags, seemed only to add validity to their alleged experience.

The two men had reportedly left their 4x4 camper at Boya Lake Provincial Park, about sixty miles north of Cassiar, off Highway 37. There, they had switched to snowmobiles for the long trek up the frozen Four Mile River bottom in search of 'game.' *Any bloody thing that moved,* their Canadian counterparts had ventured dryly, revealing an inherent distrust of any south-of-the-border yarn that brinked on *braggadocio.* Still, Elliot reasoned, if their story was to be believed at all, it would be well beyond the river's source, up into the shadowy northern slopes of Dark Mountain, where the sighting would have occurred.

They had doubled up on one machine for the day, they said, to conserve fuel, and had just rounded a low ridge at the bottom of an easy draw; a blind draw, they soon discovered, and while manoeuvring to get the sled turned around and headed back out, they were assailed by a stench so pervasive and vile they paused to investigate. On foot, and about a hundred and fifty feet from the idling snowmobile, they suddenly froze in their tracks. Directly ahead, and for no apparent cause, a large drift of snow began to disintegrate. They looked on in awe, then in paralysing fear, as the tawny form of a long-haired man-like beast began to emerge from the drift, straightening up out of its snowy lair to a height of *"twenty friggin' feet, fur'n all!"*

"How high?" someone had sniggered.

"Twenty feet, man. *An' that's a friggin' fact.*"

And when it turned its head (they freely admitted), to bend its brute face in their direction, seeking them out with fierce yellow eyes and a malevolent deep-throated growl, they found their legs and fled in terror.

The mindless panic, in Elliot's view, was unnecessary. The creature would have been as equally startled as the two hunters, and, given time to react, would likely have slunk away of its own accord, into the forested shelter of the surrounding hillside.

But whatever it was they had seen that day, man or beast, or something of both, it had so terrorized the two Americans, they left behind the idling snowmobile in their haste to get away. Elliot had remembered; and on the flight in to Cry Lake, with some grudging assistance from the pilot, he had spotted the abandoned snowmobile from the air.

Not conclusive proof, Elliot conceded, that Sasquatch was alive and well and roaming the remote slopes of Dark Mountain; but it was obvious that the Americans had seen *something,* something horrendous enough to make them flee in a state of fear, and Elliot was more determined than ever to find out what that something was.

The anticipated delay due to weather did not endure; at least, not beyond 10 AM that same morning. The bitter wind had ebbed and died as suddenly as it had begun, the sun reappearing like a pale pearl in a cold uncluttered sky. By 10:30, Elliot was dressed, fully equipped, and ready to leave the campsite.

"You'll be all right," he said to Liz. "there's plenty of food, and wood. If I'm not back by nightfall, don't get to worrying. Just stay put."

"Don't go, Elliot. I don't want to be alone out here."

"There's nothing to be afraid of. Good God, Liz. Just keep the fire going, okay?"

"What if an animal -- a bear -- a grizzly -- ?"

"You'd have to wake it up first," he told her patiently, "they're all in hibernation."

"I don't even have a gun," she whined, oblivious to his logic.

"As if you'll bloody need one."

Still, he shrugged the sling off his shoulder and propped the Remington against the pile of wood beside his wife. He rummaged in one of the packs for the .45 Colt revolver he knew to be there, checking the cylinder for a full load before strapping the holster to his belt.

"The rifle's loaded," he said as he slipped a handful of live .45 rounds into an outer pocket, "and there's one in the breach. Just flip off the safety--"

"Please don't go."

"I can't *not* go, Liz. It's why were here, remember? Besides, if we allow ourselves three days to get back to Cry Lake, the same time it took us coming in, it only leaves me today and tomorrow to do what I've come to do." He ducked out of the tent. "I'll be back as soon as I can."

Liz moved to the open flap to watch him go, her eyes brooding on his retreating back until he disappeared into a stand of snow-laden conifers.

Elliot headed due west, his snowshoes sinking to an awkward depth in the heavy drifts of new snow. He had pegged his position at roughly the same level on the mountains' northern flank as the discarded snowmobile, and should he maintain his initial pace, he fully expected to intercept the vehicle sometime before nightfall. In fact, with a bit of luck, he might even meet up with the creature itself. He dropped a reassuring hand to his waist where his camera was warmly couched in its insulated leather case, primed for instant use.

By noon, he had begun to flag a little; he had not reckoned too well with the subzero Arctic air and the debilitating effects it could have on mortal flesh and blood. He had dressed warmly enough, but, he could not totally escape the cold's crippling grip, nor avoid inhaling the frozen fire that burned his lungs with every breath. Now and then, he would have to pause to slow his breathing, and he utilized those precious moments to check for frostbite, and to munch on chunks of frozen chocolate, the manna of the north.

The sun had passed its winter's apogee when Elliot thought to uncover his watch. The time was 2:17 PM. He had begun to notice a subtle change in the lay of the terrain and as he topped a momentary rise, he was not surprised to see the distant inclination of the Four Mile River bottom winding away to the north. He was right on track. And a half mile farther along, in an open clearing, he stumbled onto the abandoned snowmobile, half buried in a wind-whipped wreath of snow.

He cleared the surplus snow from the vehicle, then began a thorough check. The fuel tank was better than half full, the motor having apparently stalled soon after being abandoned, and there was plenty of extra gas in a couple of jerricans secured to the pillion rack. And the oil had been topped up. In the saddlebags, he found an assortment of tools, extra oil, spare goggles and a balaclava (which he donned, then and there), emergency rations (bully beef and hardtack), matches and a small pressurized can of ether, no doubt for cold morning starts. There was also a well-detailed contour map of the entire Four Mile River area and a wide stretch of Dark Mountain's northern slopes. To their credit, the Americans had come well prepared.

Without the can of ether, there would have been little hope of resurrecting a fragile spark from the all but frozen battery. And the oil, which had chilled to the viscosity of cold tar, further exacerbated his attempts to get the motor running. But tinkering with old cars had been something of a hobby with Elliot in his adolescent years, and the basic skills acquired then boded well for him now as, after a spate of testy frustrations, he finally managed to coax the reluctant motor to life.

To Elliot, the sweet sound of the smoothly running motor was a symphony of renewed hope and liberation. He now had a whole new time frame in which to function. Not only could he freely come and go to this same area where Sasquatch had been sighted (or most any other area, for that matter), but the scheduled trip back to Cry Lake for their rendezvous with the airplane, could now be safely delayed by at least two full days.

And there was yet another bonus to warm his gelid blood, one he had not foreseen; once running, the snowmobile became a small but welcome oasis of warmth in an otherwise unrelieving desert of bitter cold.

The long northern twilight was already well advanced when he began the return trip. He followed his own trail, keeping the speed of the snowmobile down to a cautious easy glide. Shadows fled before the headlamp as he navigated the dark and eerie stands of timber, and in the clearings, a scintilla of icy diamonds littered the open path ahead; it was an endless alternating witchery of gloom and glitter. He was within a mile of the campsite when he heard the scream.

It was a blood-chilling shriek of terror. Even over the whine of the snowmobile, Elliot was certain he had recognized the voice of his wife. He shut down the motor and coasted to standstill. He waited, harking into the brittle hush of night for the sound to come again. But seconds later, it was the hollow crack of a rifle that rent the air, and then, before *that* sound had time to die, another scream came careening across the mountain slope like a demented banshee fleeing the wrath of hell.

In spite of the echoes that ricocheted about from tree to tree, from bluff to snowy bluff, Elliot had little doubt the screams and the rifle shot had come from the same direction. The campsite, dead ahead. He put the snowmobile in motion and raced forward, coolly indifferent to the threat of hidden rocks or windfalls.

He shot out of the stand of conifers that fringed the campsite, onto a scene that left him numb with shock. He could see no sign of life, but the camp was in total disarray. The tent lay flat against the snow and only a faint wisp of blue smoke rose from the smouldering bed of the fire. On drawing closer, he could make out the heavily trodden snow around the tangle of the tent, and some twenty feet beyond, in the swath of white light from the headlamp, he caught a flash from the polished metal of the Remington rifle, embedded muzzle first, deep into the trunk of a giant fir.

It was a pantomime of utter chaos.

And there was more. As he groped beneath the sprawling canvas to retrieve a flashlight, then to ensure that Liz was not still there in some grisly state of collapse, he spotted a small pool of blood, still warm to the touch. It marked the beginning of a thin red trail leading out of the tent, west, then south, up into the snow-laden jungle above the campsite.

But even more disconcerting, was a single set of gargantuan footprints that appeared to have meandered into the camp from the west, only to double back in a deeper and more direct path, with the foreboding trail of blood in their wake. Elliot stood long and silent over one snowy imprint;

from the clear indentation of a round narrow heel to the fanning out of five well-defined humanoid toes, he guessed the foot that made it to be a full eighteen inches in length.

And the creature to which the foot belonged? He could only speculate.

Elliot's first concern was understandably the welfare of his wife. From what he had pieced together, he could only assume that either she had fled the tragic scene and was presently hiding somewhere in the surrounding forest, or, she had been carried off bodily by the beast to its lair, out of reach of rescue, at least until daylight. He saw no alternative but to act on the assumption that she had fled the camp, and was out there even now, waiting for some sign of his return.

He began at once to build a roaring fire, far in excess of his own needs; a beacon Liz would be able to spot from miles off. And he set about restoring some order to the ravaged camp. With splints hewn from the firewood, he lashed together the fractured tent poles and retied or replaced guy ropes that had been violently torn strand from strand. Luckily, the tent's canvas had not been breached.

Later that evening, while nursing a dollop of medicinal brandy from the first aid kit, Elliot sat ruminating before the fire. He had spent an hour reclaiming the use of the tent, and another circling the open northern sector of the campsite with the flashlight, looking for some sign, anything, to strengthen the premise that Liz had left of her own accord. But the only trail in the snow that had intersected his own, other than the track of the snowmobile, was the one he had already seen of the beast, coming and going from a point just west and south of the campsite. Then, to add to his growing despair, when he went to retrieve the rifle, his attempts to pull it from the tree had been tantamount to withdrawing Excalibur from the Stone. Even with his full body weight suspended from the jutting stock, the rifle had not budged a hair.

What manner of brute force, he wondered, could have driven the rifle barrel so deeply into the vice-like grip of living hardwood?

Then, he felt the hair on his head lift in a prickly sweat as another piercing scream suddenly cleaved the dark beyond the fire. It seemed to come spilling down the mountain from somewhere behind him; a sonic avalanche of unspeakable torment and terror. And before the last echoes of the scream had died, it came again. He covered his ears to shut it out but it was already pealing through his skull. And through the long dark hours, it came again to haunt him, and again, and again. By dawn the screams had stopped, but the harrowing night had left him physically and emotionally drained.

The frigid temperatures had not abated and the light of day did little to lessen the raw chill of the mountain air beyond the fire. There had been no new snow, and the tracks, and the trails, and the blood, were even more foreboding now than they had been by flashlight. Elliot's first thoughts were of Liz, but the snowmobile became his priority. He coaxed the mulish motor to life with a healthy dose of TLC and ether, then left it idling while he breakfasted on beef jerky, hardtack and coffee.

He struck camp with the snowmobile loaded and ready to travel well before noon. The day, he knew, would be short; a prolonged sunless dawn for the most part, and a lingering twilight, with only a brief pale sun intervening, low in the winter sky. The monstrous footprints, the blood trail and the impaled rifle had already been duly committed to film. He had juxtaposed a number of everyday articles beside and within the footprints, leaving no doubt as to their comparative dimensions. And he had set the camera on time-lag to show himself hanging bodily from the stock of the rifle while it remained firmly embedded in the giant fir. Whatever the exigencies of the moment, he had no intention of going back to a scoffing public empty-handed, without some evidence to support the circumstances that had given rise to Liz's bizarre abduction.

Where is it written, he mused, that he should be morally bound to go charging up the mountain in a one-man-cavalry rescue mission (without a rifle) in what could well be an exercise in utter futility? And was it reasonable to expect, after last night's appalling ordeal, that an attempt to rescue Liz now, would amount to anything more than a token show of manly heroics? Still, a simple compromise, he fudged, with a wry twist of logic, a cursory look about for instance, might go a long way to ensure the retention of both his perceived gallantry and his elitist skin.

It was with this mind-set that Elliot mounted the snowmobile and headed cautiously up the mountain, vowing to himself that he would not venture beyond an apparent point of safe return. He followed the blood trail, winding through the trees and along a narrow path strewn with half-hidden deadfalls and rocky outcrops. It became increasingly more difficult to manoeuvre as the slope steepened and after covering less than a mile, he made the decision to terminate the arduous ascent.

The trail ahead was virtually impassable by snowmobile and the thought of parking the vehicle and proceeding on foot was an option that Elliot found quite untenable. He had no desire to put himself at further risk, to offer himself up on a platter for the beast's engorgement. Any doubts he might have once entertained of the Sasquatch's inherent bent to evil, he now acknowledged freely. How could he forget that long night of his wife's torment, or even his own demeaning role in the same ugly spectacle?

He spat a foul invective into the bitter cold as he struggled to jockey the heavy sled into a tight U-turn. The motor coughed, stalled and died. The silence that ensued was overwhelming. An irrational rush of panic seized him, and in his haste to restart the motor, he caused it to flood. The acrid stench of raw gas drifted up to heighten his alarm, and his mind gravitated darkly and at once, to thoughts of the beast.

Why, he fretted, could he not deny this goading need of his eyes to sweep the dimly-lit depths of the surrounding forest? There was nothing there, he told himself, nothing but phantoms and shadows. Phantoms, indeed, and shadows, *he knew inwardly,* that would loom larger, lurk more darkly, be infinitely more menacing than anything he might ordinarily encounter, even here, in the sinister haunts of the beast's own habitat. And could *they* be real, he wondered, those abominable sounds he was hearing? The faint whisper of some*thing* moving just beyond his vision; footsteps (heel then toe, *crunch, squeak)* in the deep untrodden snow?

He tried the starter again, applying full throttle in an attempt to blow the residue of gas from the flooded head. The motor ground over slowly, interminably, while icy chills of doubt and dread crept down his spine. When finally the vehicle roared to life, he sent it careening off in a fusillade of backfires and billowy black smoke.

Coasting down the mountain was noticeably smoother than the climb; he was able to follow his own tracks and the snowmobile surged effortlessly ahead without the uphill grade to contend with. In his haste, he allowed his speed to creep up on him and he frequently had to brake back hard to make a turn or avoid a rocky crag. On one such manoeuvre, Elliot failed to correct in time.

It was midway through a tight curve, as he tried to avoid a knife-like extrusion of solid granite, where the snowmobile made critical contact, ripping away the front skid from its umbilical moorings. The vehicle came to a jarring stop and Elliot went soaring over the windscreen, into the arms of a resilient sapling. Unhurt, but shaken with dismay, he surveyed the damage.

The sled was beyond repair. Even with a modern shop at his disposal, he could not have made it serviceable without the luxury of new parts. Grimly, he built a backpack of bare essentials from the supplies he had loaded onto the snowmobile, then, back on snowshoes, he started off down the mountain.

With *shank's mare* now his only means of locomotion, he thought it prudent to strike out at once for Cry Lake. There was no way of knowing when the weather might again turn ugly, and, even more compelling, was the desire to put distance between himself and an unpredictable creature that had suddenly become an even greater threat since his loss of the snowmobile.

As he passed through their deserted camp, he tried again to dislodge the rifle from the tree, without success. It would have been a comfort to him, a means of protection he could have administered from a distance, without having to risk an encounter at close quarters, a distressing requisite for the .45 to be effective.

Still, he had no regrets on leaving. He had the photographs and a story to go with them; at least as much as he would care to tell. There would be plenty of time to decide on a credible account of what had happened; how Liz had been abducted by the beast, how he had risked his life to try to save her--

He smiled wanly. In three days he would be long gone; the mountain, the beast, Liz--yes, even Liz--would be nothing more than a macabre memory. But as he turned to begin the long trek back to Cry Lake, a sudden piercing shriek came cascading down from the murky heights of the mountain, and he felt his stomach tighten in a knot of terror.

She was still alive! Holy Christ. But what was it doing to her? *It* was a brute beast, he reminded himself, a *brute beast,* nothing more. It was *not* a thinking, scheming creature intent on evil and mayhem. And yet, he could not but wonder, *would it now come after him?* And if it did, would the fact that Liz was female - and he was not - ? He shrugged the ugly thought from his mind and with one final, fearful glance behind, he moved hastily away, but he could not so easily shrug away a visceral tug of regret and guilt.

He did not cover the distance he had hoped, that first day. Frequent backward glances and a preoccupation with a nervous peripheral vigilance, did not make for rapid flight. Still, he'd had a late start, and so he carried on deep into the gathering twilight before stopping to make camp.

A fire was his first priority, for protection as well as warmth, then the rounding up of enough fuel to see him through the night. He had left the tent behind, opting for a lighter backpack in lieu of comfort, but there was still the need for shelter of a kind. He set about weaving together a rough bivouac from boughs of long-needled bull pine, then finally anchoring the finished lattice in against a steep of solid granite. With the rock wall at his back, the fire at his threshold, and the .45 at his side, he felt relatively secure.

Nevertheless, he lay awake for hours, wrapped snugly in his eider-down, listening to the nocturnal sounds of the northern forest; a night owl hooting hauntingly, a vagrant breeze whispering softly in his ear, and more than once being startled by the explosive crack of heartwood freezing in the subzero cold. But at some point during the long dark hours, those same sounds lulled him into fitful slumber.

He was not certain when he woke, what had aroused him; the sinister sounds of animal-like snuffling close at hand, or the reeking stench of some putrid presence lurking just beyond the darkened fire? There was no moon; the only light came dimly off the snow. Yet it was enough to reveal to Elliot a monstrous looming shadow, deeper, darker than the rest, inching toward him.

He snapped suddenly, fully alert. What *else* could it be? So huge? Smelling like that? His hand moved to the .45 and he drew it soundlessly from under the eiderdown, to point it directly at the encroaching shadow. It could not have been more than twenty feet from him when he fired.

The report was deafening. It rent the night like a clap of thunder and sent ear-piercing shards of alarm ricocheting off in all directions. And above it all, he heard a guttural yelp of pain. The shadow seemed to dissolve then before his eyes, and as he lowered the smoking gun, Elliot could hear the noisy retreat of something, some *thing*, as it hastily sought the safety of distance.

Only when the quiet of the winter night had once more closed in around him, did Elliot experience any reaction. He began to violently tremble. With nervous fingers, he fumbled with the cylinder of the gun to eject the spent cartridge, then to reload with a live round from his pocket. He could still smell the vile creature, hear its sudden cry of pain. Was he rid of it now, he wondered? Or would it pursue him still, wounded, more dangerous than ever?

The tracks of the beast could be seen at early light, along with a small showing of blood. He did not linger over the mute testimony of the footprints, identical in every way to those he had seen at the Dark Mountain campsite. Just a few quick photographs while he brewed coffee to fill his thermos, and then he struck camp. He could hardly wait to get the place well behind him. What if he hadn't woken up? What if that damn thing had gotten to him?

The first few miles were easy going. He munched on jerky and chocolate, and paused occasionally for a gulp of hot coffee. By mid-afternoon he began to feel more at ease. He had come upon some open ground where the snow was less deep, having been whipped away by the wind and piled in against the tree line. And he began to make better progress. The threat of the beast at his back seemed less imminent as he traversed the rock-strewn treeless slopes, where visibility was almost a mile on either side and the trail ahead lay open and inviting.

But he knew he could not evade the concealment of the trees indefinitely. He would be needing the wood the forest provided to build and sustain another fire, soon, and he kept alert for a likely campsite. The light of the day had almost deserted him before he saw what he wanted. It was a shallow east-west draw that was wreathed on three sides by a dense growth of spindly lodgepole pine, an almost impenetrable tangle of brittle limbs and rotting deadfalls. The likelihood of being surprised by anything larger than a squirrel, that would not first be heard approaching, or seen coming up the draw, was remote. It was, he decided, the perfect refuge, with only one proviso in the guarantee of a safe sojourn. He would have to remain awake.

There was no time, nor any suitable material with which to build a bivouac, even had he wanted to. Instead, he carved a sloping bed for his eiderdown into the deep snow, with his back to the lodgepole and his elevated head facing the open draw. There, in the glare of the fire, he had visibility and audibility both, and the .45 at the ready should either fail.

The night was long. The flickering fire reconnoitred the darkness around him like a curious hand with a spread of glowing fingers, fingers frustratingly too short or too dimly lit to reveal the evil that lurked just beyond their reach. He fought the desire to sleep, to close his heavy eyelids, to succumb to the overwhelming fatigue of his body, until, at long last, the sky in the east began to lighten.

He rose from his bed and began to gather his gear. Lightheaded from lack of sleep, he chuckled wryly as he filled the thermos, slid into his snowshoes and shouldered his pack. Was he free at last, he wondered? Free to keep his rendezvous at Cry Lake? Free, finally, to fly out of this frozen Hell -- ?

And then, before he'd taken a single step toward the east and freedom, he heard the cracking and crunching of something unaccountably large moving through the withered jungle of lodgepole pine, slowly closing the distance between them with an almost laughably awkward caution

It could not be anything but Sasquatch. No other forest creature would have any point or purpose in tearing its winter hide to shreds for the sake of a short detour through so painful a gauntlet. Could it be delirious from loss of blood, running rabid with infection? Or was it so obsessed with the hate of its prey that its inherent animal instincts had begun to malfunction? And what of Liz? Where was she now, he wondered? *How* was she? How long had it been since he'd heard that tormented scream?

He turned to face the gray new day with a troubled heart, only minutes ahead of his pursuer.

By midmorning, the open rocky slopes had petered out, and an old-growth stand of towering conifers stood before him. He paused at the edge of the tree line for a few swallows of coffee, a lump of frozen chocolate, and as he looked behind him, he could see nothing but his own tracks winding back over an endless stretch of snow.

There was something about the sky that bothered him. It had been coming on slowly through the morning; a sameness of sky and snowpack that made one indistinguishable from the other. Where there was no backdrop of trees or rocky outcrop, there was no horizon. To seasoned denizens of the Canadian north, Elliot knew, it was a phenomenon known as a 'snow sky,' an infallible precursor to a significant fall of snow.

Nothing seemed to be boding well for him. He was no longer sure of what day it was in the ten-day time frame he had planned so meticulously, or how many days were left before the plane was due to land on Cry Lake. And even in the event that he got there on time, would the plane be able to make it down in this atrocious weather?

Still, what choice was there but to press on? He capped the thermos and shoved it back into his pack, and as he turned, one final backward glance made him freeze in his tracks. In the midst of the unbroken whiteness that now lay behind him, a black object suddenly appeared, like a fly on a sheet of blank paper; then as quickly, it shrank from sight. The distance was too great for him to ascribe to it a silhouette that was certain or even vaguely familiar, but there was no doubt in Elliot's mind as to what it was.

He wasted no time in idle speculation. He simply had to stay ahead of that damnable creature if he was ever to get out alive. But the snow was deep in the forest and the going was slow. He no longer looked over his shoulder; his world had shrunk around him to a few dozen feet in any direction.

He would *hear* the cursed thing before he saw it.

By noon, the snow had begun to fall, a virtual fog of small dry flakes that reduced his visibility even further. He had to rely on his compass to keep him on a straight easterly path, and he wondered idly how the beast would fare in this new arena. It probably had a compass of blood and guts built into its ugly head. He had little doubt that the new snow would cover his tracks, but he could only guess at the *modus operandi* of the stalker. Sight, scent, or naked animal instinct - what did it matter?

His lack of sleep began to tell on him. Every bone in his body was a source of agony; every step forward, a harrowing nexus in the ritual of survival. There was no end to the trees, and the snow, and the pain, and the maniacal vision of the beast at his back, impelling him on, and on, and on--

And then suddenly he was falling. The snowy mantle on which he trod had given way under his feet, and he was tumbling down in an awkward forward roll, in a fog of swirling snow. He came to an abrupt halt with his right leg twisted under him. His head flew back and struck something solid, and the white fog of snow turned suddenly dark.

Elliot opened his eyes to a cloudless slate-colored sky. Above him, a small vapid sun peeked down through the snow-laden branches of a giant fir. The air was a thin vapor of fire and ice. His head throbbed oppressively and a dull pervasive pain seemed to emanate from somewhere in the vicinity of his right leg. He could see now where he had fallen; a chute-like furrow down the face of a precipitous bluff, where a small avalanche of snow and forest debris had fallen with him, and into which he now lay buried. Only his head and his left arm were clear of the snow.

He must have been out for hours. By the height of the sun, he guessed it to be mid-morning of the following day. He checked for frostbite, but apart from a throbbing headache and a mildly sprained ankle, he seemed in moderately good fettle. The cocoon of snow into which he had slid had surely saved him from a frozen death.

He had little difficulty in extricating himself from his snowy prison. He had landed facing the steep bluff and when he turned to see what lay behind him, he was mildly surprised to see there were no trees, just a vast expanse of level snow for as far as he could see. Of course - it was Cry Lake! He had fallen from a bluff on the lake's southern shoreline. He was elated! Had it not been for the blinding snowfall--

And it was then he heard it.

At first, he thought it was nothing more than the painful throbbing of his head, but as it grew louder, he realized it was the sound of a motor. Sweet Jesus --*it was the plane!* He could not see it, but as the minutes passed, the whine and the whir of the motor became more distinct and recognizable.

And then he saw something else that was also distinct and recogniz-able. Atop the same buff from which he had fallen, but farther along the lake edge, there stood a dark, hulking silhouette, its hirsute anthropoid head tilted skyward, apparently listening to the approaching aircraft but, as yet, seemingly unaware of his own presence.

Elliot crouched there, motionless, heart pounding, within sight and sound of his dreaded pursuer. Perhaps it was the proximity of the brute, the visual reality of the *Myth,* that made something stir deep within him, something that was beginning to transcend the raw craven fear that had driven him so blindly into such a total funk. *The cursed thing had not only taken his wife from him, it had almost robbed him of his self respect--*

his very manhood, every decent thing he had ever stood for. Live or die, he was now as much a victim of this frigid Hell as poor Liz.

He could feel a livid anger rising in his gorge, an overwhelming surge of venom that he could not swallow back, and on sheer impulse, he leapt suddenly to his feet with a mindless roar of unspeakable rage. A silence followed that was so intense, even the sound of the approaching aircraft was momentarily stilled. And as the ugly head turned toward him, seeing him, Elliot straightened, body weak with fatigue and pain, and he met the eyes of the beast with a calm, if somewhat fearsome loathing.

The plane screamed by, sideslipping to lose height, to shorten its approach, directly over the bizarre tableau on the ground. Elliot saw the creature duck, then bolt in panic as the aircraft skimmed the tree tops. He could see the pilot at the controls as the plane glided by, then settled down onto the frozen surface of the lake. As he hobbled wearily toward it, his thoughts were no longer of the beast, but of Liz.

''Where's the woman?'' the pilot asked as he stepped from the plane. He looked to be in the same incipient state of inebriation as when he had dropped them off ten days ago.

''Had a bit of trouble,'' Elliot told him. He nodded toward the plane. ''You got a rifle in there?''

''Yeah. Why? Where's your woman?''

''Back at Dark Mountain,'' Elliot said. He had no intention of going into detail. ''I'm going to need some help to get her out. I'd like you to get Search and Rescue in there as soon as possible.''

''Sure. I'll radio ahead.'' He hesitated. ''You mean you ain't coming out with me?''

''I'm staying.''

''It might help if they had someone to guide them in.''

''They'll spot the camp easily enough. A large clearing, north of Dark Mountain. Plenty of room to land a chopper. A trail leads up the mountain, south from the camp.''

''That where she is? Is she hurt?''

''Could be. What about that rifle?''

The pilot climbed back into the plane and reappeared with an old Lee-Enfield 303, the wood barrel casing and shoulder sling still intact.

''My old man brought it back from WW2. I ain't fired it myself, mind, but the way he tells it, it sure helped send a mess of them Nazis off to

Glory.'' He handed the rifle and a clip of eight rounds to Elliot. ''That's all the ammo I got.''

''That ought to do.'' Elliot took the rifle and slid the eight rounds into the magazine, snapping it back up in place. He worked the bolt to lever one round into the breach. ''Any spare rations?''

Once again the pilot made a sally into the plane's cabin. He returned with a small canvas-wrapped bundle. ''Emergency tuck. Last you a week.''

Elliot stuffed the bundle into his knapsack. ''Thanks,'' he said, ''I owe you.''

''You don't owe me nothin'.'' The man seemed suddenly, sadly sober. ''Your lady hurt bad back there?''

Elliot turned away so the man could not see the moisture that had risen to his eyes. ''Let's hope not.''

''Well,'' the pilot said lamely, ''good luck.'' Then, in afterthought, ''I spotted a bear, or something, up on the ridge as I was coming in. Best watch your back.''

''No bear about this time of year,'' Elliot said offhandedly.

''Yeah--guess you're right, but you never know--big bugger, though, whatever it was.''

A few moments later, Elliot heard the plane's door slam shut, and only then, through misted eyes, did he turn to watch the aircraft gather speed across the lake, sending a rooster-tail of snow billowing in its wake.

He thought again of Liz. Oddly, he felt closer to her now than he ever had. Was she still alive, he wondered? What, in fact, had the creature done to her? And what hope was there now for *him,* even with the rifle and the .45? At this moment, a mess of Nazis seemed somehow less formidable than the seemingly unrelenting fury of the Sasquatch--the mythical mountain monster he had come to find, intending to shoot only with his camera.

He waited until the plane had dwindled to a black speck in the northern sky before he turned and headed directly toward the spot where he had last seen the beast. If he could just keep the creature busy until the S & R team got to Liz.

Here, he thought, was the moment of truth. It would be either him, or it. There was not enough room in this God-forsaken land for both of them. He hurried forward. There would be tracks in the new snow.

———————— ✳ ————————

Grist for the Mills of Christmas
JAMES POWELL

"For some time now," James Powell confesses, "I've tried to wrtie a Christmas story in December as my way to survive the intrusion of the holiday. Those who think Christmas doesn't have its dark side should remember that Childermas isn't far behind with its commemoration of the Holy Innocents whom Herod murdered in his vain hope to cancel Christmas altogether."

A Christmas story in a dark fantasy anthology? Not to worry. This one's by Jim Powell, who contributed the delightfully offbeat "Code of the Poodles" to Northern Frights 2. *Let's just say that "Grist" is to Santa Claus yarns what "Code" was to dog stories.*

The tabloid press dubbed the corner of southern Ontario bounded by Windsor, Sarnia and St. Thomas "The Christmas Triangle" after holiday travelers began vanishing there in substantial numbers. When the disappearances reached twenty-seven, Wayne Sorley, editor-at-large of *The Traveling Gourmet* magazine, ever on the alert for off-beat articles, pencilled in a story on "Bed-and-Breakfasting Through the Triangle of Death" for an upcoming Christmas number, intending to combine seasonal decorations and homey breakfast recipes (including a side article on "Muffins from Hell") with whatever details of the mysterious triangle came his way.

So when the middle of December rolled around Sorley flew to Detroit, rented a car and drove across the border into snow, wind and falling temperatures.

He quickly discovered the bed-and-breakfast people weren't really crazy about the Christmas Triangle slant. Some thought it bad for business. Few took the disappearances as lightly as Sorley did. To make matters worse, his reputation had preceded him. The current issue of *The Traveling Gourmet* contained his "Haunted Inns of the Coast of Maine," and his side article "Cod Cakes from Hell," marking him as a dangerous guest to have around. Some places on Sorley's itinerary received him grudgingly. Others claimed no record of his reservation and threatened to loose the dog on him if he didn't go away.

On the evening of the 23rd of December and well behind schedule Sorley arrived at the last bed-and-breakfast on his rearranged itinerary to find a hand-written notice on the door. "Closed by the Board of Health." Shaking his fist at the dark windows Sorley decided, then and there, to throw in the towel. To hell with the damn Christmas Triangle! So he found a motel for the night, resolving to get back across the border and catch the first available flight for New York City. But he awoke late to find a fresh fall of snow and a dead car battery.

It was mid-afternoon before Sorley, determined as ever, was on the road again. By six o'clock the snow was coming down heavily and aslant and he was still far from his destination. He drove on wearily. What he really needed now, he told himself, was a couple of weeks in Hawaii. How about an article on "The Twelve Luaus of Christmas"? This late they'd have to fake it. But what the hell, in Hawaii they have to fake the holidays anyway.

Finally Sorley couldn't take the driving anymore and turned off the highway to find a place for the night. That's when he saw the "Double Kay B. and B." sign with the shingle hanging under it that said "Vacancy." On the front lawn beside the sign stood a fine old pickle-dish sleigh decorated with Christmas tree lights. Plastic reindeer lit electrically from within stood in the traces. Sorley pulled into the driveway and a moment later was up on the porch ringing the bell.

Mrs. Kay, a short, stoutish, white-haired woman with a pleasant face which, except for a old scar from a sharp-edged instrument across the left cheekbone, seemed untouched by care. She ushered Sorley inside and down a carpeted hallway and up the stairs. The house was small, tidy, bright and comfortably arranged. Sorley couldn't quite find the word to describe it until Mrs. Kay showed him the available bedroom. The framed naval charts on the walls, the boat in a bottle and the scrim-shawed narwhal tusk on the mantel gave him the word he was looking for. The house was "ship-shape."

Sorley took the room. But when he asked Mrs. Kay to recommend a place to eat nearby she insisted he share their dinner. "After all, it's Christmas Eve," she said. "You just freshen up, then, and come down stairs." Sorley smiled his thanks. The kitchen smells when she led him through the house had been delicious.

Sorley went back out to his car for his suitcase. The wind had ratcheted up its howl by several notches and was chasing streamers of snow down the road and across the drifts. But that was all right. He wasn't going anywhere. As he started back up the walk someone inside the house switched off the light on the bed-and-breakfast sign.

Sorley came out of his room pleased with his luck. Here he was settled in for the night with a roof over his head and a hot meal and a warm bed in the bargain. Suddenly Sorley felt eyes watching him, a sensation as strong as a touch on the nape of his neck. But when he looked back over his shoulder the hall was empty. Or had something tiny just disappeared behind the lowboy against the wall? Frowning, he turned his head around. As he did he caught the glimpse of a scurry, not the thing itself but the turbulence of air left in the wake of some small creature vanishing down the stairs ahead of him. A mouse, perhaps. Or, if they were sea-going people, maybe the Kays keep rats. Sorley made a face. Then, shaking his head at his over-heated imagination, he went down stairs.

Mrs. Kay fed him at a dining-room table of polished wood with a single place setting. "I've already eaten," she explained. "I like my supper early. And Father, Mr. Kay, never takes anything before he goes to work. He'll just heat his up in the microwave when he gets home." The meal was baked *finnan haddie*. Creamed smoked haddock was a favorite Sorley had not seen for a long time. She served it with a half bottle of Alsatian Gewurtztraminer. There was Stilton cheese and a fresh pear for dessert. "Father hopes you'll join him later in the study for an after-dinner drink," said Mrs. Kay.

The study was a book-lined room decorated once again with relics and artifacts of the sea. The light came from a small lamp on the desk by the door and the fire burning in the grate. A painting of a brigantine under sail in a gray sea hung above the mantel. Mr. Kay, a tall, thin man with a long, sallow clean-shaven face, heavy white eye-brows and patches of white hair around his ears, rose from one of two wing-backed chairs facing the fire. As he shook his guest's hand he examined him and seemed pleased with what he saw. "Welcome, Mr. Sorley." Here was a voice that might once have boomed in the teeth of a gale. "Come sit by the fire."

Before sitting Sorley paused to admire a grouping of three small statues on the mantel. They were realistic representation of pirates, each with a tarred pig-tail and a brace of pistols, all three as ugly as sin and none more than six inches tall. A peg-legged pirate. Another with a hook for a hand. The third wore a black eye-patch. Seeing his interest Mr. Kay took peg-leg down and displayed it in his palm. "Nicely done, are they not? I'm something of a collector in the buccaneer line. Most people's family trees are hung about with horse thieves. Pirates swing from mine." He set the statue back on the mantel. "And I'm not ashamed of it. With all this what-do-you-call-it going round, this historical revisionism, who knows what's next? Take Christopher Columbus, eh? He started out a saint. Today he's worse than a pirate. Some call him a devil. And Geronimo has gone from devil incarnate to the noble leader of his people. But here, Mr. Sorley. Forgive my running on. Sit down and join me in a hot grog."

Sorley's host poured several fingers of a thick dark rum from a heavy green bottle by his foot, added water from the electric tea-kettle steaming on the hearth, urging as he passed him the glass, "Wrap yourself around that."

The drink was strong. It warmed Sorley's body like the sun on a cold spring day. "Thank you," he said. "And thanks for the excellent meal."

"Oh, we keep a good table, Mother and I. We live well. Not from the bed-and-breakfast business, I can tell you that. After all, we only open one night a year and accept only a single guest."

When Sorley expressed his surprise Mr. Kay explained, "Call it a tradition. I mean, we certainly don't need the money. I deal in gold coins-- you know, doubloons, moidore-- obtained when the price was right. A steal, you might say. So, yes, we live well." He looked at his guest. "And what do you do for a living, Mr. Sorley?"

Sorley wasn't listening. A moment he thought he'd noticed something small move behind Mr. Kay, back there in the corner where two eight-foot-long bamboo poles were leaning and was watching to catch sight of it again. When Mr. Kay repeated his question Sorley told him what he did and briefly related his adventures connected with the aborted article.

Mr. Kay laughed like thunder, slapped his knees and said, "Then we are indeed well met. If you like I'll tell you the whole story about the Christmas Triangle. What an evening we have ahead of us, Mr. Sorley. Outside a storm howls and butts against the windows. And here we sit snug by the fire with hot drinks in our fists, a willing tale-teller and...."

"...an eager listener," said Sorley, congratulating himself once again on how well things had worked out. He might get his article yet.

Mr. Kay toasted his guest silently, thought for a moment and then began. "Now years ago when piracy was in flower a gangly young Canadian boy named Scattergood Crandal who had run off to join the pirate trade in the Caribbean finally earned his master-pirate papers and set out on a life's journey in buccaneering. But no panty-waist warm-water pirating for him, no rummy palm-tree days under blue skies. Young Crandal dreamed of home, of cool gray summers plundering the shipping lanes of the Great Lakes, of frosty winter raiding parties skating up frozen rivers with mufflers around their necks and cutlasses in their teeth surprising sleeping townspeople under their eiderdowns.

"So with his wife's dowry Crandal bought a ship, the Olson Nickelhouse, and sailed north with his bride, arriving in the Thousand Islands just as winter was closing the St. Lawrence. The captain and his wife and crew spent a desperate four months caught in the ice. Crandal gave the men daily skating lessons. But they were slow learners and there were to be no raiding parties that winter. By the end of February with supplies running low the men ate the Captain's parrot. And once having eaten talkative flesh it was a small step to utter cannibalism. One snowy day Crandal came upon them dividing up the carcasses of three ice fishermen. He warned them: 'Don't do it, you fellows. Eating human flesh'll stunt your growth and curl your toes!' But he was too late. Those men already slaves to that vile dish whose name no menu dare speak."

As Mr. Kay elaborated on the hardships of that first year he took his guest's glass, busied himself with the rum and hot water and made them both fresh drinks. For his part Sorley was distracted by bits of movement on the edges of his vision. But when he turned to look there was never anything there. He decided it was only the jitters brought on by fatigue from his long drive in bad weather. That and the play of light from the fire.

"Now Crandal knew terror was half the pirate game," continued Mr. Kay. "So the loss of the parrot hit him hard. You see, Mr. Sorley, this Canadian lad had never mastered the strong language expected from pirate captains and counted on the parrot to hold up that end of things. The blue jay he later trained to stride his shoulder wasn't quite the same effect and was incredibly messy. Still, pirates know to go with the best they have. So he had these flyers printed up announcing that Captain Crandal, his wife (for Mrs. Crandal was no slouch with the cutlass on boarding parties) and his cannibal crew, pirates late of the Caribbean, were now operating locally, vowing Death and Destruction to all offering resistance. At the bottom he included a drawing of his flag, a skeleton with a cutlass in one bony hand and in the other a frying pan to underscore the cannibal reference.

"Well, the flyer and flag made Crandal the hit of the season when things started up again on the Lakes that spring. In fact, the frying pan and Crandal's pale, bean-pole appearance and his outfit of pirate black earned him the nickname, Death-Warmed-Over. And, as Death-Warmed-Over the Pirate, he so terrorized the shipping lanes that soon the cold booty was just rolling in: cargoes of mittens and headcheese, sensible swag of potatoes and shoes, and vast plunder in the hardware line, anvils, door hinges and barrels of three-penny nails which Crandal sold for gold in the colorful and clamorous thieves' bazaars of Rochester and Detroit."

"How about Niagara Falls?" asked Sorley, to show he knew how to play along with a tall tale. He was amused to detect a slur in his voice from the rum.

"What indeed?" smiled Mr. Kay, happy with the question. He rose and lifted the painting down from its nail above the mantel and rested it across Sorley's knees. "See those iron rings along the water line? We fitted long poles through them, hoisted the Olson Nickelhouse out of the water and made heavy portage of her around the Falls."

As Mr. Kay replaced the painting Sorley noticed the group of three pirates on the mantel had rearranged themselves. Or was the strong drink and the heat from the fire effecting his concentration?

"Well," said Mr. Kay, "as cream rises soon Crandal was Pirate King with a pirate fleet at his back.   And there was no man-jack on land or sea that didn't tremble at the mention of Death-Warmed-Over.   Or any city either.   Except for one.

"One city on the Canadian side sat smugly behind the islands in its bay and resisted Crandal's assaults.   It's long indian name with a broadside of o's in it translated out as 'Gathering Place for Virtuous Moccasins.'   But Crandal called it 'Goody Two-Shoes City' because of its reek of self-righteousness.   Oh, he hated the world as a pirate must and wished to do creation all the harm he could.   But Goody Two-Shoes City he hated with a special passion.   Early on he even tried a Sunday attack to catch the city by surprise.   But the inhabitants came boiling out of the churches and up onto the battlements to pepper him with cannon balls with such a will that, if their elected officials hadn't decided they were enjoying themselves too much on the Sabbath and ordered a cease fire, they might have blown the Olson Nickelhouse out of the water."

Here Mr. Kay broke off his narrative to poke the fire and then to stare into the flames.   As he did, Sorley once again had the distinct impression he was being watched.   He turned and was startled to find another grouping of little pirate statues he hadn't noticed before on a shelf right at the level of his eye in the bookcase beside the fireplace.   They held drawn dirks and cutlasses in their earnest little hands and had pistols stuck in their belts.   And, oh, what ugly little specimens they were!

"Then early one December," Mr. Kay continued, "Crandal captured a cargo of novelty items from the toy mines of Bavaria.   Of course in those days toys were quite unknown.   Parents gave their children sensible gifts like socks or celluloid collars or pencil boxes at Christmas.   Suddenly Crandal broke into a happy hornpipe on the frosty deck for it had come to him how he could harm Goody Two-Shoes City and make it curse his name forever.   But he would need a disguise to get by the guards at the city gate who had strict orders to keep a sharp eye out for Death-Warmed-Over.   So he changed his black outfit for a red one with a pillow for fatness, rouge for his gray cheeks, a white beard to make him look older and a jolly laugh to cover his pirate gloom.   Then on Christmas Eve he put the Olson Nickelhouse in close to shore and sneaked into Goody Two-Shoes City with a wagon load of toys crated up like hymnals.   That night he crept across the rooftops and down chimneys and by morning every boy and girl had a real toy under the Christmas tree.

"Well, of course the parents knew right away who'd done the deed and what Crandal was up to. Next Christmas, they knew, they'd have to go and buy a toy in case Crandal didn't show up again or risk a disappointed child. But suppose he came next year, too? Well, that would mean that the following year the parents would have to buy two toys. Then three. And on and on until children no longer knew the meaning of the word 'enough'.

"'Curse Crandal and the visit from the Olson Nickelhouse,' the parents muttered through clenched teeth. But their eavesdropping children misheard and thought they said 'Kris Kingle' and something about a visit from 'Old Saint Nicholas.'' As if a saint would give a boy a toy drum or saxophone to drive his father mad with, as if a saint would give a girl a Little Dolly Clotheshorse doll and set her dreaming over fashion magazines when she should be helping her mother in the kitchen.'' Mr. Kay laughed until the tears came to his eyes. "Well, the Pirate King knew he'd hit upon a better game than making fat landlubbers walk an icy gangplank over cold gray water. And since the Crandals had salted away a fortune in gold coins they settled down here and started a reindeer farm so Crandal could Kringle full time with the Missus as Mrs. Kringle and the crew as his little helpers.'' Mr. Kay looked up. "Isn't that right, Mother?''

Mrs. Kay had appeared in the doorway with a red costume and a white beard over her arm and a pair of boots in her hand. "That's right, Father. But it's time to get ready. I've loaded the sleigh and harnessed the reindeer.''

Mr. Kay got to his feet. "And here's the wonderfully strange and miraculous thing, Mr. Sorley. As the years passed we didn't age. Not one bit. What did you call it, Mother?''

"The Tinker Bell Effect,'' said Mrs. Kay, putting down the boots and holding up the heavily-padded red jump-suit trimmed with white for Mr. Kay to step into.

"If children believe in you,'' explained Mr. Kay, as he did up the velcro fasteners, "why then you're eternal and evergreen. Plus you can fly through the air and so can your damn livestock!''

Mrs. Kay laughed a fine contralto laugh. "And somewhere along the line children must have started believing in Santa's little helpers, too,'' she said. "Because our pirate crew didn't age either. They just got shorter.''

Mr. Kay nodded. "Which fitted in real well with their end of the operation."

"The toy workshop?" asked Sorley.

Mr. Kay smiled and shook his head. "No, that's only a myth. We buy our toys, you see. Not that Mother and I were going to spend our own hard-earned money for the damn stuff. No, the crew's little fingers make the counterfeit plates to print what cash we need to buy the toys. Electronic ones, mostly. Wonderful for stunting the brain, cramping the soul and making ugly noises that just won't quit."

"Hold it." Sorley wagged a disbelieving finger. "You're telling me you started out as Death-Warmed-Over the Pirate and now you're Santa Claus?"

"Mr. Sorley, I'm as surprised as you how things worked out. Talk about revisionism, eh? Yesterday's yo-ho-ho is today's ho-ho-ho." Mr. Kay stood back and let his wife attach his white beard with it's built-in red plastic cheeks.

"But where does the Christmas Triangle business fit in?" demanded Sorley. "We've got twenty-seven people who disappeared around here last year alone."

"Copy-cats," insisted Mr. Kay. "As I said, Mother and I only take one a year, what we call our Gift from the Night. But of course when the media got onto it the copy-cats weren't far behind. Little Mary Housewife can't think of a present for Tommy Tiresome who has everything so she gives him a slug from a .38 between the eyes and buries him in the basement, telling the neighbors he went to visit his mother in Sarnia. Little Billy Bank Manager with shortages in the books and a yen for high living in warmer climes vanishes into the Christmas Triangle with a suitcase of money from the vault and re-emerges under another name in Rio. And so on and so on. Copy-cats.

"Father's right. We only take one," said Mrs. Kay. "That's what our agreement calls for."

Father nodded. "Last year it was an arrogant young bastard from the SPCA investigating reports of mistreated reindeer. Tell me my business, would he?" Mr. Kay's chest swelled and his eyes flashed. "Well, Mother and I harnessed him to the sleigh right between Dancer and Prancer. And his sluggard backside got more than its share of the lash that Christmas

Eve, let me tell you. He was blubbering like a baby by the time I turned him over to my scurvy crew.''

"I don't understand," said Sorley. But he was beginning to. He stood up slowly, utterly clear-headed and sober. "You mean your cannibal crew *ate* him?" he demanded in a horrified voice.

"Consider the fool from the SPCA part of our employee benefits package," shrugged Mr. Kay. "Oh, all right," he conceded when he saw Sorley's outrage, "so my little shipmates are evil. Evil. They've got wolfish little teeth and pointed carnivore ears. And don't think those missing legs and arms were honestly come by in pirate combat? Not a bit of it. There's this card game they play. Like strip poker but without the clothes. They're terrible, there's no denying it. But you know, few of us get to pick the people we work with. Besides, I don't like to be judgmental. No matter what you've heard, Santa doesn't give a damn about naughty or nice.''

Sorley's voice was shrill and outraged. "But this is hideous. Hideous. I'll go to the police.''

"Go, then," said Mr. Kay. "Be our guest. Mother and I won't stand in your way.''

"You'd better not try!" warned Sorley defiantly, intending to storm from the room. But when he tried he found his shoelaces were tied together. He fell forward like a dead weight and struck his head, blacking out for a moment. When he regained consciousness he was lying on his stomach with his thumbs lashed together behind his back. Before Sorley's head cleared he felt something being shoved up the back of his pant legs, over his buttocks and up under his belt. When they emerged out beyond the back of his shirt collar he saw they were the bamboo poles that had been leaning in the corner.

Before Sorley could try to struggle free a little pirate appeared close to his face, a grizzled thing with a hook for an arm, little curly-toed shoes and a bandanna pulled down over the pointed tops of its ears. With a cruel smile it placed the point of its cutlass a menacing fraction of an inch from Sorley's left eyeball and, in language no less vile because of the tiny voice that uttered it, the creature warned him not to move.

Mrs. Kay was smiling down at him. "Now don't trouble yourself over your car, Mr. Sorley. I'll drive into the city later tonight and park it where the car strippers can't miss it. Father'll pick me up in the sleigh on his way back.''

Mr. Kay had been stamping his boots to get them on properly. Now he said, "Give us a kiss, Mother. I'm on my way." Then the toes of the boots hove into view on the edge of Sorley's vision. "Goodbye, Mr. Sorley," said his host. "Thanks for coming. Consider yourself grist for the mills of Christmas.''

As soon as Mr. Kay left the room Sorley heard little feet scramble around him and more little pirates rushed to man the ends of the bamboo poles in front of him. At a tiny command the crew put their cutlasses in their teeth and, holding their arms over their heads, hoisted Sorley up off the floor. He hung there helplessly, suspended front and back.

The little pirates lugged Sorley out into the hall and headed down the carpet toward the front door. He didn't know where they were taking him. But their progress was funereally slow, and, swaying there, Sorley conceived a frantic plan of escape. He knew his captors were tiring under their load. If they had to set him down to rest he would dig in with his toes and, somehow, somehow, work his way to his knees. At least there he'd stand a chance.

Sorley heard sleigh bells. He raised his chin. Through the pane of beveled glass in the front door he saw the sleigh on the lawn rise steeply into the night, Christmas tree lights and all, and he heard Mr. Kay's booming "Yo-ho-ho-ho."

Suddenly Sorley's caravan stopped. He got ready, waiting for them to put him down. But they were only adjusting their grips. The little pirates turned him sideways and Sorley saw the open door and the top of the cellar steps and smelled the darkness as musty as a tomb. Then he felt the beginning of their big heave-ho. It was too damn late to escape now. Grist for the mills of Christmas? Hell, he was meat for the stew pots of elfdom.

Tamar's Leather Pouch
DAVID SHTOGRYN

In order to pay the mortgage, Toronto author David Shtogryn works as a radiation technologist, as yet being unable to convince his wife (understandably so) to allow him to write full time.

Currently, he is working his way through a novel, taking a break for the occasional short story. Since 1991 he has had considerable success getting mainstream stories published, as well as science fiction, fantasy, and horror, in journals ranging from Crossroads *to* Midnight Zoo. *He reports that his main passions are dreaming, writing, and cooking*

Her emaciated body scarcely causes a ripple in the heavy blankets that cover her. I can see the motion of shallow breathing only if I watch intently. I fear it will stop while I'm here.

The room reeks with that acrid stink which so often precedes death. There has been no effort to mask the smell. Darkness will soon displace the grayness of a despairing autumn day, so maybe I should go now, come back in the morning when there may be sunshine, and perhaps she'll show some sign of improvement.

Janice's mother glares at me while I make preparations to leave. She barely tolerated my presence when Janice first came to me for help; I was too old, too filthy, and in love. The wisdom of the aged spotted this easily. Janice could not. She was ill, and my potions were the only medicines left to help her.

"I s'pose you'll be back with the sunrise."

I whirl around, startled. The hatred in her black eyes crackles more intensely than I have ever seen. "Yes, M', with your permission." I must remain humble in my thoughts and words.

"I wish you wouldn't," the elderly woman mumbles as she shuffles away and lights two thick candles set on a low table at the foot of the bed.

"Tamar might answer my call tonight, and Janice can be saved," I respond hoarsely.

She scowls. I don't think she is a cold woman. Maybe she has resigned herself totally to Janice's condition in a way I cannot. Perhaps she is too acquainted with death ... her husband and two sons, gone in the past year. Does she have anything left to give?

"It's too late for your friend to come," she says, her voice tailing off into silence.

I paint Janice's lips with the last of my herbal balm and return the empty container to my medicine bag. "I'm not the only one who failed her," I try to explain. "You tried the physicians."

She looks down at Janice. "I can tell your feelings. Do you really think she would have returned your love?"

Of course, I think, but cannot say it. "You helped me at first. We fed her together. I was the only hope left."

"Yes." She pulls a handkerchief from the pocket of her apron and wipes the balm off. "I only went along with it for Janice."

"I took no money."

"I would give no money to a fraud."

"My feelings for her only helped me to try harder."

"For what? To have her reject you if you succeeded. Perhaps your idea of love is to share coldness with a corpse."

I leave without another word, pulling on the thick black coat that Mr. Mayfair the undertaker gave me. I live in a corner of his basement. He took me in when I was very young, many years ago. I think I lived in an orphanage before that. I don't remember. Mr. Mayfair and his wife never showed me much affection, and after she died, he became even more distant. But I really didn't care. Janice brought me love though we never touched. Her eyes told me in their innocent ways. It could not have been the love of desperation. I could sense it too, in her voice, when she could still speak.

Before Janice, Tamar was my only friend. He is dead now. I met him in the wood behind the church cemetery. He taught me the arts of healing that our physicians do not practice. Sometimes people would come to me for a cure when all other hope was gone. For some I succeeded, for others I did not. People feared dealing with me ... I frightened them ... but desperation continued to bring them. Janice came to me, and I fell in love with her. I should have been able to help her.

Mr. Mayfair has removed the candle from over the door to the basement. Its light has been the only welcome beacon left. I think my time here nears its end.

I am crying now as I have been for most of the night. My tiny bottles of herbs, spices, oils, and ingredients taken from the dead who constantly pass through this house lie scattered in their uselessness on the floor. I cannot shake the damp cold, though the snows of winter have yet to fall. Maybe I'm just too old. Even the warmth radiating from the bright flame of my lantern feels cold on my hands.

My heart suddenly races. Breathing becomes difficult and I feel faint. A buzzing in my ears sounds a warning as my being slips away. I find myself in a world of shadows flitting about in a silent, grey mist. The fingers at the end of my outstretched arm are scarcely visible. Faces appear to me. I should recognize them, but don't. Then Tamar approaches. He hands me a tiny leather pouch. His fingers are ice. Words enter my mind and take the form of sound in Tamar's voice.

"You were my one friend," he says. "This is the favor I owe." Then he vanishes.

I wake and my body aches with the stiffness of cramped muscles. I didn't realize that I'd fallen asleep. I feel a growth of stubble on my face. Three, maybe four days have passed.

Outside, the full moon brightens the darkness. I run, clutching the leather pouch, to Janice's home. Her mother must have seen me, for she intercepts me in front of the house.

"Come no more." She smiles through rotted teeth. "Janice is dead."

I cannot collapse, though I wish I would, to blot out the meaning of her words. Janice's image aches in my mind; not what she had become through the ravages of sickness, but the beauty she radiated only a few short months before.

"Where?" I gasp not knowing what I really ask.

"In the cemetery, fool," she spits. "For two days now."

I stagger back to the home of the undertaker. I visualize Janice in the silk of her coffin, and I and curl up into my corner of the basement. Her lips shine full, moist. The ravages of disease vanish as my mind watches.

The leather pouch comes alive in my clutching hand. I open it and reel backwards as a metallic spider, beautiful in its grotesqueness, crawls out. Shiny spindly legs hold a pulsing silver body. An emerald, faceted eye stares at me.

"I am for Janice," it whispers and leaps onto my forehead, "and for you."

A gold stinger vibrates menacingly over my left eye. I freeze in terror. Then the spider hops back to my hand and into the pouch, leaving me shaking but hopeful. Perhaps this thing will bring Janice life, and with her, love will return again.

I stuff the leather pouch into my pocket, pull on my coat, and grasp the rusted shovel and lantern. No one sees me walk to the cemetery.

I find Janice's grave under a tormented tree that seems ill able to survive until spring. I set down the lantern and begin to dig. The going is easy, the soil as yet unpacked. Suddenly I am afraid. This is evil. I stand, gasping for air, and lean on the shovel. The spider bolts out from the pouch and lands on my forehead again. I sense the deadliness of its stinger.

"Are you truly for Janice?" I ask.

"I'm death for you, or life for her. You are to choose."

I start digging again. The shovel strikes the coffin and I stop. I cannot decide. To join her in life ... or death.

The spider waits.

Snow Angel

NANCY KILPATRICK

Nancy Kilpatrick has published the vampire novel Near Death, *in addition to five pseudonymous erotic horror novels. A prolific short story writer, she has one collection in print and two more coming soon, as well as a signed limited edition hardcover from Transylvania Press (all vampire tales).*

About "Snow Angel," Nancy writes: "I've always wanted to visit the Yukon, and every year for a decade have gotten maps and promo material on travel up there (summer, of course), but so far I haven't made it. Snow Angel came out of a writing exercise I do with a short story class I teach. It's a kind of word-association exercise, and while I was demonstrating it on the board, three words jumped out at me. (I won't say what they were, because it will give the plot away). I took them home and thought about them and this story flowed from there."

They'd been warned in Whitehorse. By several people. And again in Dawson City. But Joe never listened. He called himself a 'free-floating spirit'. Coleen thought of him as somebody who needed to be nailed firmly to the earth.

Joe's death had come as a complete shock. Coleen was just finishing drying and putting away dinner dishes in the Winnebago's little cupboards. He stepped out of the one-man shower that also functioned as the toilet. She pushed aside the pink and white curtain above the sink to watch the odd snowflake drift onto the frozen tundra, thinking again how much she did not share his love of or trust in this barren land. It had been his idea to come way up here in the Fall, "when there's no tourists," he'd said, adding in his poetic way, "so we can nourish the snow spirits and they can nourish us."

She folded the dish towel. "We're almost out of food, Joey. We'd better head back to Dawson City--that'll take us half a day. Didn't that guy on the CB say something about a low pressure system building?"

When he didn't answer, Coleen turned. Joe sat on one of the benches at the table, a deck of cards before him. His chunky six foot frame slumped back towards the front of the vehicle. His pale green eyes looked as cold as the crevices in a glacier. In his right hand he held two mismatched socks.

Coleen performed mouth to mouth resuscitation. It didn't work. She got out the first aid kit and found some smelling salts. When everything else failed, she pounded hard on his chest, first in desperation, then in hysteria.

All that had happened yesterday. Today she had a different problem--what to do with her husband's rotting corpse.

She stared out the window. The storm she feared had magically eaten its way across the landscape while she'd struggled last night to revive Joe. She had judged the weather too bad to drive in but now she realized she'd made a mistake by not trying. Eight hours had done damage. Swirling gusts of snow clouded her view beyond a couple of yards. Every so often the wind banshee-howled as it buffeted the two-ton camper, threatening to hurl everything far above the permafrost and into another dimension. It made her think of Dorothy being swept away by the tornado and ending up disoriented in Oz.

Coleen's eyes automatically went to Joe's body. She had wrapped him in the two sheets they'd brought along and secured the sheets with rope. He lay on the floor like a tacky Halloween ghost, or a silly husband playing ghost. Any moment she expected him to rise with a 'Boo!'. Then he'd laugh and admit to another of his practical jokes. But the form refused to play its part. It did not sit up. She had an urge to kick it in the side.

"It's all your fault." Furious tears streaked down her face. She snatched at the box of Kleenex and blew her nose long and loudly. "*You* wanted to go into debt to buy this stupid camper. *You* wanted to drive all the way to the Arctic Circle. *You* wanted to stop at this dumb lake. You never plan anything. Why do you have to be so damn spontaneous?" She yanked open the small door beneath the sink and hurled the tissue into a paper bag of burnable trash.

Suddenly her shoulders caved in and she let loose. The weeping turned to a wailing that frightened her all the more because it made her aware that she was alone. She stopped abruptly and the silence hurt her eardrums. When had the snow and wind expired? Outside it looked like some kind of perverse fairy land, white on white merging with a colorless sky. Although the Winnebago was warm, she shivered. This place. It was so...empty. Nothing could live here.

Coleen knew she needed to act to break this mood. She washed her face in the kitchen sink, dried it with her shirt tail and tried the radio again.

Last night the storm had smothered signals coming and probably going too. For the first time since Joe's death, she was getting some static; she reread the part in the manual about broadcasting. She picked up the microphone and sent out a distress call and gave their location, as recorded by her in the log--three hundred kilometres north east of Dawson City, on Hungry Lake. She repeated the call for over an hour until she needed a break. Coleen sat at the table with her coffee. She felt disheartened and lifted the cup to inhale the comforting sweet-roasted scent. Sweet-sour noxiousness clotted her nostrils and she gagged. "Oh my God." Setting the cup down spilled its contents. Joe was starting to stink.

Primal fear raked a nerve. She jumped up and lifted the seat of the bench. Among the tools inside she found a small shovel and the ice ax she'd insisted on buying. She threw on her parka, stepped into her boots and grabbed the fur-lined mitts.

Once she was dressed she turned the knob of the back door. The door wouldn't budge. The glass had frosted so she couldn't see the problem. Panicked, Coleen threw her weight against the door, finally creating an inch gap that let in freezing air. She peered through the slender opening. Snow drifts had climbed half way up the camper. She jammed the shovel handle between the door and the frame and used it as a lever to pry another inch, then another; finally it was wide enough to get the ax through. Hacking and plowing gave her a one foot opening she could lean around.

Crystalline whiteness extended as far as she could see. The banks must have been four feet high, the lowest drifts two feet deep. The realization dawned that the truck would not get through this. Even if she managed to connect the chains to the snow tires--and there was a good chance she couldn't do it by herself--no way would the camper make it.

Despite warm clothing, the air nipped at the skin on her face until it numbed. A bad sign, she knew. She pulled the door shut and made herself another cup of coffee.

While Coleen drank it, she thought about her situation. The weather might warm. The snow could melt enough in a week or so that she could drive. She'd keep working the radio; eventually somebody would hear her. The thought came, *maybe a snowmobile will drive by, or a dogsled,* but she knew that's the way Joe would think. There were only 25,000 people in the whole of the Yukon and Hungry Lake was a good hundred kilometres from the nearest highway.

Thank God she'd bought that book on surviving in the Yukon when they'd passed through Dawson City. Joe, of course, had laughed at her. There was a checklist at the front--*What to do While Waiting for Help to Arrive.* She'd torn it out and tacked it to the wall. Joe had found such practicality even more amusing.

Joe. She knew she'd been avoiding thinking about him. She sighed but it sounded more like a moan. Her heart felt both too full and empty. She looked at the body on the floor, wrapped like a mummy. Even now the smell was there, under everything, seeping into the air like poison spreading through water. She'd have to take him outside.

After trying the radio again, Coleen dressed in the heavy clothes-- this time wearing a ski mask as well. She continued chopping and digging into the crusty snow. By five o'clock she had the door wide open and the bar locked so it would stay that way. The landscape looked the same now as it had at ten a.m., as it would look at ten p.m.. With only six hours of darkness, even the underside of the clouds reflected white luminosity-- snowblink, they called it. This almost endless brightness was unnatural. She remembered near-death stories she'd read about, of white light and how departed souls float down the tunnel towards that blinding light. Coleen wondered if Joe had gone down a tunnel. She squinted. She couldn't imagine anything brighter than this.

Dense cold filled the Winnebago, which numbed her nose and anesthetized her emotions, making the second part of the job easier.

She grabbed Joe's ankles. Despite the gloves, she was aware of the hardness of his cadaver. Coleen clamped her teeth together; this was no time to let grief and fear overwhelm her. Grunting, heaving, she dragged his dead weight along the brick-red linoleum to the back door.

There were snowshoes--she'd seen to that--and she strapped a pair onto her boots. She'd never walked in them and had no idea how she'd manage. They weren't like skis; they were feather light but the racket part up front was so wide that she couldn't help tripping herself.

Her big fear was that the snow wouldn't be solid enough to hold her up, but it did. She backed out of the camper and, once sure she was balanced, bent over and grabbed Joe's feet again. She pulled and the rigid body slid over the door frame easily. All but the head. It caught on the frame. When she yanked, it plummeted into the trench she'd created around the door.

Joe was so stiff that when his head went down into that pit, it jarred her hold and the rest of his body popped straight up into the air.

Look, Collie, a human popsicle!

Fear slid up her spine. Coleen looked around. Nothing. No one. Only the corpse.

She knew he was dead but still she said, "Joey?" and waited. It had to have been the wind. She steeled herself and jumped up to grab his feet. Her body weight pulled them down. He leveled like a board and, stepping backwards carefully, she slid him along the compacted snow.

Somehow she didn't want to leave him just outside the door. The dry cold was exhausting, and deceptive--she knew it was colder than it felt and she had to be careful of frostbite--but she dragged him away from the camper, tripping once, having a hell of a time getting back up on the snowshoes. The air burned its way down her throat and the pain in her lungs became ferocious, making her fear pneumonia.

Finally he was far enough away that she wouldn't smell him every time she opened the door, yet he'd still be within sight.

Coleen struggled back. By the time she got inside, her entire body was numb. That desensitization was preferable to the defrosting that followed. A hot shower brought pins and needles pain that made her cry out loud. Trembling, she bundled up in Joe's two bulky sweaters, pulled open the bed and crawled in. She couldn't see Joe from here. She drifted into what turned out to be a nightmare. A frozen animal carcass with Joe's face grinned down at her. He was sucking on a decaying popsicle.

When Coleen woke it was still light outside. She checked the battery-operated clock radio and could hardly believe she'd slept nearly twenty-four hours until she moved and her muscles screamed and she remembered having been up for thirty-six hours doing exhausting work in sub-zero temperatures.

Joe's death, her being stranded, all of it suffocated her with despair. It was only the thought, *I could die here*, that got her out of bed.

She ate, played with the radio--now even the static was gone--reread the survival list, and went about doing what was necessary. She checked all propane hookups and turned the heater down--she'd have to use the gas sparingly. Thanks to Joe, the extra tank had been gobbled up when he'd insisted they extend their stay.

Next she tried the engine. It wouldn't kick over; the fuel line had to be de-iced first. She'd need to do that twice a day to keep the battery charged. The gas gauge needle pointed to three quarters full and there was a five gallon container for emergencies. Two of the three hundred kilometres back to Dawson City would be through the mountains where the snow could avalanche and put out the road. But at least there was a road. Making it to Highway No. 5 was the problem. They'd had a hell of a time getting through the spruce and poplars to the lake from there and, under these conditions, there'd be double hell to pay to get out. And all of it depended on enough of a thaw to drive the camper.

The snow, she realized with a bitter laugh, had at least one benefit-- there would be plenty of snowbroth; fresh water wouldn't be a problem. She checked flashlight batteries, matches, candles, flares and medical supplies. The cupboard held a big jar of instant coffee and a box of tea bags, but even at half rations, the food would only last one person one day. They should have been back in Dawson City five days ago but Joe had insisted on this side trip. She'd argued against it but he'd fixed on some crazy idea he'd read about in a magazine that he could fish in the lake and catch char and they'd "negotiate with the Eskimo gods to live off the land," a concept that now struck her as insane.

Most of their fifteen year marriage she had, in her way, loved Joe, although their relationship was not the fulfilling one she'd hoped for. She had to admit that because of him she'd been places and done things she wouldn't have, left to her own devices. Early on she'd seen him as a welcome contrast: devilish to her seriousness, adventurous to her timidity.

But it wasn't long before she admitted that what had once been charming traits in Joe turned to juvenile habits that gnawed away at her patience; divorce had crossed her mind.

Still, he was her husband, till death did them part. He had died, if not in her arms at least in her presence, and he had died as he'd lived-- impulsively. On some level she missed him dearly.

But she was also angry. Angry that he'd brought her to this God-forsaken place and left her, maybe to slowly starve, or freeze to death like a character in a Jack London story. And why? Because he claimed his destiny was to see the "Good and Great White North." And he had too much childish faith that life would support him to worry about freak storms. If he wasn't already dead, she might have entertained murderous thoughts.

She pressed her face against the chilled glass in the back door. White. Everywhere. So pure, so foreboding. The wind had erased her tracks. She couldn't see Joe's body. Suddenly she felt guilty for leaving him out there all alone in an icy grave. The thought struck, *maybe he's not dead. Maybe he's in a coma or something.* She tried to talk herself out of that notion but soon Coleen was putting on the parka and the snowshoes and trudging across the hardened snow in the direction she thought she'd taken her husband.

The air had a peculiar and enticing quality. The cold felt almost warm. As she crunched along, the beauty of the snowscape struck her. Everything was elementally pure, pristine. Blameless. Almost spiritual. In the darkening sky a faint aurora borealis flickered green and blue, like some kind of signals emanating from heaven. She understood how Joe's soul could soar here. Suddenly, the incredible glare on the horizon temporarily snowblinded her.

From behind, the wind resurrected itself and knocked Coleen off her feet. She plunged straight forward as if her body were jointless. Her face crashed into the frost and knocked out her breath. As she struggled to her knees, little puppy yaps came out of her mouth. Pain shot through her nose and forehead. She squeezed her eyes shut hard and opened them slowly to regain her vision. The snow beneath her was red. She touched the ski mask over her nose; the glove was stained.

Coleen looked around wildly, trying to orient herself. Joe's body lay six feet away. She started to think, *why didn't I notice it before...* and then

stopped. The body looked the same, but the snow surrounding it appeared scraped. It reminded her of being a child and lying flat, making snow angels by opening and closing her legs, and raising and lowering her arms above her head. *He can't be alive*, she thought. *The sheets are still tied around his body. There's no way he could move his arms and legs.*
Coleen crawled to the body. Instinctively she felt afraid to touch it, but forced herself. It was iceberg hard. When she tried to shake him, she discovered that the sheets had adhered to the snow crust.

"Joe! Joey!"

Freezing in Spirit Land, honey.

"My God!" She tore at the sheets but her gloves were too bulky so she yanked them off. Still, the cotton was more like ice and she had to use a key to gouge through it. She wedged her fingers between the fabric and his neck and ripped the fabric up over his chin. The cotton peeled away from the familiar face to reveal chunks of torn flesh and exposed frozen muscle. Coleen gasped, horrified. His face was a pallid death mask. "Joe!" Her hands had numbed and were turning blue and she stuffed them back into the gloves before slapping his cheeks. "Can you hear me?"

She sobbed and gulped stabbing air. The storm was getting bad again; she could hardly see the Winnebago through the frozen fog of ice crystals. If she didn't go back now she might be stranded here. She glanced down at Joe. If he hadn't been dead when she'd brought him out, he certainly had suffered hypothermia and died of exposure. The wind whispered and Coleen accepted the fact that Joe had not spoken to her.

She left him and clumped her way back. By the time she shut the door and peered through the glass, the camper was enshrouded in white air.

Coleen devoured the rest of a tin of sardines in mustard with the last two saltines and drank another cup of coffee. The coffee had her edgy and she decided to switch to tea, although she didn't like it as well. But now that the solid food was gone, she'd need to keep her head.

All day she'd tried the radio and reread the *Survival in the Yukon Guide*. She'd just finished an improbable chapter on snaring rabbits by locating their breath holes in the snow and was about to close the book when the section on leaving food outdoors caught her eye. The three paragraphs warned about wolves, bears, caribou and other wild animals being attracted to food. She lay the book in her lap for a moment and rubbed her sore eyes. Human bodies were food. She recalled seeing the movie *Alive* and how the survivors turned to cannibalism. She shivered and hugged herself.

Coleen went to the door. Snow, the voracious deity of this land, lay quiet and pallid, waiting. Somewhere out there was her husband's body. Those marks in the snow crust could have been made by something that was hungry. Something that might at this moment be gnawing on Joe's remains.

She shuddered. He deserved better than that. Maybe she should bring him back indoors. But that thought was so bizarre it led to the toilet and her vomiting up sardines.

By the time Coleen felt steady enough to put on the heavy outdoor clothing, she knew what she had to do. She gathered the supplies she'd need and went to Joe.

The snowscape had turned into an icescape--the Winnebago was icebound. That should have scared her but she felt strangely invincible and coherent, her mind as crystal clear as the air. There were no tracks; she found him by instinct.

She opened the cap on the lighter fluid and doused his body. It was hard to believe that under this frozen earth lay huge oil deposits; the nauseatingly sweet combustible reeked. She struck a match and dropped it onto the pyre. Flames sprang upward and black smoke fouled the air. She hoped the snow gods did not feel defiled.

Coleen stared at the fire charring her husband's remains. Flesh crackled and a familiar scent wafted up; she realized that she had never known anyone who'd been cremated. It came to her that maybe his spirit was trapped in his frozen flesh. If any body possessed a spirit, it would have been Joey's.

As the inky cloud danced heavenward, she panicked. Maybe she was doing the wrong thing. Maybe the flames would not just cook his flesh but would burn his soul. Maybe hell was...but something caught her eye.

A pale spectre appeared in the dark smoke. The face was luminous, the form familiar. She watched Joe ascend like a snow angel. He smiled down at her and waved. Coleen sobbed and waved back. Tears welled over her eyelids and froze on her lower lashes and she stepped closer to the fire's warmth. *We all do what we have to, Collie.* He'd said that often enough, but this was the first time she understood it.

She felt bone chilled. The wind confided in her--the northern demons were still hungry.

Coleen shovelled snow onto the flames and they sizzled into silence. As darkness crawled up the sky, she worked quickly with the ice ax. There was plenty of meat. It would take time to pack it in ice and store it safely before the storm returned.

The Perseids

ROBERT CHARLES WILSON

Robert Charles Wilson is a native Californian who now resides in To-ronto with his wife and son. He has published a number of outstanding science fiction novels, including A Bridge of Years, A Hidden Place, Memory Wire, The Divide, The Harvest, *and* Mysterium.

He writes: "'The Perseids' is a personal mile-marker: my first short work in some years, and my first serious work of dark fantasy. Mind you, elements of dark fantasy have found their way into my science fiction novels, and there are certainly elements of sf in this particular horror story. My favorite stories in either genre are often balancing acts: light vs. *dark, knowledge* vs. *mystery, awe* vs. *terror. Sf and dark fantasy writers both have a thumb on the scale; they just lean in different directions.*

"'The Perseids' is also a small act of homage to the original master of the astronomical horor story, the late Fritz Leiber. No one can hope to emulate him but he certainly had the power to inspire. This one's for him."

The divorce was finalized in the spring; I was alone that summer.

I took an apartment over a roti shop on Bathurst Street in Toronto. My landlords were a pair of ebullient Jamaican immigrants, husband and wife, who charged a reasonable rent and periodically offered to sell me grams of resinous, potent *ganja*. The shop closed at nine, but most summer nights the couple joined friends on a patio off the alley behind the store, and the sound of music and patois, cadences smooth as river pebbles, would drift up through my kitchen window. The apartment was a living room facing the street, a bedroom and kitchen at the rear; wooden floors and plaster ceilings with rusting metal caps where the gas fixtures had been removed. There was not much natural light, and the smell of goat curry from the kitchen downstairs was sometimes overwhelming. But taken all in all, it suited my means and needs.

I worked days at a second-hand book shop, sorting and shelving stock, operating the antiquated cash register, and brewing cups of yerba mate for the owner, a myopic aesthete of some sixty years who subsisted on whatever dribble of profit he squeezed from the business. I was his only employee. It was not the work I had ever imagined myself doing, but such is the fortune of a blithe thirty-something who stumbles into the recession with a B.A. and negligible computer skills. I had inherited a little money from my parents, dead five years ago in a collision with a lumber truck on Vancouver Island; I hoarded the principal and supplemented my income with the interest.

I was alone and nearly friendless and my free time seemed to stretch to the horizon, as daunting and inviting as a desert highway. One day in the bookshop I opened a copy of *Confessions of an English Opium-Eater* to the passage where de Quincey talks about his isolation from his fellow students at Manchester Grammar School: "for, whilst liking the society of some amongst them, I also had a deadly liking (perhaps a morbid liking) for solitude." Me, too, Thomas, I thought. Is it that the Devil finds work for idle hands, or that idle hands seek out the Devil's work? But I don't think the Devil had anything to do with it. (Other invisible entities, perhaps.) Alone, de Quincy discovered opium. I discovered Robin Slattery, and the stars.

We met prosaically enough: she sold me a telescope.

Amateur astronomy had been my teenage passion. When I lived with my parents on their country property north of Port Moody I had fallen in love with the night sky. City people don't understand. The city sky is as gray and blank as slate, faintly luminous, like a smouldering trash fire. The few celestial bodies that glisten through the pollution are about as inspiring as beached fish. But travel far enough from the city and you can still see the sky the way our ancestors saw it, as a chasm beyond the end of the world in which the stars move as implacably and unapproachably as the souls of the ancient dead.

I found Robin working the show floor at a retail shop called *Scopes & Lenses* in the suburban flatlands north of the city. If you're like me you often have a powerful reaction to people even before you speak to them: like or dislike, trust or fear. Robin was in the *like* column as soon as she spotted me and smiled. Her smile seemed genuine, though there was no earthly reason it should be: we were strangers, after all; I was a customer; we had these roles to play. She wore her hair short. Long, retro paisley skirt and two earrings in each ear. Sort of an art-school look. Her face was narrow, elfin, Mediterranean-dark. I guessed she was about twenty-five.

Of course the only thing to talk about was telescopes. I wanted to buy one, a good one, something substantial, not a toy. I lived frugally, but every couple of years I would squeeze a little money out of my investments and buy myself an expensive present. Last year, my van. This year, I had decided, a telescope. (The divorce had been expensive but that was a necessity, not a luxury.)

There was plenty to talk about. 'Scopes had changed since I was teenager. Bewilderingly. It was all Dobsonians, CCD imagers, object-acquisition software.... I took a handful of literature and told her I'd think about it. She smiled and said, "But you're serious, right? I mean, some people come in and look around and then do mail order from the States...." And then laughed at her own presumption, as if it were a joke, between us.

I said, "You'll get your commission. Promise."

"Oh, God, I wasn't *angling*...but here's my card...I'm in the store most afternoons."

That was how I learned her name.

Next week I put a 10-inch Meade Starfinder on my Visa card. I was back two days later for accessory eyepieces and a camera adapter. That was when I asked her out for coffee.

She didn't even blink. "Store closes in ten minutes," she said, "but I have to do some paperwork and make a deposit. I could meet you in an hour or so."

"Fine. I'll buy dinner."

"No, let me buy. You already paid for it. The commission-- remember?"

She was like that.

Sometime during our dinner conversation she told me she had never looked through a telescope.

"You have to be kidding."

"Really!"

"But you know more about these things than I do, and I've looked through a lot of lenses."

She poked her fork at a plate of goat cheese torta as if wondering how much to say. "Well, I know telescopes. I don't know much astronomy. See, my father was into *telescopes*. He took photographs, 35mm long exposures, deep-sky stuff. I looked at the pictures; the pictures were great. But never, you know, through the eyepiece."

"Why not?" I imagined a jealous parent guarding his investment from curious fingers.

But Robin frowned as if I had asked a difficult question. "It's hard to explain. I just didn't want to. Refused to, really. Mmm...have you ever been alone somewhere on a windy night, maybe a dark night in winter? And you kind of get spooked? And you want to look out a window and see how bad the snow is but you get this idea in your head that if you open the curtain something truly horrible is going to be out there staring right back at you? And you know it's childish, but you still don't open the curtain. Just can't bring yourself to do it. You know that feeling?"

I said I'd had similar experiences.

"I think it's a primate thing," Robin meditated. "Stay close to the fire or the leopard'll get you. Anyway, that's the way I feel about telescopes. Irrational, I know. But there it is. Here we are on this cozy planet, and out there are all kinds of things--vast, blazing suns and frigid planets and the dust of dead stars and whole galaxies dying. I always had this feeling that if you looked too close something might look back. Like, don't open the curtain. Don't look through the 'scope. Because something might look back."

Almost certainly someone or something was looking back. The arithmetic is plain: a hundred billion stars in the galaxy alone, many times that number of planets, and even if life is uncommon and intelligence an evolutionary trick shot, odds are that when you gaze at the stars, somewhere in that horizonless infinity another eye is turned back at you.

But that wasn't what Robin meant.

I knew what she meant. Set against the scale of even a single galaxy, a human life is brief and human beings less than microscopic. Small things survive because, taken singly, they're inconsequential. They escape notice. The ant is invisible in the shadow of a spruce bud or a clover leaf. Insects survive because, by and large, we only kill what we can see. The insect prayer: *Don't see me*!

Now consider those wide roads between the stars, where the only wind is a few dry grains of hydrogen and the dust of exploded suns. What if something walked there? Something unseen, invisible, immaterial-- vaster than planets?

I think that's what Robin felt: her own frailty against the abysses of distance and time. *Don't look. Don't see me. Don't look.*

It was a friend of Robin's, a man who had been her lover, who first explained to me the concept of "domains."

By mid-September Robin and I were a couple. It was a relationship we walked into blindly, hypnotized by the sheer unlikeliness of it. I was ten years older, divorced, drifting like a swamped canoe toward the rapids of mid-life; she was a tattooed Gen-Xer (the Worm Oroborous circling her left ankle in blue repose) for whom the death of Kurt Cobain had been a meaningful event. I think we aroused each other's exogamous instincts. We liked to marvel at the chasm between us, that deep and defining gulf: Wynona Ryder vs. Humbert Humbert.

She threw a party to introduce me to her friends. The prospect was daunting but I knew this was one of those hurdles every relationship has to jump or kick the traces. So I came early and helped her clean and cook. Her apartment was the top of a subdivided house in Parkdale off Queen Street. Not the fashionable end of Queen Street; the hooker and junkie turf east of Roncesvalles Avenue. Rent was cheap. She had decorated the rambling attic space with religious bric-a-brac from Goodwill thrift shops and the East Indian dollar store around the corner: ankhs, crosses, bleeding hearts, gaudy Hindu iconography. "Cultural stew," she said. "Artifacts from the new domain. You can ask Roger about that."

I thought: Roger?

Her friends arrived by ones and twos. Lots of students, a few musicians, the creatively unemployed. Many of them thought black was a party colour. I wondered when the tonsure and the goatee had come back into style. Felt set apart in jeans and sweatshirt, the wardrobe-for-all-occasions of another generation. But the people (beneath these appurtenances: people) were mostly friendly. Robin put on a CD of bhangra music and brought out a tall blue plastic water pipe, which circulated with that conspiratorial grace the cannabis culture inherits from its ancestors in Kennedy-era prehistory. This, at least, I recognized. Like Kennedy (they say), unlike Bill Clinton, I inhaled. But only a little. I wanted a clear head to get through the evening.

Robin covered a trestle table with bowls of kasha, rice cooked in miso (her own invention), a curry of beef, curry of eggplant, curry of chicken; chutneys from Kensington Market, loaves of sourdough and French bread and chapatis. Cheap red wine. There was a collective murmur of appreciation and Robin gave me more credit than I deserved--all I had done was stir the pots.

For an hour after dinner I was cornered by a U. of T. poli-sci student from Ethiopia who wanted me to understand how Mao had been betrayed by the revisionists who inherited his empire. He was, of course, the son of a well-to-do bureaucrat, and brutally earnest. I played vague until he gave up on me. Then, cut loose, I trawled through the room picking up fragments of conversation, names dropped: Alice in Chains, Kate Moss, Michaelangelo Signorile. Robin took me by the elbow. "I'm making tea. Talk to Roger!"

Roger was tall and pale, with a shock of bleached hair threatening to obscure the vision in his right eye. He had the emaciated frame of a heroin addict, but it was willful, an aesthetic statement, and he dressed expensively.

Roger. "Domains." Fortunately I didn't have to ask; he was already explaining it to a pair of globe-eyed identical twins.

"It's McCluhanesque," one twin said; the other: "No, *ecological....*"

Roger smiled, a little condescendingly, I thought, but I was already wondering what he meant to Robin, or Robin to him. He put out his hand: "You must be Michael. Robin told me about you."

But not me about Roger. At least not much. I said, "She mentioned something about 'domains'--"

"Well, Robin just likes to hear me bullshit."

"No!" (The twins.) "Roger is *original.*"

It didn't take much coaxing. I can't reproduce his voice--cool fluid, slightly nasal--but what he said, basically, was this:

Life, the biological phenomenon, colonizes domains and turns them into ecologies. In the domain of the ocean, the first ecologies evolved. The dry surface of the continents was a dead domain until the first plants (lichens or molds, I suppose) took root. The air was an empty domain until the evolution of the wing.

But domain theory, Roger said, wasn't just a matter of biology versus geology. A living system could *itself* become a domain. In fact, once the geological domains were fully colonized, living systems became the last terrestrial domain and a kind of intensive recomplication followed: treetops, colonizing the air, were colonized in turn by insects, by birds; animal life by bacteria, viruses, parasites, each new array creating its own new domain, and so *ad infinitum.*

What made Roger's notion original was that he believed human beings had--for the first time in millenia--begun to colonize a wholly new domain, which he called the gnososphere: the domain of culture, art, religion, language. Because we were the first aboard, the gnososphere felt more like geology than ecology: a body of artifacts, lifeless as a brick. But that appearance was already beginning to change. We had seen in the last decade the first glimmerings of competition, specifically from the kind of computer program called "artificial life," entities that live--and evolve-- entirely in the logarithms of computers, the high alps of the gnososphere. Not competing for *our* ground, obviously, but that time might come (consider computer "viruses"), and--who knows?--the gnososphere might eventually evolve its own independent entities. Maybe already had. When the gnososphere was "made of" campfire stories and cave paintings it was clearly not complex enough to support life. But the gnososphere at the end of the twentieth century had grown vast and intricate, a landscape both cerebral and electronic, born at the juncture of technology and human population, in which crude self-replicating structures (Nazism, say; Communism) had already proven their ability to grow, feed, reproduce and die. Ideologies were like primitive DNA floating in a nutrient soup of radio waves, television images, words. Who could say what a more highly evolved creature--with protein coat, nucleus, mitochondria; with eyes and genitals--might be like? We might not be able to experience it at all, since no single human being could be its host; it would live through our collectivity, as immense as it was unknowable.

"Amazing," the twins said, when Roger finished. "*Awesome.*"

And suddenly Robin was beside me, handing out tea, taking my arm in a proprietary gesture meant, I hoped, for Roger, who smiled tolerantly. "He is amazing, isn't he? Or else completely insane."

"Not for me to say," Roger obliged. (The twins laughed.)

"Roger used to be a Fine Arts T.A. at the University," Robin said, "until he dropped out. Now he builds things."

"Sculpture?" I asked.

"*Things.* Maybe he'll show you sometime."

Roger nodded, but I doubted he'd extend the invitation. We were circling each other like wary animals. I read him as bright, smug, and subtly hostile. He obviously felt a powerful need to impress an audience. Probably he had once impressed Robin--she confirmed this later--and I imagined him abandoning her because, as audience, she had grown a little cynical. The twins (young, female) clearly delighted him. Just as clearly, I didn't.

But we were polite. We talked a little more. He knew the book store where I worked. "Been there often," he said. And it was easy to imagine him posed against the philosophy shelves, long fingers opening Kierkegaard, the critical frown fixed in place. After a while I left him to the twins, who waved me goodbye: "Nice meeting you!" "*Really!*"

When I was younger I read a lot of science fiction. Through my interest in astronomy I came to sf, and through both I happened across an astronomer's puzzle, a cosmological version of Pascal's Wager. It goes like this: If life can spread through the galaxy, then, logically, it already has. Our neighbours should be here. Should have been here for millennia. Where are they?

I discussed it, while the party ran down, with the only guest older than I was, a greying science-fiction writer who had been hitting the pipe with a certain bleak determination. "The Oort cloud," he declared, "*that's* where they are. I mean, why bother with planets? For dedicated space technologies--and I assume they would send machines, not something as short-lived and finicky as a biological organism--a planet's not a really attractive place. Planets are heavy, corrosive, too hot for superconductors. Interesting places, maybe, because planets are where cultures grow, and why slog across all those light years unless you're looking for something as complex and unpredictable as a sentient culture? But you don't, for God's sake, fill up their sky with spaceships. You stick around the Oort cloud, where it's nice and cold and there are cometary bodies to draw resources from. You hang out, you listen. If you want to talk, you pick your own time.''

The Oort cloud is that nebulous ring around the solar system, well beyond the orbit of Pluto, composed of small bodies of dust and water ice. Gravitational perturbation periodically knocks a few of these bodies into elliptical orbits; traversing the inner solar system, they become comets. Our annual meteor showers--the Perseids, the Geminids, the Quadrantids-- are the remnants of ancient, fractured comets. Oort cloud visitors, old beyond memory.

But in light of Roger's thesis I wondered if the question was too narrowly posed, the science fiction writer's answer too pat. Maybe our neighbors had already arrived, not in silver ships but in metaphysics, informing the very construction and representation of our lives. The cave paintings at Lascaux, Chartres Cathedral, the Fox Broadcasting System: not their physicality (and they become less physical as our technology advances) but their intangible *grammar*--maybe this is the evidence they left us, a ruined archeology of cognition, invisible because pervasive, inescapable: they are both here, in other words, and not here; they are us and not-us.

When the last guest was gone, the last dish stacked, Robin pulled off her shirt and walked through the apartment, coolly unselfconscious, turning off lights.

The heat of the party lingered. She opened the bedroom window to let in a breeze from the lakeshore. It was past two in the morning and the city was relatively quiet. I paid attention to the sounds she made, the rustle as she stepped out of her skirt, the easing of springs in the thrift-shop bed. She wore a ring through each nipple, delicate turquoise rings that gave back glimmers of ambient light. I remembered how unfamiliar her piercings had seemed the first time I encountered them with my tongue, the polished circles, their chilly, perfect geometry set against the warmer and more complex terrain of breast and aureole.

We made love in that distracted after-a-party way, while the room was still alive with the musk of the crowd, feeling like exhibitionists (I think she felt that way too) even though we were alone.

It was afterward, in a round of sleepy pillow talk, that she told me Roger had been her lover. I put a finger gently through one of her rings and she said Roger had piercings, too: one nipple and under the scrotum, penetrating the area between the testicles and the anus. Some men had the head of the penis pierced (a "Prince Albert") but Roger hadn't gone for that.

I was jealous. Jealous, I suppose, of this extra dimension of intimacy from which I was excluded. I had no wounds to show her.

She said, "You never talk about your divorce."

"It's not much fun to talk about."

"You left Carolyn, or she left you?"

"It's not that simple. But, ultimately, I guess she left me."

"Lots of fighting?"

"No fighting."

"What, then?"

I thought about it. "Continental drift."

"What was her problem?"

"I'm not so sure it *was* her problem."

"She must have had a reason, though--or thought she did."

"She said I was never there." Robin waited patiently. I went on, "Even when I was with her, I was never *there*--or so she claimed. I'm not sure I know what she meant. I suppose, that I wasn't completely engaged. That I was apart. Held back. With her, with her friends, with her family-- with anybody."

"Do you think that's true?"

It was a question I'd asked myself too often.

Sure, in a sense it *was* true. I'm one of those people who are often called loners. Crowds don't have much allure for me. I don't confide easily and I don't have many friends.

That much I would admit to. The idea (which had come to obsess Carolyn during our divorce) that I was congenitally, hopelessly *set apart*, a kind of pariah dog, incapable of real intimacy...that was a whole 'nother thing.

We talked it around. Robin was solemn in the dark, propped on one elbow. Through the window, past the halo of her hair, I could see the setting moon. Far away down the dark street someone laughed.

Robin, who had studied a little anthropology, liked to see things in evolutionary terms. "You have a night watch personality," she decided, closing her eyes.

"Night watch?"

"Mm-hm. Primates...you know...proto-hominids...it's where all our personality styles come from. We're social animals, basically, but the group is more versatile if you have maybe a couple of hyperthymic types for cheerleaders, some dysthymics to sit home and mumble, and the one guy--you--who edges away from the crowd, who sits up when everybody else is asleep, who basically keeps the watches of the night. The one who sees the lions coming. Good night vision and lousy social skills. Every tribe should have one."

"Is that what I am?"

"It's reassuring, actually." She patted my ass and said, "Keep watch for me, okay?"

I kept the watch a few minutes more.

In the morning, on the way to lunch, we visited one of those East Indian/ West Indian shops, the kind with the impossibly gaudy portraits of Shiva and Ganesh in chrome-flash plastic frames, a cooler full of ginger beer and coconut pop, shelves of sandalwood incense and patchouli oil and bottles of magic potions (Robin pointed them out): St. John Conqueror Root, Ghost Away, Luck Finder, with labels claiming the contents were an Excellent Floor Polish, which I suppose made them legal to sell. Robin was delighted: "Flotsam from the gnososphere," she laughed, and it was easy to imagine one of Roger's gnostic creatures made manifest in this shop--for that matter, in this city, this English-speaking, Cantonese-speaking, Urdu-speaking, Farsi-speaking city--a slouching, ethereal beast of which one cell might be Ganesh the Elephant-Headed Boy and another Madonna, the Cone-Breasted Woman.

A city, for obvious reasons, is a lousy place to do astronomy. I worked the 'scope from the back deck of my apartment, shielded from streetlights, and Robin gave me a selection of broadband lens filters to cut the urban scatter. But I was interested in deep-sky observing and I knew I wasn't getting everything I'd paid for.

In October I arranged to truck the 'scope up north for a weekend. I rented a van and Robin reserved us a cabin at a private campground near Algonquin Park. It was way past tourist season, but Robin knew the woman who owned the property; we would have the place virtually to ourselves and we could cancel, no problem, if the weather didn't look right.

But the weather cooperated. It was the end of the month--coincidentally, the weekend of the Orionid meteor shower--and we were in the middle of a clean high-pressure cell that stretched from Alberta to Labrador. The air was brisk but cloudless, transparent as creek water. We arrived at the camp site Friday afternoon and I spent a couple of hours setting up the scope, calibrating it, and running an extension cord out to the automatic guider. I attached a 35mm SLR camera loaded with hypersensitized Tech Pan film, and I did all this despite the accompaniment of the owner's five barking Yorkshire Terrier pups. The ground under my feet was glacier-scarred Laurentian Shield rock; the meadow I set up in was broad and flat; highway lights were pale and distant. Perfect. By the time I finished setting up it was dusk. Robin had started a fire in the pit outside our cabin and was roasting chicken and bell peppers. The cabin overlooked a marshy lake thick with duckweed; the air was cool and moist and I fretted about ground mist.

But the night was clear. After dinner Robin smoked marijuana in a tiny carved soapstone pipe (I didn't) and then we went out to the meadow, bundled in winter jackets.

I worked the scope. Robin wouldn't look through the eyepiece--her old phobia--but took a great, grinning pleasure in the Orionids, exclaiming at each brief etching of the cave-dark, star-scattered sky. Her laughter was almost giddy.

After a time, though, she complained of the cold, and I sent her back to the cabin (we had borrowed a space heater from the owner) and told her to get some sleep. I was cold, too, but intoxicated by the sky. It was my first attempt at deep-sky photography and surprisingly successful: when the photos were developed later that week I had a clean, hard shot of M100 in Coma Berenices, a spiral galaxy in full disk, arms sweeping toward the bright center; a city of stars beyond counting, alive, perhaps, with civilizations, so impossibly distant that the photons hoarded by the lens of the telescope were already millions of years old.

When I finally came to bed Robin was asleep under two quilted blankets. She stirred at my pressure on the mattress and turned to me, opened her eyes briefly, then folded her cinnamon-scented warmth against my chest, and I lay awake smelling the hot coils of the space heater and the faint pungency of the marijuana she had smoked and the pine-resinous air that had swept in behind me, these night odors mysteriously familiar, intimate as memory.

We made love in the morning, lazy and a little tired, and I thought there was something new in the way she looked at me, a certain calculating distance, but I wasn't sure; it might just be the slant of light through the dusty window. In the afternoon we hiked out to a wild blueberry patch she knew about, but the season was over; frost had shrivelled the last of the berries. (The Yorkshire Terriers were at our heels, there and back.)

That night was much the same as the first except that Robin decided to stay back at the cabin reading an Anne Rice novel. I remembered that her father was an amateur astronomer and wondered if the parallel wasn't a little unsettling for her: there are limits to the pleasures of symbolic incest. I photographed M33 in Triangulum, another elliptical galaxy, its arms luminous with stars, and in the morning we packed up the telescope and began the long drive south.

She was moodier than usual. In the cabin of the van, huddled by the passenger door with her knees against her chest, she said, "We never talk about relationship things."

"Relationship things?"

"For instance, monogamy."

That hung in the air for a while.

Then she said, "Do you believe in it?"

I said it didn't really matter whether I "believed in" it; it just seemed to be something I did. I had never been unfaithful to Carolyn, unless you counted Robin; I had never been unfaithful to Robin.

But she was twenty-five years old and hadn't taken the measure of these things. "I think it's a sexual preference," she said. "Some people are, some people aren't."

I said--carefully neutral--"Where do you stand?"

"I don't know." She gazed out the window at October farms, brown fields, wind-canted barns. "I haven't decided."

We left it at that.

She threw a Halloween party, costumes optional--I wore street clothes, but most of her crowd welcomed the opportunity to dress up. Strange hair and body paint, mainly. Roger (I had learned his last name: Roger Russo) showed up wearing a feathered headdress, green dye, kohl circles around his eyes. He said he was Sacha Runa, the jungle spirit of the Peruvian *ayahuasqueros*. Robin said he had been investigating the idea of shamanic spirit creatures as the first entities cohabiting the gnososphere: she thought the costume was perfect for him. She hugged him carefully, pecked his green-dyed cheek, merely friendly, but he glanced reflexively at me and quickly away, as if to confirm that I had seen her touch him.

I had one of my photographs, the galaxy M33, enlarged and framed; I gave it to Robin as a gift.

She hung it in her bedroom. I remember--it might have been November, maybe as late as the Leonids, mid-month--a night when she stared at it while we made love: she on her knees on the bed, head upturned, raw-cut hair darkly stubbled on her scalp, and me behind her, gripping her thin, almost fragile hips, knowing she was looking at the stars.

Three optical illusions:

1) Retinal floaters. Those delicate, crystalline motes, like rainbow-hued diatoms, that swim through the field of vision.

Some nights, when I've been too long at the 'scope, I see them drifting up from the horizon, a terrestrial commerce with the sky.

2) In 1877, Giovanni Schiaparelli mapped what he believed were the canals of Mars. Mars has no canals; it is an airless desert. But for decades the educated world believed in a decadent Martian civilization, doomed to extinction when its water evaporated to the frigid poles.

It was Schiaparelli who first suggested that meteor showers represent the remains of ancient, shattered comets.

3) Computer-generated three-dimensional pictures--they were everywhere that summer, a fad. You know the kind? The picture looks like so much visual hash, until you focus your eyes well beyond it; then the image lofts out, a hidden *bas-relief*: ether sculpture.

Robin believed TV worked the same way. "If you turn to a blank channel," she told me (December: first snow outside the window), "you can see pictures in the static. Three-dee. And they move."

What kind of pictures?

"Strange." She was clearly uncomfortable talking about it. "Kind of like animals. Or bugs. Lots of arms. The eyes are very...strange." She gave me a shy look. "Am I crazy?"

"No." Everyone has a soft spot or two. "You look at these pictures often?"

"Hardly ever. Frankly, it's kind of scary. But it's also...."

"What?"

"*Tempting.*"

I don't own a television set. One summer Carolyn and I had taken a trip to Mexico and we had seen the famous murals at Teotihuacan. Disembodied eyes everywhere: plants with eyes for flowers, flowers exuding eyes, eyes floating through the convolute images like lost balloons. Whenever people talk about television, I'm reminded of Teotihuacan.

Like Robin, I was afraid to look through certain lenses for fear of what might be looking back.

That winter, I learned more about Roger Russo.

He was wealthy. At least, his family was wealthy. The family owned Russo Precision Parts, an electronics distributor with a near-monopoly of the Canadian manufacturing market. Roger's older brother was the corporate heir-designate; Roger himself, I gather, was considered "creative" (i.e, unemployable) and allowed a generous annual remittance to do with as he pleased.

Early in January (the Quadrantids, but they were disappointing that year) Robin took me to Roger's place. He lived in a house off Queen West--leased it from a cousin--a three-story brick Edwardian bastion in a

Chinese neighborhood where the houses on each side had been painted cherry red. We trekked from the streetcar through fresh, ankle-high snow; the snow was still falling, cold and granular. Robin had made the date: we were supposed to have lunch, the three of us. I think she liked bringing Roger and me together, liked those faint proprietary sparks that passed between us; I think it flattered her. Myself, I didn't enjoy it. I doubted Roger took much pleasure in it, either.

He answered the door wearing nothing but jogging pants. His solitary silver nipple ring dangled on his hairless chest; it reminded me-- sorry--of a pull-tab on a soft drink can. He shooed us in and latched the door. Inside, the air was warm and moist.

The house was a shrine to his eccentricity: books everywhere, not only shelved but stacked in corners, an assortment too random to catego- rize, but I spotted early editions of William James (*Psychology*, the com- plete work) and Karl Jung; a ponderous hardcover *Phenomenology of the Mind*, Heidegger's *Being and Time*. We adjourned to a big wood-and-tile kitchen and made conversation while Roger chopped kohlrabi at a butcher- block counter. He had seen *Natural Born Killers* at a review theatre and was impressed by it: "It's completely post-post--a deconstruction of *itself*-- very image-intensive and, you know, florid, like early church iconogra- phy...."

The talk went on like this. High-toned media gossip, basically. After lunch, I excused myself and hunted down the bathroom.

On the way back I paused at the kitchen door when I heard Roger mention my name.

"Michael's not much of a watcher, is he?"

Robin: "Well, he is, actually--a certain kind of watcher."

"Oh--the astronomy...."

"Yes."

"That photograph you showed me."

"Yes, right."

That photograph, I thought. The one on her bedroom wall.

Later, in the winter-afternoon lull that softens outdoor sounds and amplifies the rumble of the furnace, Robin asked Roger to show me around the house. "The upstairs," she said, and to me: "It's so weird!"

"Thanks," Roger said.

"You know what I mean! Don't pretend to be insulted. Weird is your middle name."

I followed Roger's pale back up the narrow stairway, creaking risers lined with faded red carpet. Then, suddenly, we were in another world: a cavernous space--walls must have been knocked out--crowded with electronic kibble. Video screens, raw circuit boards, ribbon wire snaking through the clutter like eels through a gloomy reef. He threw a wall switch, and it all came to life.

"A dozen cathode ray tubes," Roger said, "mostly yard-sale and electronic-jobber trash." Some were black and white, some crenellated with noise bars. "Each one cycles through every channel you can get from cable. I wired in my own decoder for the scrambled channels. The cycles are staggered, so mostly you get chaos, but every so often they fall into sync and for a split second the same image is all around you. I meant to install a satellite dish, feed in another hundred channels, but the mixer would have been...complex. Anyway, I lost interest."

"Not to sound like a Philistine," I said, "but what is it--a work of art?"

Roger smiled loftily. "In a way. Actually, it was meant to be a ghost trap."

"Ghost trap?"

"In the Hegelian sense. The *weltgeist*."

"Summoned from the gnososphere," Robin added.

I asked about the music. The music had commenced when he threw the switch: a strange nasal melody, sometimes hummed, sometimes chanted. It filled the air like incense. The words, when I could make them out, were foreign and punctuated with thick glottal stops. There were insect sounds in the background; I supposed it was a field recording, the kind of anthropological oddity a company called Nonesuch used to release on vinyl, years ago.

"It's called an *icaro*," Roger said. "A supernatural melody. Certain Peruvian Indians drink *ayahuasca* and produce these songs. *Icaros*. They learn them from the spirit world."

Ayahuasca is a hallucinogenic potion made from a mixture of *Banisteriopsis caapi* vines and the leaves of *Psychotria viridis*, both rainforest plants. (I spent a day at the Robarts looking it up.) Apparently it can be made from a variety of more common plant sources, and *ayahuasca* churches like the *Uniao do Vegetal* have popularised its use in the urban centres of Brazil.

"And the third floor," Robin said, waving at the stairs dimly visible across the room, "that's amazing, too. Roger built an addition over what used to be the roof of the building. There's a greenhouse, an actual greenhouse! You can't see it from the street because the facade hides it, but it's huge. And there's a big open-air deck. Show him, Roger."

Roger shook his head: "I don't think it's necessary."

We were about to leave the room when three of the video screens suddenly radiated the same image: waterfall and ferns in soft focus, and a pale woman in a white skirt standing beside a Datsun that matched her blue-green eyes. It snagged Roger's attention. He stopped in his tracks.

"*Rainha da Floresta*," he murmured, looking from Robin to me and back again, his face obscure in the flickering light. "The lunar aspect."

The winter sky performed its long procession. One clear night in February, hungry for starlight, I zipped myself into my parka and drove a little distance west of the city--not with the telescope but with a pair of 10X50 Zeiss binoculars. Hardly Mount Palomar, but not far removed from the simple optics Galileo ground for himself some few centuries ago.

I parked off an access road along the ridge-top of Rattlesnake Point, with a clear view to the frozen rim of Lake Ontario. Sirius hung above the dark water, a little obscured by rising mist. Capella was high overhead, and to the west I was able to distinguish the faint oval of the Andromeda galaxy, two-million-odd light years away. East, the sky was vague with city glare and etched by the running lights of airliners orbiting Pearson International.

Alone in the van, breathing steam and balancing the binoculars on the rim of a half-open window, I found myself thinking about the E.T. paradox. They ought to be here...where are they?

The science fiction writer at Robin's party had said they wouldn't come in person. Organic life is too brief and too fragile for the eons-long journeys between stars. They would send machines. Maybe self-replicating machines. Maybe sentient machines.

But, I thought, why machines at all? If the thing that travels most efficiently between stars is light (and all its avatars: X-rays, radio waves), then why not send *light itself*? Light *modulated*, of course; light alive with information. Light as medium. Sentient light.

Light as domain, perhaps put in place by organic civilizations, but inherited by--something else.

And if human beings are truly latecomers to the galaxy, then the network must already be ancient, a web of modulated signals stitching together the stars. A domain in which things--entities--creatures perhaps as diffuse and large as the galaxy itself, creatures made solely of information-- live and compete and maybe even hunt.

An ecology of starlight, or better: a *jungle* of starlight.

The next day I called up Robin's sf-writer friend and tried out the idea on him. He said, "Well, it's interesting...."

"But is it possible?"

"Sure it's possible. Anything's possible. Possible is my line of work. But you have to keep in mind the difference between a possibility and a likelihood." He hesitated. "Are you thinking of becoming a writer, or just a career paranoid?"

I laughed. "Neither one." Though the laughter was a little forced.

"Well, then, since we're only playing, here's another notion for you. Living things--species capable of evolving--don't just live. They eat." (Hunt, I thought.) "They die. And most important of all: they reproduce."

You've probably heard of the hunting wasp. The hunting wasp paralyses insects (the tarantula is a popular choice) and uses the still-living bodies to incubate and feed its young.

It's everybody's favorite Hymenoptera horror story. You can't help imagining how the tarantula must feel, immobilized but for its frantic heartbeat, the wasp larvae beginning to stir inside it...stir, and feed.

But maybe the tarantula isn't only paralysed. Maybe it's entranced. Maybe wasp venom is a kind of insect ambrosia--*soma, amrta, kykeon*. Maybe the tarantula sees God, feels God turning in hungry spirals deep inside it.

I think that would be worse--don't you?

Was I in love with Robin Slattery? I think this narrative doesn't make that absolutely clear--too many second thoughts since--but yes, I was in love with Robin. In love with the way she looked at me (that mix of deference and pity), the way she moved, her strange blend of erudition and ignorance (the only Shakespeare she had read was *The Tempest*, but she had read it five times and attended a performance at Stratford), her skinny legs, her pyrotechnic fashion sense (one day black Goth, next day tartan miniskirt and knee socks).

I paid her the close attention of a lover, and because I did I knew by spring (the Eta Aquarids...early May) that things had changed.

She spent a night at my place, something she had been doing less often lately. We went into the bedroom with the sound of *soca* tapes pulsing like a heartbeat from the shop downstairs. I had covered one wall with astronomical photographs, stuck to the plaster with push pins. She looked at the wall and said, "This is why men shouldn't be allowed to live alone--they do things like this."

"Is that a proposition?" I was feeling, I guess, reckless.

"No," she said, looking worried, "I only meant...."

"I know."

"I mean, it's not exactly *Good Housekeeping*."

"Right."

We went to bed troubled. We made love, but tentatively, and later, when she had turned on her side and her breathing was night-quiet, I left the bed and walked naked to the kitchen.

I didn't need to turn on lights. The moon cast a gray radiance through the rippled glass of the kitchen window. I only wanted to sit a while in the cool of an empty room.

But I guess Robin hadn't been sleeping after all, because she came to the kitchen wrapped in my bath robe, standing in the silver light like a quizzical, barefoot monk.

"Keeping the night watch," I said.

She leaned against a wall. "It's lonely, isn't it?"

I just looked at her. Wished I could see her eyes.

"Lonely," she said, "out here on the African plains."

I wondered if her intuition was right, if there was a gene, a defective sequence of DNA, that marked me and set me apart from everyone else.

The image of the watchman-hominid was a powerful one. I pictured that theoretical ancestor of mine. Our hominid ancestors were small, vulnerable, as much animal as human. The tribe sleeps. The watchman doesn't. I imagine him awake in the long exile of the night, rump against a rock in a sea of wild grasses, shivering when the wind blows, watching the horizon for danger. The horizon and the sky.

What does he see?

The stars in their silent migrations. The annual meteor showers. A comet, perhaps, falling sunward from the far reefs of the solar system.

What does he feel?

Yes: lonely.

And often afraid.

In the morning, Robin said, "As a relationship, I don't think we're working. There's this *distance*...I mean, it's lonely for me, too...."

But she didn't really want to talk about it and I didn't really want to press her. The dynamic was clear enough.

She was kinder than Carolyn had been, and for that I was grateful.

I won't chronicle the history of our break-up. You know how this goes. Phone calls less often, fewer visits; then times when the messages I left on her machine went unreturned, and a penultimate moment of drawing-room comedy when Roger picked up her phone and kindly summoned her from the shower for me. (I pictured her in a towel, hair dripping while she made her vague apologies--and Roger watching.)

No hostility, just drift; and finally silence.

Another spring, another summer--the Eta Aquarids, the Delta Aquarids, at last the Perseids in the sweltering heat of a humid, cicada-buzzing August, two and half months since the last time we talked.

I was on the back deck of my apartment when the phone rang. It was still too hot to sleep, but *mirabile dictu*, the air was clear, and I kept the night watch in a lawn chair with my binoculars beside me. I heard the ring but ignored it--most of my phone calls lately had been sales pitches or marketing surveys, and the sky, even in the city (if you knew how to look), was alive with meteors, the best display in years. I thought about rock fragments old as the solar system, incinerated in the high atmosphere. The ash, I supposed, must eventually sift down through the air; we must breathe it, in some part; molecules of ancient carbon lodging in the soft tissue of the lung.

Two hours after midnight I went inside, brushed my teeth, thought about bed--then played the message on my answering machine.

It was from Robin.

"Mike? Are you there? If you can hear me, pick up...come on, *pick up*! [Pause.] Well, okay. I guess it's not really important. Shit. It's only that...there's something I'm not sure about. I just wanted to talk about it with someone. With you. [Pause.] You were always so *solid*. It thought it would be good to hear your voice again. Not tonight, huh? I guess not. Hey, don't worry about me. I'll be okay. But if you--"

The machine cut her off.

I tried calling back, but nobody answered the phone.

I knew her well enough to hear the anxiety in her voice. And she wouldn't have called me unless she was in some kind of trouble.

Robin, I thought, what lens did you look through? And what looked back?

I drove through the empty city to Parkdale, where there was no traffic but cabs and a few bad-tempered hookers; parked and pounded on Robin's door until her downstairs neighbors complained. She wasn't home, she'd gone out earlier, and I should fuck off and die.

I drove to Roger's.

The tall brick house was full of light.

When I knocked, the twins answered. They had shaved their heads since the last time I saw them. The effect was to make them even less distinguishable. Both were naked, their skin glistening with a light sheen of sweat and something else: spatters of green paint. Drops of it hung in their wiry, short pubic hair.

They blinked at me a moment before recognition set in. I couldn't recall their names (I thought of them as Alpha and Beta)--but they remembered mine.

"Michael!"

"Robin's friend!"

"What are *you* doing here?"

I told them I wanted to talk to Robin.

"She's real busy right now--"

"I'd like to come in."

They looked at each other as if in mute consultation. Then (one a fraction of a second after the other) they smiled and nodded.

Every downstairs light had been turned on, but the rooms I could see from the foyer were empty. One of Roger's *icaros* was playing somewhere; the chanting coiled through the air like the winding of a spring. I heard other voices, faintly, elsewhere in the house--upstairs.

Alpha and Beta looked alarmed when I headed for the stairs. "Maybe you shouldn't go up there, Michael."

"You weren't *invited*."

I ignored them and took the steps two at a time. The twins hurried up behind me.

Roger's gnostic ghost trap was switched on, its video screens flashing faster than the last time I had seen it. No image lingered long enough to resolve, but the flickering light was more than random; I felt presences in it, the kind of motion that alerts the peripheral vision. The icaro was louder and more insinuating in this warehouse-like space, a sound that invaded the body through the pores.

But the room was empty.

The twins regarded me, smiling blandly, pupils big as half-dollars. "Of course, all this isn't *necessary*--"

"You don't have to *summon* something that's already *inside you*--"

"But it's *out there*, too--"

"In the images--"

"In the *gnososphere*..."

"Everywhere...."

The third floor: more stairs at the opposite end of the room. I moved that way with the maddening sensation that time itself had slowed, that I was embedded in some invisible, congealed substance that made every footstep a labor. The twins were right behind me, still performing their mad Baedeker.

"The greenhouse!" (Alpha.)

"Yes, you should see it." (Beta.)

The stairs led to a door; the door opened into a jungle humidity lit by ranks of fluorescent bars. Plants were everywhere; I had to blink before I could make sense of it.

"*Psychotria viridis,*" Alpha said.

"And other plants--"

"Common grasses--"

"*Desmanthus illinoensis--*"

"*Phalaris arundinacea--*"

It was as Robin had described it, a greenhouse built over an expansion of the house, concealed from the street by an attic riser. The ceiling and the far walls were of glass, dripping with moisture. The air was thick and hard to breathe.

"Plants that contain DMT." (The twins, still babbling.)

"It's a drug--"

"And a *neurotransmitter.*"

"N,N-dimethyltryptamine...."

"It's what dreams are made of, Michael."

"Dreams and imagination."

"Culture."

"Religion!"

"It's the *opening--*"

I said, "Is she drugged? For Christ's sake, where is she?"

But the twins didn't answer.

I saw motion through the glass. The deck extended beyond the greenhouse, but there was no obvious door. I stumbled down a corridor of slim-leaved potted plants and put my hands against the dripping glass.

People out there.

"She's the *Rainha da Floresta--*"

"And Roger is *Santo Daime!*"

"All the archetypes, really...."

"Male and female, sun and moon...."

I swiped away the condensation with my sleeve. A group of maybe a dozen people had gathered on the wooden decking outside, night wind tugging at their hair. I recognized faces from Robin's parties, dimly illuminated by the emerald glow of the greenhouse. They formed a semicircle with Robin at the centre of it--Robin and Roger.

She wore a white t-shirt but was naked below the waist. Roger was entirely naked and covered with glistening green dye. They held each other at arm's length, as if performing some elaborate dance, but they were motionless, eyes fixed on one another.

Sometime earlier the embrace must have been more intimate; his paint was smeared on Robin's shirt and thighs. She was thinner than I remembered, almost anorexic.

Alpha said, "It's sort of a wedding--"

"An *alchemical* wedding."

"And sort of a birth."

There had to be a door. I kicked over a brick and board platform, spilling plants and potting soil as I followed the wall. The door, when I found it, was glass in a metal frame, and there was a padlock across the clasp.

I rattled it, banged my palm against it. Where my hand had been I could see through the smear of humidity. A few heads turned at the noise-- including, I recognized, the science fiction writer I had talked to long ago. But there was no curiosity in his gaze, only a desultory puzzlement. Roger and Robin remained locked in their peculiar trance, touching but apart, as if making room between them for...what?

No, something *had* changed: now their eyes were closed. Robin was breathing in short, stertorous gasps that made me think of a woman in labor. (A *birth*, the twins had said.)

I looked for something to break the glass--a brick, a pot.

Alpha stepped forward, shaking her head. "Too late for that, Michael."

And I knew--with a flood of grief that seemed to well up from some neglected, swollen wound--that she was right.

I turned back. To watch.

Past understanding, there is only observation. All I know is what I saw. What I saw, with the glass between myself and Robin. With my cheek against the dripping glass.

Something came out of her.

Something came out of her.

Something came out of her and Roger, like ectoplasm; but especially from their eyes, flowing like hot blue smoke.

I thought their heads were on fire.

Then the smoke condensed between them, took on a solid form, suspended weightless in the space between their tensed bodies.

The shape it took was complex, barbed, hard-edged, luminous, with the infolded symmetries of a star coral and the thousand facets of a geode. Suddenly translucent, it seemed made of frozen light. Strange as it was, it looked almost obscenely organic. I thought of a seed, an *achene*, the dense nucleus of something potentially enormous: a foetal god.

I don't know how long it hovered between their two tensed bodies. I was distantly aware of my own breathing. Of the hot moisture of my skin against the greenhouse glass. The *icaro* had stopped. I thought the world itself had fallen silent.

Then the thing that had appeared between them, the bright impossibility they had given birth to, began to rise, at first almost imperceptibly, then accelerating until it was suddenly gone, transiting the sky at, I guessed, the speed of light.

Commerce with the stars.

Then Robin collapsed.

I kicked at the door until, finally, the clasp gave way; then there were hands on me, restraining me, and I closed my eyes and let them carry me away.

She was alive.

I had seen her led down the stairs, groggy and emaciated but moving under her own volition. She needed sleep, the twins said. That was all.

They brought me to a room and left me alone with my friend the science fiction writer.

He poured a drink.

"Do you know," he asked, "can you even begin to grasp what you saw here tonight?"

I shook my head.

"But you've thought about it," he said. "We talked. You've drawn some conclusions. And, as a matter of fact, in this territory, we're all ignorant. In the gnososphere, Michael, intuition counts for more than knowledge. My intuition is that what you've seen here won't be at all uncommon in the next few years. It may become a daily event--a part, maybe even the central part, of the human experience.''

I stared at him.

He said, ''Your best move, Michael, and I mean this quite sincerely, would be to just get over it and get on with your life.''

''Or else?''

''No 'or else.' No threats. It doesn't matter what you do. One human being...we amount to nothing, you know. Maybe we dive into the future, like Roger, or we hang back, dig in our heels, but it doesn't matter. It really doesn't. In the end you'll do what you want.''

''I want to leave.''

''Then leave. I don't have an explanation to offer. Only a few ideas of my own, if you care to hear them.''

I stayed a while longer.

The Orionids, the Leonids: the stars go on falling with their serene implacability, but I confess, it's hard to look at them now. Bitter and hard.

Consider, he said, living things as large as the galaxy itself. Consider their slow ecology, their evolution across spans of time in which history counts for much less than a heartbeat.

Consider spores that lie dormant, perhaps for millennia, in the planetary clouds of newborn stars. Spores carried by cometary impact into the fresh biosphere (the *domain*) of a life-bearing world.

Consider our own evolution, human evolution, as one stage in a reproductive process in which *human culture itself* is the flower: literally, a flower, gaudy and fertile, from which fresh seed is generated and broadcast.

''Robin is a flower,'' he said, ''but there's nothing special about that. Roger hastened the process with his drugs and paraphernalia and symbolic magic. So he could be among the first. The *avante-garde*. But the time is coming for all of us, Michael, and soon we won't need props. The thing that's haunted us as a species, the thing we painted on our cave walls and carved into our pillars and cornices and worshipped on our bloody altars and movie screens, it's almost here. We'll all be flowers, I think, before long.''

Unless the flower is sterile--set apart, functionally alone, a genetic fluke.

But in another sense the flower is our culture itself, and I can't help wondering what happens to that flower after it broadcasts its seed. Maybe it wilts. Maybe it dies.

Maybe that's already happening. Have you looked at a newspaper lately?

Or maybe, like every other process in the slow ecology of the stars, it'll take a few centuries more.

I cashed in my investments and bought a house in rural British Columbia. Fled the city for reasons I preferred not to consider.

The night sky is dark here, the stars as close as the rooftop and the tall pines--but I seldom look at the sky.

When I do, I focus my telescope on the moon. It seems to me that sparks of light are gathering and moving in the Reiner Gamma area of Oceanus Procellarum. Faintly, almost furtively. Look for yourself. But there's been nothing in the journals about it. So it might be an optical illusion. Or my imagination.

The imagination is also a place where things live.

I'm alone.

It gets cold here in winter.

Robin called once. She said she'd tracked down my new number, that she wanted to talk. She had broken up with Roger. Whatever had happened that night in the city, she said, it was finished now. Life goes on.

Life goes on.

She said she got lonely these days and maybe she understood how it was for me, out there looking at the sky while everyone else sleeps.

(And maybe the watchman sees something coming, Robin, something large and terrible and indistinct in the darkness, but he knows he can't stop it and he can't wake anyone up....)

She said we weren't finished. She said she wanted to see me. She had a little money, she said, and she wanted to fly out. Please, she said. Please, Michael. Please.

God help me, I hung up the phone.

———————— ✳ ————————

Widow's Walk

CAROLYN CLINK

Her spirit walks each evening as the moon rises.
Salt spray passes through her. Looking out to sea,
she wonders, Which ship will carry my husband home?

Her hair, a charcoal mist framing a stark white face,
looks windblown though no breeze touches her.
As she moves, the ancient grey dress shimmers.

The sea shrieks with sympathy for her endless tears.
Surf blasts the shoreline, scouring the driftwood bones
of capsized vessels finally returned to land.

The distant lighthouse beacon shines no more.
Behind her, the abandoned harbor town sleeps on.
She watches the endless horizon, waiting.

Other sailors' wives paced up and down this path,
but that was long ago. Now only she remains to walk
and wonder, Which ship will carry my husband home?

If You Know Where To Look
Chris Wiggins

Chris Wiggins is one of Canada's most accomplished actors. Fans of dark fantasy will recognize Chris for his starring role as Jack Marshak in the Friday The 13th *TV Series, but his other impressive credits in television, radio, motion pictures and stage would be longer than the following story if we were to detail them here.*

What is less known about Chris is that he is also a writer -- chiefly for radio, television and the stage. But recently he has been busy turning out a number of excellent short stories, of which this is the first to be published.

"If You Know Where To Look" impressed us not only for the writer/actor's ear for dialog, but also for the fact that it deals with storytelling itself -- with the power *of storytelling. The* power *to chill and thrill....and perhaps even kill.*

Driving a coast-road through rolling sea-mist is the most isolated feeling in the world. Time suspended. Time to think in a world of your own.

I should have stopped long before. How can you look for film locations in a sea mist? And yet, the feeling was so right, the very mood of the film itself...folding and unfolding, things seen, half seen and not seen...nature took the hand of the unreal. If only I could bottle the atmosphere and release it later onto film!

We had the money, at last. All the planning, writing, re-writing, all the meetings, convincing, persuading and figuring but, at last, we had the money! Even the Canadian Film Development Corporation were persuaded to invest and we were sure we could do it on the highest level. A good story, too, right from the salt and soul of Nova Scotia and the seed that grew there.

The lonely spell was broken as a transport truck boomed out of the mist, horn blaring. I swerved tightly.

Almost at once, the road swung inland and away from the cliffs, climbing like a hump-backed cat. The mist retreated from my headlights and soon was gone. I half-cursed at having driven so far through veiled scenery which I would have to go back and see properly for its possible use in the film.

A distant sign gloomed into the beam of my lights and I kicked up the high beam to read:

The Cormorant Inn
Next left, nine miles.

The road levelled off, the turning came, I took it and the road climbed again.

The Inn nestled in folds of hills like a brown field-mouse in a furrow. Trees, all but their last leaves fallen, stood around like protecting hands.

I cut the engine and the sudden silence was made deeper by the soft sussuration of the distant sea. A good film location, perhaps. I determined to take some still photos in the morning.

I booked a room with a smiling but silent old lady who answered me with shy nods and shakes but made it seem warm and friendly. I asked if I could get a drink and was nodded to a door with two steps descending to a small and charming bar.

Ducking my head under beams, I saw a man seated behind the bar, smoking a pipe and polishing glasses with a meticulous care that a brain-surgeon might apply to his work. He did not look up as I spoke.

"Good evening."

"Fog?"

"I--beg your pardon?"

"Fog? Good?"

"Oh, I see what you mean. Yes, It's a bit misty all right but, hey, sometimes that can be pleasant."

"Depends what you're doing!" he said flatly.

"I suppose that's true," I said with a laugh.

"It is!"

What a face the man had, carved out of weathered granite in which were set two bright, beady eyes. I tried a different tack. "You sound Scottish."

"Got to sound something."

"I thought Nova Scotians had a sort of --Irish sound...!"

"Did you."

"Well, yes. But then, I guess, some communities were settled by Scots? And the accent sort of held on? After all this time? Eh?"

"Aye."

I was fascinated by that craggy face and wondered if I could get his into the film. Not the easiest guy to talk to, though. I tried again, "Not too many guests this time of the year?"

"You're it!"

"Oh."

"Summer."

"Summer?"

"Lots."

"What?"

"Guests."

"Oh."

Damn the man, he must have worked for a telegraph. He startled me with a sudden question.

"Drink?"

"Yes."

"What?"

"Scotch."

"And?"

"Ice."

"Right."

"You?"

"Yes."

"Good."

"Thanks."

Now I'd caught the disease. Talking to him was like verbal ping-pong. I used to be an interviewer on television but I couldn't think of a single thing to ask him that wouldn't be flattened by a one-word answer. As it happened, the problem disappeared after he downed his drink and, surprisingly, started to talk.

"Y'know, that's all right!"

"What is? the drink?"

"Tourists! Summer, you see? Sun, grass, leaves, sea's warm. Pretty. All over the place!"

"Oh?" I said, in complete bewilderment, "What is?"

"Tourists, man, tourists!" He leaned close and spoke confidentially, "But when the wind blows through the crags, the sea heaves and the bare bones of the trees rattle against your window-pane - ah-hah! Scoot!"

"Er - scoot?"

"Tourists! And that's all right"

"Is it?" I asked, losing the thread again.

Aye. 'Cos Nova Scotia was made for Nova Scotians! Not tourists!"

He could talk, after all. I offered him another drink, to which he assented with a dignified nod.

"Isn't it a strange thing for you to be saying? I asked, "About tourists?"

"Why?"

"Well, I mean...you own an Inn, don't you...?"

"No."

"Oh."

"It's my sister's."

That, apparently made a difference regarding tourists but I decided not to pursue it. We drank, silently for a few moments.

"What d'you do here in winter-time?" I asked.

"Do?"

"Yes. I mean, you're pretty remote here. D'you have television, movies...?"

He looked at me, pityingly, "Now, what's a man got need for that?"

"What's a what?" I mumbled.

He looked at me with strained patience then suddenly, darted a question, "Tell you a story?"

"A story?" I almost spilled my drink, "You're a man of many surprises, Mr....?"

"Stuart."

"I'm Ericson, and you're the last person I'd have expected to be a story-teller, Mr. Stuart - but I'm delighted, I'd love to hear it..."

"So you will if you'll be quiet for a minute!" he said, sharply.

"Sorry," I said, "Have another drink!" It was the correct answer. He poured, drank, pushed back on straight arms and paused dramatically before launching.

"I mind one time when we had a city feller, like you, up here when the leaves were down and the fog rolling over them. He came in here alone --like you--sat in this bar. Pale, he was, thin, artist-type lad, looked like a piece of chewed string..."

"What was he doing here?" I asked.

After a thundering pause, Stuart said heavily, "Am I telling the story?"

"Sorry. I just wondered...."

"I was about to say!! He wanted to paint the lake out at the back..."

"Lake?" I asked, surprised.

"There was another pause for me to be shrivelled before Stuart continued through his strained patience, "A spring-fed tarn, more than a pond and less than a lake! Now, would you care to open your ears and put your glass to your mouth!"

"Sorry--sorry...!" I mumbled.

"All *right*! Now...it's a pictureful tarn and he wanted to paint it with the naked trees around it, for some reason. Whatever, he came in here and sat down one night..." Stuart paused, considering, "No--he didn't *sit*, like folks...he more--went to a chair and fainted! City-type feller!"

I couldn't resist it, "Like me, huh?" I said, and immediately regretted it.

"He asked fool questions like you!" said Stuart, his eyes flashing and then, to my surprise, he imitated a mincing falsetto with splendid exaggeration, "'Do you not have television?' he says, 'Or radio or the moving pictures and the like?' I told him we dang-fired didn't! 'Oh,' says he, 'What in the world do you do?' I was near minded to tell him to mind his own business, but I was raised polite..."

I coughed into my drink.

"I was raised *polite*!...and I says, 'Laddie, laddie, what's a man got need for that? There's good, simple pleasures to be had everywhere, if you know where to look!' Well, he laughs!"

I laughed.

"Laughed at *me*!" said Stuart, heavily.

I stopped laughing.

"Thought I was being funny. I'm not funny."

"No, no," I murmured, "Of course not."

He ignored me and went on, "But I had an idea to give him a taste of local entertainment. The Crone!"

"Er--Crone?"

"Crone! Granny! Old hag, she is! No teeth! Chin curves to her nose! Warts! Old!"

After a pause, I had to ask, "She's the local entertainment?"

"The best," he replied proudly.

"Wasn't the lad--a bit young?"

"Young or old, they all love her. You never heard the like. Nightmares! Make your skin crawl! Hair winds off your neck like a salted worm. Voice like a rusted door. Smokes a pipe!"

"Wait a minute," I asked, desperately, "What, exactly does she *do*?"

"It's all she *can* do, man!"

"*What*?"

"Tell tales! What else?"

I was vastly relieved - but still..."She's a - a story teller?"

"The finest ever to bless your ears!"

Perhaps it was the drink but I was still not very clear about all this. "Yes, but where? And who's listening?"

"Everyone who can get there, I'll tell you!" he said, eyes glistening with triumphant relish.

"Where?" I asked.

"MacTarran's, man, MacTarran's! Where have you been?"

"Well - I dunno...in the city, I guess."

"But you must have heard of *Mactarran's*?"

"Uh-uh."

Stuart shook his head in disbelief, "Back of Moenangle Rise? Below the crag? Abandoned since the mid-sixteen hundreds!"

"What--a ruin of some sort?"

"Some sort, aye. But what sort?" His voice fell to a hush, "Some say a fort or a mansion. Solid stone walls, three feet thick!"

"Still standing?" I asked, surprised.

"We make sure of that!" he said with finality, "all of us. If a stone falls, we hear the Piper, louder every night 'til it's fixed."

"Piper? What piper?"

His voice was a whisper, "MacTarran Piper. Playing a pibroch, "MacTarran Will Never Return" It comes at you from all sides. Hurting your ears on the drones!"

"Now, wait a minute..." I said, thoroughly exasperated, "I'm getting lost..."

"It's easily done," he nodded.

"You say there's this old place near here, abandoned for more than three hundred years...?"

"And like to remain so," agreed Stuart, grimly.

"...but people go there...and this old woman ..."

"Aye, the Crone. It's the only place she'll tell a tale. Never speaks a word anywhere else. When she tells a tale, people come from miles around."

"The same tale?"

"Och, no, man! Lots of them, for all occasions. Funerals, births, anniversaries, weddings..."

"*Weddings*?" I said, with a yelp.

"Aye! I mind one time she told a tale that kept the bride and groom apart for the first two weeks of their honeymoon!"

How many weeks did they have, I wondered, but Stuart went on in fond reminiscence.

"Her favorite is 'The MacTarran Headsman' --the story of the place itself. Good for any occasion. I thought it just right for the young painter-feller. So I sent the sign for the Crone to come to MacTarran's the following night and passed the word to the neighbors."

"What was the sign?" I asked.

He looked at me suspiciously, "Never you mind. She came. I walked the lad over there. He needed the exercise. Moenangle Rise is quite a climb, you see."

"What's MacTarran's like?" I asked, now completely fascinated.

"I was about to tell you! It's a thick, heavy building. Roofs long gone but all the walls grow out of the ground like a part of the Rise itself. A huge fireplace, there in the main hall where we all meet. We had a big fire roaring there with a poker stuck in it and a big mug of ale ready for the mulling beside the Crone's chair."

"Chair? Is there furniture, then?"

"The Crone's chair is a throne of rock, carved from a single slab of granite..."

"Who carved the ...?"

"Och, peace, man! Or I'll not tell you the story, you prattling natterjay!"

"Another drink?" I asked softly. Again, I had understood him quite well as he soothed his ruffled feathers and poured for us both. He drank, wiped his mouth and decided to continue.

"There was a big crowd. Near fifteen or sixteen of us seated on the rocks, hearth or grass, huddled close to the fire...but we could feel her approaching. The artist-lad was sprawled on a big rock, but he sat up sharp when Granny came." Stuart chortled at the memory.

"His eyes near popped out of his head when he saw her hobble in, her whisps of hair patching corners of her wrinkled skull, bits of shawl jigging about her sparrow shoulders in the night breeze as she labored to her chair. She climbed onto the great stone slab--nobody helped, she won't be touched--and she flopped into place with the noise that a little dead bird might make as it fell to earth.

"She sat still, eyes shut, to recover from the effort. He waited. She raised her thin, crooked forefinger in a sign and I plunged the red-hot poker into her mug of ale until it frothed over in steam and bubbles. She took it and drank hard and deep. Her straggle beard dripped when she raised her head. She fumbled for her stump of a clay pipe, filled it, and I held a brand for her as she made little, gasping puffs. Then we were all still and waiting. Och, I can hear that crushed and wheezing voice even now as she cleared her stringy windpipe..."

I was so caught up in the story that Stuart was telling me that I couldn't say if he imitated the Crone's voice or my imagination did the job, but it seemed to me that I, too, was hearing a voice that seemed to speak through dust...

"MacTarran! Can ye hear me, Devil? It's your tale I'm telling!

"I speak of years long gone, of terrors past and some forgot ... of screams from throats long dead that are still heard. The night is old! Listen! The Piper plays across the years... and who shall pay?

"The Stuart Kings of Scotland sit on England's throne. Scotland and England, Catholic and Protestant, King and Commoner...*Writhe* together! And the Jackal of France prowls and watches, breathing heavy. Listen!

"To be alive is danger. Listen with your old ears. The pad of foot behind you. Feel the *fear*!

"The Star Chamber is the King's Court where anything may be proved. The King needs money for his wars with France and tax grows heavy on the rich and fat. Those who hide their gold and will not speak in the Chamber of Stars are taken *below*--to the *vaults* to have their tongues loosened - or stretched with hot pincers...Listen!

"Hah! The King may rule the Star Chamber--but in the slippery, green stench of the Vaults, all are ruled by *MacTarran*, the King's master torturer. Close your eyes and see him in his lair! MacTarran! Lord of the Rack! Sceptered with a white-hot iron. Prince of Pain!

"As Satan punishes for God, so MacTarran for his King, and all is proved for Good King Charles.

"And so my tale begins! MacTarran's Piper plays to drown the shriek and shuddered moans of maiming flesh and cracking bone. Listen! Hear the vats of bubbling oil, hear the hiss of steam, the lick of flames over the long years as they glint on thumbscrew, spike and dripping whip! *Feel the fear*!

"MacTarran curses the body of an old man who broke and died without telling where his fortune was hid. The old man's daughter is sent for.

"MacTarran strips his sweat-soaked body and has his Piper drench him from a water-bucket, washing off the gore and sweat to mingle with the floor's filth.

"'Twas then the strange, wild girl, Bess Ptarmigan, was thrust into the room. She took one look at her father, dead upon the rack, and then her great eyes fixed upon MacTarran's thick nakedness.

"Some say she was a witch with toad in hand, her dark beauty not of this world. Some say her eyes held swords that no-one could combat. Some say her simple beauty held the power of light. But sure it is, whatever spell she cast, MacTarran and Bess were gone when the guards returned to find MacTarran's Piper, his hair turned snow-white, playing a crazed and skirling tune.

"How he got her from the Vaults and out of London, how he found a boat without King Charles' men catching them is a mystery that only darkest forces could conceive, and sure, MacTarran and Bess spoke scarce a word to any living soul.

"Across the cold Atlantic to New Scotland--Nova Scotia did he bring her! *Here*, to Moenangle Rise. He built for her his place we're in. Some say no man could have done such work alone, no matter how strong. But others know how!

"When all was finished, she stood there--right where you are, city lad--and he sat here. She held out her arms, at last offering him his promised reward and he stood from this great, carved seat...slowly.

"A smile was on her lips but, as she watched, he seemed to grow taller, his huge frame stretching. Then, on either side of his head, the skin split and two sharp growths appeared. Bess recoiled in horror as the splitting skin spread round his face and began to slide down the brow like a snake shedding its coat. When it reached the eyes, the staring eyeballs rolled from their sockets and tumbled to the floor!"

"The growths on the top now were the horns of a goat and, as MacTarran's face slid away it uncovered another head, dripping with slime, bestial and foul, green-gray and pouched with warts, the eyes slitted and no more than dark holes, reaching into eternity. The goat-like mouth, fanged and frothing, opened in a silent laugh and a foul stench filled the room and *still* the skin slid and folded down to the floor.

"Bess tried to scream. She crumpled and fell, staring at the creature being uncovered before her. the scaled body sprouted black hair, the fur of the legs was clotted with filth and the feet were heavy, cleft hooves.

"Then the creature's laugh sounded as though from far off, louder and louder... Listen!

"At last, Bess was able to scream, and the nightmare before her danced with glee, pointed a blackened finger at the folds of skin that lay around its hooves and, to Bess' horror, the shape that had been MacTarran filled out as though with puffs of air and then stood and started to gambol and flap, eyeless and terrible.

"The horned creature laughed the harder, pointed another finger in the air, and the sound of MacTarran's Piper filled the night as the empty skin danced to the tune of a lurching reel, coming toward Bess as she cringed against the fireplace, here--its arms outstretched, inviting her to dance.

"Bess could feel her face crawl and crease, her hair move on her scalp and, with desperation, she flung herself from the fireplace and ran into the night, hands clawing at the darkness.

"They found her the next morning, floating in the lake, under-water, face up. Her youth and beauty had returned to her but her hair was snow-white and she was very, very dead!"

"Another drink, Mr. Ericson?"

I was shocked to find myself still standing by the bar in the Cormorant Inn.

"Good God, yes!" I said, and never meant it more.

"So you see," said Stuart, a flicker of amusement crossing his face, "The old Crone could tell a fair story, wouldn't you say?"

"I don't know what to say," I answered and drank deeply.

"Aye, so! And the young artist-type feller--och y'should've seen him, white as his drawing paper. Sensitive sort, I suppose. He sat there, shaking and twitching like he was laying an egg. And Granny gone by the time he focussed his eyes again."

"What a story!" I said, shakily.

"But that's not the all of it," said Stuart with a big grin, "Here's the best part, y'see. I led the lad back to the Inn, here, and him shying at every bush on the way. Then, as I lay in bed that night, I thought I could hear the MacTarran Piper coming closer--and even the far off scream of poor Bess. And I chuckled to myself and thought, 'Well, Granny really told it well this time.'"

He leaned toward me, beaming, "I wondered how the lad was sleeping! In the morning I didn't see him and I thought he'd maybe not slept much in the night so I kept pretty quiet down here. A bit later, my sister came running in all upset and told me what had happened. I went to take a look...'' He shook his head, remembering fondly.

"*What*?'' I demanded.

"Why out at the Tarn--the wee lake,'' he said, as though it was obvious. "Right enough, there he was, floating under the surface, face up...''

"The *artist*?'' I asked, gaping, "He was *dead*?''

"Och, very, very dead!'' smiled Stuart, "He must've been quite a sensitive soul, y'see.''

I stared at him for a long moment. "What did you do?''

"Nothing at first,'' he said, with a shrug, "I was just looking at him and thinking when I heard a sound and there was old Granny come along for a look.''

"For a *look*!'' I cried.

"Aye, So I said to her 'That was a fair old story you told the night, Granny...' and she said, 'Aye, I know!' And I told her that I'd heard it often enough before but it'd really got to me this time, in fact I could almost believe I'd heard the MacTarran Piper in the night. Well, she laughed at that and told me I probably had and that she'd brought her pipes down to the Inn in the middle of the night to give the city-lad a wee thrill. Said she screamed a bit, too. Out in the dark, of course.''

"You mean she ... she...'' I gasped.

"Och, she's got a rare humor in her y'know. But I said, 'Look here, though, Granny. Have you not heard what happened. Look at him. there in the water!' And she cackled and said, 'Aye, I know. And I've not had a success with a story like that in many a year.'''

Stuart finished his drink then looked up, his expression softening. "Och, she's a good soul, really. Aye, there's good simple pleasures to be had everywhere, if you know where to look.''

We shot the film in New Brunswick.

The Bleeding Tree
SEAN DOOLITTLE

Sean Doolittle's short stories have appeared in such anthologies as The Year's Best Horror XXII, Young Blood, *and* Northern Frights 2. *His magazine appearances include* Cavalier, Death Realm, Palace Corbie, Kinesis, *and others. He lives in Lincoln, Nebraska with his wife Jessica, and recently received his Master's degree in English from the Univerisity of Nebraska at Lincoln. Sean is currently at work on his first novel, titled* Holy Man.

On the day they finally talked sense into Pomie Fauquet, authorities excavated the skeletal remains of a family of four from the west embankment of the border crossing at I-5. The incidents were unrelated, occurring at different times and eighty miles away from each other.

Men in coveralls tilled up the bones; a man and a woman. Two small children, girl and boy. A cat, and what was later discovered to be the skeleton of a good-sized coho salmon. The bodies had been planted strangely at distances from each other, a configuration which spanned a radius of nearly thirty feet.

The afternoon was overcast and crisp; they were working on convincing information from an anonymous tip on a case that had been left yawningly open nearly seven years before. A hand trowel, handle rotted away, still protruded from between the third and fourth ribs of the adult male. Broken necks for wife, kids and cat. The cat, whose ID collar was still intact, had gone by the name of ''Clovis.'' The fish was truly a mystery. Bumpers and chrome snaked into the distance beneath the gloom, four lanes on either side of the line who'd decided to stay for the show.

It was little wonder the grass above the graves seemed so terribly green and plush, the letters BC rendered in bas-relief by lawnmower for the pleasure of incoming travellers. Welcome to British Columbia, we hope you enjoy your stay.

All of this could have seemed ominous. At the very least, symbolic: human beings sacrificed unto the earth, offering back that which the earth itself had given. Symbiosis in a grand cycle, a joining of the ends of some great organic loop. Except for the fish, which was incongrous to the whole thing, but could be ignored for lack of relevance in the first place.

Judson Ventura and Rainey Kio wouldn't hear the news, however, until later. Even when they did, the poignancy would be lost, news being news and irony for pussies.

"Why don't you try carrying the goddamn thing for awhile then?" Rainey said. He was skinny and smoked Luckies like they were going off the market any day, and he hadn't stopped yapping since they'd left the truck.

"Chrissakes, give it to me," Judson told him, planting on a heel and snatching the chainsaw with one hand. It was hard enough navigating in the dark to begin with, and all the whining was making his head pound.

"Thanks," Rainey said, and wiped his nose with a sleeve. Judson gave him a look and pushed on, dodging a stump at the last second and grinning when Kio stumbled blindly into it from behind.

Not the way he'd have picked to spend a Friday night, but the boys from Northeastern were paying high. Regardless of it being a weekend, some jobs were just too good to pass up.

There was a full moon tonight, but the cloud-cover was thick and the light was eerie and dim. Flashlights were risky this close, and Judson had to pop his zippo to check the compass against the map Erikson had drawn him. Rainey kept asking questions and running into Judson's back every time he stopped to get his bearings; he was about three seconds from pounding the guy a good one.

Lucky for Kio, they'd reached the treeline. Judson could see the cabin from where they stood.

"Okay," he whispered, pointing. I'm gonna bust in the front, hear? You go around back."

Rainey nodded enthusiastically and started off. Judson grabbed his elbow.

"And try not trippin all over yourself, okay?" Rainey rolled his eyes and grimaced, jerked his arm free and told Judson to kiss his ass. Then he was off, circling wide through the trees, hunching like he had the bends.

Judson watched him for a few moments, scratching his beard and wondering why he ever hung around with the guy in the first place.

Then he stashed the saw and made a beeline for the door.

Pomie Fauquet had himself a genuine zoning anomaly on his hands, some kind of purchase made by great-grandfathers back when Port Alberni still had just a single sawmill to its name. Times had changed since then, and Fauquet was pissing off Northeastern's big guns to beat the band; the development on Alberni's northern end was already reaching into the next few miles of the forest, Fauqet's little plot the only thing standing in the way. Hounded the cutters every step of the way, screaming about his tree and being a general insect about things.

Judson put one big shoulder into the front door of the cabin and felt buckshot chew through the doorframe next to his head before he even got ahold of his balance.

The darkened cabin suddenly flooded, yellow light chasing the shadows away. And Pomie was waiting in the middle of the small front room, leveling a Winchester at Judson's brain. He was a grizzled little bastard, gray beard sprawling over his jaw like wire. He was standing there in his boxers, knobby knees set firmly apart.

"You get out," he said, squinting through the sights and thrusting the barrel forward. "You just get the hell out, you hear me? Tell your boys they ain't touching a goddam thing!"

Judson got himself together and stood straight; six-five and starting to get annoyed. He sighed heavily and put his hands on his hips.

"Old man," he said, "you can't win and you know it. Now why don't you put that thing down 'fore I prong you with it."

Fauquet jerked his arm, shucking a fresh shell into the chamber. "I mean it!" he screamed. "I mean it, you get out! *I'll blow your goddamn head clean off, you take one more step!*"

Judson kept his eyes on Fauquet's, folded his arms sternly across his chest. Fauquet looked just about ready to spout off again when Rainey reached around from behind to knock the gun from his hands. He slapped a hand across the old man's forehead and swiped the big knife across his throat.

Then he cradled Fauquet, who was gurgling, to the floorboards.

After a few minutes, he wiped his hands on his butt and looked up to Judson for approval.

Judson grinned and gave him a nod.

Always knew that Kio had to be good for something.

The deal was that they'd cut down Fauquet's tree to signify the job was done. Judson and Rainey burned good time taking care of the old man's body, back in the trees where the logging crew would be by Tuesday.

Then Judson got the saw, and the two of them got to work.

It was a gigantic old Douglas Fir, right in the middle of everything.

It took a few pulls before the saw finally roared to life, cleaving the cool stillness like a banshee. Judson grinned and squeezed the trigger, goosing it and feeding from the power in his hands.

Rainey was getting weird on him, shouting something over the screaming chain.

Judson ignored him, goosed the saw again and sank the blade into the old boy's skin.

Son of a bitch, he was thinking then, oh sweet son of a bitch.

Judson would have never believed it, but the goddamn thing really bled after all. The splatters were warm on his face.

He wrangled the sawblade free and cut the power, stumbling back into Rainey. They stood together and stared, watched the blood flow like syrup from the cut, down the bark and over the ground, glistening blackly in the muted silver light of a covered moon.

Rainey was gasping. "Holy shit," he hissed. "Jud, holy shit! Holy goddamn shit!"

"Shut up," Judson told him, and watched.

You don't understand, none of you, the old man had screamed at them, said Erikson and his fellows from Northeastern, with grins. You can't cut down the bleeding tree.

They stood together, and watched.

After a long while, Judson shook his head. "Deal's a deal," he said. He pulled the cord.

Rainey was grabbing his sleeve. "Jud, *Jesus Christ.*"

Judson shoved him off and pulled the cord again. This time the motor caught. He gunned it. "Your gonna help me, too," he yelled over the noise. Rainey's eyes were wide. "Goddamn if you ain't. Deal's a deal."

He stepped back in.

It took them a very long time. Switching turns, not wanting to take a break. It was a bitch of a big tree, and by the time they were finished both of them were covered head to toe in gore, standing knee-deep in slime.

When the tree gave way at last, it was with a wet kind of sucking sound. Not a crack at all, and nothing you felt like yelling "Timber!" about. It crushed the roof of the cabin beneath it.

Beyond the outer bark, the stump was ragged meat. It steamed in the chill in smoky white waves, and the center of it pulsed like a heartbeat.

When they were through, Judson and Rainey ran. Slipping and sliding in the goo, then like rabbits toward the truck.

If they drove fast enough, they could maybe get back across to Vancouver, shower and change, be at Jimmie's before last call.

Neither of them could recall from recent memory ever needing a drink so bad.

It could have been considered poetic justice, the stuff that happened on the day after they cut down the bleeding tree.

The Canadian national hockey team went down in Kyuquot Sound on their way home from Nagano, Japan, putting a dismal cap on the '98 Olympics and leaving everybody in Jimmie's Wonder Bar dumbstruck when the special bulletin came over the tube. Emotion descended on the patrons like a shroud.

Most fatal accidents are known to occur within a few blocks of home.

The bar was later struck by lightning. Judson Ventura and Rainey Kio were the first to burn.

A naked faction of the men's movement who called themselves "For Members Only," getting in touch with their primal roots while pounding drums in the wilderness of Port MacNeill, were suddenly ambushed from the trees and eaten by wolves. The wolves left the scene in a funk, having found more fat than meat.

Sasquatch and Ogopogo tag-teamed the hell out of the Kelowna Community Theatre. Survivors lost their hair within hours and wandered the streets, bug-eyed and insane.

Everything had gotten loopy.

When the nine o'clock cannon boomed loud across Vancouver Harbor, several diners were killed when the cannonball smashed through the bay windows of the Cloud 9 revolving restaurant. No one could remember the last time in Vancouver history the cannon had been loaded, or if it was pointed toward the Cloud 9 at all.

Bald eagles dive-bombed pedestrians at random, and fourteen-thousand people commited suicide for no apparent reason in the greater British Columbia area.

All of it could have been considered poetic justice. Like the irony of the skeletal remains on the border, the earth taking back that which it had given.

It could have been considered poetic justice, except for the simple fact that none of those things really happened, the day after they cut down the bleeding tree.

Not only did the Canadian national team arrive home safely, but they trounced Germany by five goals in the final match to bring the Gold along home with them. Jimmie's Wonder Bar was a bacchic frenzy; Judson Ventura and Rainey Kio won the pool on the spread, each leaving the place that night with an extra two-hundred clams tucked safely in their underwear.

By Monday, the bleeding tree was still bleeding. The ground was a thick slick blanket of red for a hundred yards in every direction, and the stump was still pumping; Northeastern sent in a team with hip waders and acetelyne torches to cauterize the wound. Only an American tabloid covered the story; no other self-respecting journalistic institution bought any of it for even a minute.

Later in the afternoon, a heavy rain began to fall. It drenched the newly charred stump of the great Douglas Fir, as well as the mound of a fresh grave in the trees. It diluted the viscera and sluiced it away, and the Northeastern crew got to go home early.

The raindrops were fat and wet.   Poetry had nothing to do with anything--they did not fall like anvils; or tears; or pennies from heaven.

They fell like raindrops.

For chrissakes, it was only rain.

The Dead Go Shopping
STEPHANIE BEDWELL-GRIME

Stephanie Bedwell-Grime has a background in media and communications, and has worked for several Toronto television stations. She currently teaches a college course in Studio Management

Her work has appeared in After Hours, Writer's Block, Romantic Interludes, Vampire's Crypt, Just Write, Distant Horizons, *and the* Canadian Writer's Journal. *Her novelette,* Until Death *(the first in a series) was released in March '95 from Cogswell Publishing.*

Prime time on the Watch 'N Shop Channel. Bryanna Johnson stifled a yawn. Eleven thirty-two p.m., 28 minutes to go. They called it the 'save money shift' because all the stores were closed and all your friends were in bed by the time you got home.

Discount Dan was hawking a Star Voyagers Communications Pin, a Discount Dan Dandy Deal for the low, low price of $49.99 (plus shipping and handling, provincial sales tax, goods and services tax), of course.

One hundred sold, another fifty queued.

"I tell you," Discount Dan was telling his viewers, "I've had requests on the street for this thing. Why the other day this guy came to my house to fix mywindow, and he asked me..." "Oh no," moaned Mario, the audio technician. "Not this story again. Doesn't this guy ever change his material?" They were in the safety of master control, a pane of double glass between them and Dan's sensitive ears.

"Apparently not this week," Bryanna said. Over the intercom, she could hear Discount Dan badgering the relay operator for the next testimonial.

"Hurry it up will you, man. I'm dying up here!"

Through the glass window of master control she watched him jab furiously at the computer's update button. Rumor had it that Dan, while a little slow at intelligent conversation, was capable of complex calculations when it came to his commission.

Twenty minutes to go and five thousand bucks short of quota.

"...and we only have a few left..." Dan was saying. Killing his mic, he growled into the intercom. "Make it look that way, put a counter up!"

Bryanna hurried to obey, then cycled through the few shots stored in the Abekas for something to make it more interesting. Shots scrolled by on the preview monitor: Discount Dan's smiling face; the pin on his suit lapel; a close-up of his fingers pushing the button that made the high-tech beep. That would have to do. She sent the shot to air. Silently, she cursed the outdated government regulation that forced the show into a still-frame format, making the high-tech production look like a slide show.

"I have a bit of trivia for you," Discount Dan was saying on air. "The communicators they wear on the T.V. show don't make any noise. The sound is dubbed in afterward."

"No kidding, Einstein," Mario said, his professional sensibilities offended.

Twenty minutes later and Discount Dan had still to unload his last 30 Star Voyagers pins. The elusive commission was several thousand dollars short. On the screen a green box patiently counted down the last few pins.

"Only a few left," Dan was saying. "We don't know when we'll have them back in stock. So, if you want one, now's the time..."

"He's going to be in a mood tonight," Bryanna warned Mario, then wondered silently if she could beat it from the door of master control to the parking lot before Dan left the set.

She was cycling through the shots quickly, trying to keep up with the urgency Dan was trying to project, and his rapid-fire instructions off-mic. The close-up of the pin, Dan smiling broadly with the pin on his lapel. Only too happy to oblige, she thought sullenly.

On the set, Dan was practically yelling, pounding the air with his fist. "Only ten left! Oops, another sold, nine left. Get 'em now folks, 'cause we don't know when they'll be back. Eight, seven, two more sold..."

They were coming up on the top of the hour. The late night host fidgeted nervously in the wings. Stage crew hustled to get the product line-up ready for the next show.

Leaving the close-up to fill the screen, Bryanna turned to cue the promos for the upcoming break.

"Six left, only six..." Dan's voice blared monotonously in the background. "Five, we're down to

five--"

A wet gurgle erupted from the speakers.

Then silence.

Mario screamed. His foot shot out, sending his swivel-chair sailing away from the console. The cord on his headset snapped tight, then jerked from its socket.

Bryanna turned. In the sweeping arc of her vision, she took in the chaos in the network, the stage crew standing with hands over their mouths in mute horror, the communications pin still on its stand on the set, and finally, Discount Dan's body slumped lifelessly in his chair.

For an eternity it seemed, she stared at the gleaming white eyes staring silently at the ceiling and the thin line of blood that dripped from the corner of his open mouth, down into a spreading stain against the white collar of his shirt. One finger was still on the update button.

"Cut the mics!" she said, suddenly coming to her senses. Stay calm, she ordered herself. That's what good directors did under pressure. Mario seemed not to hear her.

Leaning over the console, she pulled down the fader bars. The close-up of the communications pin still filled the screen. She sent the promos to air. There was an hour's worth of them on that tape. That ought to do, she thought with dazed efficiency.

Out in the telephone network, the supervisor was on the relay operator's line. Over the intercom, they eavesdropped as he put in a call to 911. On the set, the station manager bent gingerly over Dan's body, checking for a pulse.

Bryanna grabbed the horrified audio technician by the shoulders and shook him hard. "Mario! What happened? Did you see?"

Slowly, he tore his eyes from the set, looked at her and swallowed. "No. I was looking down at the board. I heard this...choking sound. It was really loud in the headphones. When I looked up..." He pointed to the set. "He, he-- Do you think he's dead?"

She hazarded a quick glance in Dan's direction. "Looks that way."

"What do you mean you've got nothing on tape?" the female police officer demanded.

Bryanna took a deep breath. She'd explained it many times to cynical friends who complained the station was boring to watch because of its still-frame format. But this time, she was standing not ten feet away from Discount Dan's bloody corpse.

Adrenaline coursed through her body, making her veins feel like they were vibrating. She couldn't seem to stop her bottom lip from trembling.

"We take a few shots, store them electronically, then use them as we need them. When the product's been on the air for a few minutes, we take some more just to keep it interesting." She watched the police officer's eyes change from disbelief to cynicism. "Because it was the end of the show, I was using shots I'd taken earlier so I'd have time to cue up the promos and the people in staging would have a chance to set up the first product for the next show. We were working on two shows, really, wrapping up the old one and beginning the next."

Patiently, she plotted out her last steps before the *incident*, explaining how she'd been standing by the racks of VCR's in master control, with her back to the wide, glass windows. On the other side of the narrow room, Mario was going through the same motions for one of the officer's colleagues.

"I'll need to run some tests," the coroner said, coming up behind them.

"Heart attack?" one of the police officers asked hopefully.

"Let's hope so."

Dazed crew milled about the now quiet phone network. The station had been off the air for over two hours. Polite graphics broadcast apologies of technical difficulties. Discount Dan's body was wheeled away in a black, zippered bag. In the cafeteria, arrivals for the late shift drank coffee and hoped to be sent home so they could go back to bed.

The station manager clapped his hands. "Okay folks, let's get this show back on the road."

Hesitantly, the night crew filed into master control. Telephone operators signed on to their workstations. The show host looked nervously at Discount Dan's seat,then quickly wheeled it out of the way and found himself another chair.

On Sunday night, even the ladies room was quiet. Just as the station broadcast its message, the washroom broadcast news of who was sleeping with whom, who was divorcing as a result of off-hours liaisons, who made their quota last night and all the other essential information that never made it to departmental memos.

Bryanna brushed a strand of maroon hair from her eyes and touched up her black eyeliner. Her watch said two minutes to six. She'd better get out there.

Telephone operators who were forever being scolded about chatting on duty were uncustomarily quiet. Except for the whispers of operators taking orders and the supervisor's quiet footsteps, there was no sound at all in the network. It reminded her of a funeral parlor. She shivered, ran her name badge through the magnetic slot on the door and stepped into the frigid air of master control.

The temperature in master never rose above 59 degrees, even in the winter. Mario was already slouched in his chair in front of the audio board, hands in the pockets of his kangaroo sweatshirt. The expression on his face was as dismal as the rest of the crew.

"Relax," Bryanna said, taking the seat the afternoon director vacated for her. "The chances of another host expiring in the line of duty two nights in a row are extremely rare." They were in a break, promos already running. Stage crew had the next item set up. Everything was running smoothly.

Mario didn't appreciate her humor. He ran a hand through his black hair, a nervous habit. "Yeah?" he asked. "Well, I've never seen a dead body before. And Dan, he was a real bastard at times, but I knew him!"

His comment hung in the air between them. Master control, it seemed, was doomed to be as somber as the rest of the place.

On the air, Markdown Mabel was taking full advantage of Dan's prime time slot. "One hundred and ninety-nine dollars is a great price!"

Bryanna switched to the macro shot of the sapphire and diamond ring.

"But I think we can do better, ladies," Mabel teased. A black X appeared over the previous price. "How would you feel about one hundred and seventy-five dollars?"

Ten phone lines lit up.

"But..." she drawled, "I think we can do even better than that."

Another X, a new price flashed in red numbers.

"One hundred and fifty-nine dollars!" crowed Markdown Mabel.

In the telephone network, operators scrambled for their phones.

Bryanna switched to a close-up of the ring on a model's hand. The fingers were long and slender, the nails painted with crimson nail polish.

Claws, dripping blood.

She blinked away the image. *I'm getting as maudlin as the rest of them.*

Markdown Mabel had a voice that could break glass, a voice that didn't do much for the headache lancing its way through her temples. She hadn't slept well last night. The image of Dan's staring corpse projected itself on her eyelids every time she'd closed her eyes.

"Can you turn down the sound on the monitor?" she asked Mario. "Mabel's starting to grate on my nerves."

Mario smiled. Mabel got on everyone's nerves.

Minus the sound, the production became a hilarious pantomime. Mabel dyed her hair the shiny black it had been fifty years ago in her childhood and settled for no less than scarlet when it came to lipstick. To illustrate a point she had a repertoire of hand gestures made all the more flamboyant by a multitude of gaudy rings. She was entertaining to watch, Bryanna decided. As long as you didn't have to listen to her.

"I'm selling a thousand bucks a minute, can you believe it!" Mabel cooed via the intercom.

"Great!" Bryanna and Mario chorused, without much enthusiasm. Mabel, no doubt, was already making plans to spend her commission.

Bryanna looked up at the clock on the wall above the window. Still ten minutes to break, and the sapphire ring seemed to be selling itself. She saved another shot, just to be safe, leaned her feet against the console and closed her eyes.

A piercing scream shook her awake. She tore off the headset. As it fell to the console, she could still hear the scream echoing in the tiny speakers. Beside her, Mario leapt to his feet.

"Jesus God!" he said, then uttered a few more oaths in Italian.

In the network, the entire staff was on their feet, mouths open in a simultaneous scream. But in the silence of master control there was only the whir of machinery and the sounds of Mario's ragged breaths.

Please don't make me look, Bryanna prayed silently, as her head turned of its own accord toward the set.

Propped up by the high-backed chair, Mabel's corpse was still sitting upright. A thick cloak of velvet blood gushed from a ragged tear in her neck, covering not only her expensive suit, but a good deal of the set as well.

The blood, Bryanna noted, was the same shade as Mabel's lipstick.

"Bry," Mario whispered hoarsely, "we've got to get out of here. There's a killer out there."

"Well, he can't get in," she said, as much to reassure herself. "The door's security-keyed, remember?"

"What if he's one of us?"

That, she didn't want to consider.

This time the police concentrated on questioning the stage crew who'd been closest to Mabel at the time of the...incident. The station was off the air, the building sealed, and Bryanna and Mario stuck in master control until someone told them they could go home.

"It's like a bad dream," Bryanna said, mostly to herself. "Things like this don't really happen, do they?"

Mario was staring at the floor. On the preview monitor, the shot she'd been planning to use still showed the sapphire ring on its stand. Bryanna was about to look away in disgust when something caught her attention. She moved closer to the monitor, squinting to bring the television image into better focus.

In the foreground was the sparkling ring. Mabel dominated the background with her flailing hands and garish makeup. And between the ring and Mabel was a dark smear, like a cloud.

"Mario, have a look at this."

He gazed at her impatiently, as if nothing could possibly be important at a time like that, then his eyes narrowed as he noticed the smudge on the image.

"What do you think it is?"

"One of the crew," he suggested.

Bryanna scanned the stage crew who were practically pinned against the wall by a line of cops. "No one's wearing black."

Mario cocked his head. "Could be the monitor."

"Can't be," she said, "it's new. They only put it in last month." With a flick of the fader bar, she switched to the tiny monitors on the console. The smudge was still there. It was only a smear, she told herself, something on the lens perhaps, but it made her spine tingle with apprehension.

She peered at the image, but a television picture was like a newspaper photo, the closer you looked, the more blurry it got. "I've got a friend at a special effects house who could enhance this on their system."

"We should show it to the police," Mario said.

"They can look at it on the monitor." Bryanna slipped the disk into the back pocket of her jeans.

The police were unimpressed. The homicide detective squinted at the monitor, then grunted. "That could be anything," he said, dismissively. "It certainly doesn't look like a person."

She had to agree, it looked like anything but.

Bryanna stared at the fuzzy image over her friend Debbie's shoulder. "So, what do you think?"

"I don't know, Bry," she said, busily typing into the system. "It doesn't look like anything more than a shadow. Someone stepped in front of a light perhaps."

"You could be right," Bryanna said, acknowledging her own paranoia. The result of too much stress and too little sleep. "But whatever it is, it give me the creeps."

"Let's gamma warp it and see what we find." Debbie drew a box around the shadow and enlarged that part of the screen. The picture disintegrated into a series of light and dark gray boxes. With the mouse, she worked around the edge of the shadow, lightening some of the boxes and darkening others. Pixels arranged themselves, gradually taking shape, until the smear was more human looking than shadow.

"God," Debbie breathed, sitting back in her chair. "This really is spooky."

"What do you think it is?"

"I wouldn't even hazard a guess."

Strategically, Deb placed a few pixels, bringing out the shadows that could have been eyes. "That's the best I can do," she said finally. "I don't have much to work with."

"Thanks," Bryanna said, hiding the disk in the zipper pouch of her purse.

"Next time you've got something eerie," Deb said. "Don't bring it to me."

Bryanna turned to leave.

"You going to show it to the police?"

Bryanna turned back. "They practically laughed at me," she said, then stepped from the air-conditioned studio into the crushing heat outside.

Mario was waiting for her in the narrow closet they called the production suite. In those cramped quarters, the promotions crew assembled the spots that ran during the breaks. A small window overlooked an equally tiny studio where file shots were taken of the products and stored on disk.

It was Monday, the first day of their "weekend". Police had warned them not to leave town in case they were wanted for further questioning.

"So?" he asked, rubbing a hand across bleary eyes. Mario never got up before three on his day off.

Bryanna fed the disk into the Abekas and called up the file on the monitor. "Take a look at this!"

Critically, he glanced at the monitor, prepared to dismiss what he saw there. Then his eyes widened and stepped back. "Man, that's creepy."

"That's what I said." Bryanna punched him lightly on the arm. "Told you there was something there."

"Come on," Mario objected, the cynic in him restored. "Anyone with a paint program can make a monster out of a smear."

"I'd hardly call that a smear," she said, tapping her finger against the screen.

Mario was staring at the monitor, confused. "Hey, where did it go?"

Bryanna gaped at the image beneath her fingertip. The screen was blank.

She reloaded the file and gazed again at the blank spot in the image. "I've got the most awful feeling," she said. The screen reflected her face back at her, like a ghost. "I know this sounds stupid, but I think it went into the system."

"Now that," Mario said, "is total bullshit."

"Is it?" She flicked on the nearby television set. Nearly every room in the building had one, just in case one of the station's executives was wandering by and wanted to check up on how the show was going. The station manager slept with the show running in his bedroom, which might account for his recent divorce.

The station was in the middle of the afternoon china bargain-a-rama, hosted by Candy Cane, a blond, thirty-five year old host with a twelve year old voice. A giant bowl of pottery roses dominated the television screen.

"The problem with real roses," Candy was saying, "is that they die. But, for $79.99, you can enjoy the beauty of roses all year round!"

On the screen, the picture switched to a close up of a chunky, red, ceramic rose.

"I think you ought to go home and get some sleep, Bry," Mario said behind her.

"Think I'll go home and have a real stiff drink." Bryanna reached to turn the television set off.

And stopped half way.

On one of the petals a crimson bead of dew was forming. They watched, transfixed as it swelled to the point of bursting, then fell in a scarlet splash to the white velvet material below.

"This can't be happening," Mario said. "That's a still shot."

All over the flower, ruby beads burst into existence. Filling the television picture, the bowl of ceramic flowers cried tears of blood.

"Stigmata," Mario breathed. "My grandmother's always talking about stuff like this!"

"Yeah? Well's that's no statue of the virgin," Bryanna said. "And we *let* that thing into the system. Now it's trapped there. If it gets out, we could have another murder on our hands!"

In master control, a panicked director was rapidly changing shots. Images of the figurine from different angles flashed by like the flickering picture from a turn-of-the-century hand-cranked movie.

The director took safety in a long shot. But as soon as the shot went to air, a river of crimson gushed from between two flowers. Twisting like scarlet snakes, it joined others sprouting from every leaf and petal until it had dyed the white velvet background crimson.

The audio feed was silent. No doubt Candy was on the intercom regaling the already-harried director. Bryanna knew from personal experience that Ms. Cane had a good set of lungs when she chose to use them.

"And we've got another item for you," a shaken Candy said.

A doll in a frilly pink dress was the next item up.

Before their eyes, its ceramic face changed to a leering skull. Glass eyes rocked back into its cranium. Brown roaches squeezed from under its lashes, then skittered down its freckled cheeks.

"We've got to get into master control," Bryanna said. "We've got to catch that thing!"

"Catch it!" Mario said. "How?"

In answer Bryanna yanked the disk from the drive and bolted from the room.

As she tore down the carpeted corridors, she could still hear Candy's quavering voice echoing from the monitors in each office she passed.

Wisely, the director switched to promos. She reached the phone network with its sterile rows of order takers and barrelled down the aisles toward master control.

Master control was in chaos. The daytime director, John Barlow, was besieged by screaming executives. Margaret, the audio technician was staring intently at her board, desperately trying not be get involved in the fray.

If any of them noticed Bryanna as she barged through the door, they said nothing. She sat in John's abandoned chair and stuck her disk into the Abekas' disk drive.

"...how should I know?" John was practically yelling. "I've never seen anything like it in my life!"

"It's your job to find out and fix it!" a red-faced station manager bellowed.

Taking advantage of the confusion, Bryanna busied herself by loading the file. The still shot of the doll disappeared from the screen and onto her disk. Quietly, she ejected the disk and stuck it in the pocket of her jeans.

"Johnson!" the station manager hollered, seeing her for the first time. "What the hell are you doing here?"

She opened her mouth to reply, "I--"

"Well, get out! We've got enough trouble here without you under-foot!"

"Good God!" Deb exclaimed looking at the lurid still of the doll. "What do you expect me to do with this?"

"Paint it out."

Deb said, "What!" with the inflection of someone who's humoring the insane.

"Hurry," Bryanna said. "You don't want it getting into your system. Who knows what it might do."

Her friend looked to Mario, hoping he'd inject some sense into the situation. But the audio technician merely stared back at her with the same desperation as Bryanna. "Whatever you say," Debbie said, reaching for the mouse. Selecting an airbrush tool from the program's menu she began *painting* over the skull with a beige color. "That's it," she muttered between furtive looks at Bryanna and Mario. "You've gone completely crazy and so have I."

On a clear section of the screen she created two almond shaped eyes and decorated them with sparkling blue irises and long, brown lashes. With the mouse she dragged them across the screen toward the doll's face.

A flash of lightning arced between the screen to the mouse.

Deb screamed and yanked her hand away. "What the hell--?"

Bryanna gripped the back of her chair. "Be careful, Deb."

"Careful!" the paint artist shrieked. "Of what?"

On the monitor, the doll's face had decomposed into a leering skull.

"Of that," Mario said. "Whatever it is."

"The damned thing tried to electrocute me," Debbie said angrily. She drew a circle roughly the size of the doll's head and placed it over the skull.Quickly, she dragged the mouse to the *save* menu.

A torrent of slime gushed from the mouth and oozed in a greenish-black curtain down the inside of the screen.

Deb jumped to her feet, sending the chair, skidding across the floor on its side. Bryanna leapt for the mouse.

On the monitor, a demonic skull leered at her. Its face stretched, split. A mouth of jagged teeth filled the screen. She watched in amazement as the gleaming spikes pressed against the glass, attempting to chew their way past the barrier. The monitor bulged, then settled.

Time seemed to slow as she dragged the pointer to the *erase* function. She clicked the mouse button.

"Come on, come on," she chanted, impatiently drumming her fingers on the desk.

The thing on the monitor roared in fury.

Desperately, her hand trembling, she flipped through the pull-down menus until she found the command to initialize the disk.

Overhead the lights flashed, then went out. They watched, horrified, as the power lights in Deb's production suite systematically went out.

"It's sucking up all the power!" Mario said suddenly. He thrust Debbie toward the door and hauled Bryanna after him.

At the doorway she turned back long enough to see the computer's plastic casing stretch and buckle as the thing inside struggled to free itself.

For one terrible moment she thought the glass would break. A red message flashed across the screen. *Software Failure*. The power light flickered once, then went out. The fan in the back of the monitor sputtered, then stopped turning and was silent.

"We broadcast our message," Mario said and took a long pull on his beer. "But we never think about who, or what else, is listening."

"The station must be an attractive hunting ground," Bryanna added. "All that bad energy and greed to feed on. Then it learned to kill, and it would have continued, if I hadn't captured it in the still store."

"We made it stronger when we refined it in the paint program," Deb said. "Who knows what it could have done if it got loose."

"Well, it's gone now," Bryanna said.

"Right," Mario said, without much conviction.

Family Ties

EDO VAN BELKOM

Edo van Belkom is the author of the horror novel Wyrm Wolf, *and over 80 short stories of science fiction, fantasy, horror and mystery, including works that have appeared in the two previous* Northern Frights *anthologies as well as* Year's Best Horror Stories XX.

A former daily newpaper sports and police reporter, Edo became a full-time freelance wrtier in 1992. He is currently a contributing editor to the Science Fiction Writers of America's Bulletin *and writes a regular column on Canadian horror for* Horror! *the newsmagazine of the horror and dark fantasy field. He also serves as the Horror Writers Association's Canadian memebership representative. He lives in Brampton, Ontario with his wife Roberta and son Luke.*

He threw the covers off and sat bolt upright on the bed.

"Did you hear that?" he whispered.

"Mmmmm?" his wife mumbled. "What?"

"A scream. A woman's scream."

His wife rolled onto her back and looked at him. "How can you hear anything over that train?"

He strained to listen for it again, but the train was rumbling by and the roar and clang of the cars was enough to drown out any other sound.

He lay back down on the bed and pulled the covers over top of him. Their warmth was a welcome relief from the shivers that had been brought on by the scream.

There *had* been a scream, he was sure of it. A blood-curdling scream, edged with terror, sharp as a knife edge. It had come with the train. As if someone had been on the tracks, in front of the oncoming train.

But if that were the case the engineer would have tried to stop, blown its horn. Something.

"It was probably two cats fighting out on the lawn, hon. Go back to bed."

He lay awake, eyes wide and staring at the ceiling. It hadn't been a cat, that he knew for sure. He had *felt* emotion in the scream. Surprise, fear, despair, anguish, horror. They had all been there. This had been a human scream.

With his wife's breath falling into a regular rhythm next to him, he got out of bed and went to the kitchen. He looked out the window at the railroad crossing not a hundred yards from the house. The tracks looked quiet and cold, rails slicing into the darkness like twin steel blades.

Maybe I was imagining things, he thought. He glanced at the clock above the stove. Who'd be out walking the tracks at this time of night, anyway? He cracked open the refrigerator and took a few gulps of orange juice straight from the jug.

He returned to bed and spent what was left of the night trying to get back to sleep.

Gardner Shaw worked as a features reporter at *The Brampton Times*, a daily newspaper serving the half-million people who lived in the bedroom community northwest of Toronto.

He'd taken the job less than a month ago, coming from *The Cambridge Reporter* where he'd been working the police and court beats for the last three years. He'd moved into the old house at 52 Mill Street North, ready to settle in for the next little while. He'd started out ten years ago working at a tiny weekly in Kapuskasing and had moved closer to Toronto--closer to the big time -- every couple of years. Now he was so close he could taste it. But he knew he'd have to spend at least five more years working just outside Toronto before he could expect the chance at a job at the *Star* or *Globe*.

It was a good time to start a family.

He'd been reluctant at first, but the joy on his wife Susan's face every time she mentioned having a child was too persuasive. It always won out over all the logical reasons like cost, time, responsibility...

So here he was a month at a new job and a child due in four.

He'd spent the last two weeks finishing up the baby's room, papering it in a neutral design of pink ponies and powder blue clowns. It was a cozy little room that would hopefully provide his child with a sense of love and warmth.

It was already full of toys and stuffed animals.

He hated to admit it, but he was looking forward to the baby's arrival. Almost to the point of being impatient. Like most men, he was hoping for a son, but knew he would love a daughter just as much. More than anything, he was looking forward to being a father. A dad.

He sat at the kitchen table, sipping his coffee while he read the morning edition of *The Brampton Times*. He was pleased to find the night editor had liked his piece on Pinkles The Clown, a city employee who spent every Saturday visiting the children's ward at Peel Memorial Hospital, enough to place the story above the fold on page one.

Just then a freight train passed, its four diesel engines roaring so loudly that it sounded for a moment as if it were chugging down the street in front of his house.

The engines passed and the noise died down slightly as the rest of the train rattled by, every fourth of fifth car sounding as if it might fall apart rounding the next curve.

''Doesn't that bother you?'' people would say when they'd come to visit.

He had one pat answer. ''It passes so often, you don't even notice.'' It was a little cliche, but it was true. He hated the thought that such a noisy intrusion into his life could numb his mind so much as to fade into the background, but it had happened. Anyway, the proximity of the track made the house cheap enough for them to afford. That was a big consolation. As was the thought that his stay in the sleepy bedroom community was a temporary one. The next time he bought a house, when he moved into Toronto, he'd be patient enough to wait for just the right house. A reward to himself, and his family, for the long, hard work he done to climb the journalistic ladder.

He closed the paper and folded it into quarters. As he drained the last of his coffee, another train passed by.

This time, he strained to hear the scream. To his surprise it was there, muffled, faint.

He rushed over to the window to see the last car slide out of view. Nothing.

How long would he hear this... phantom scream?

He let the blinds roll back and readied himself for work. He was interviewing a falconer this morning about how his birds kept Pearson International Airport clear of pigeons and gulls. It would be an odd, quirky kind of story, and he was looking forward to flexing his creative muscles on it.

He stopped at the bedroom door to say goodbye to his wife. She was still sleeping and he decided not to wake her. He closed the door gently, then tiptoed down the hall to the front door.

As he stepped outside, his attention was again drawn to the tracks. He looked down that way often. To see what? He didn't know.

He knew the newspaper reporter part of him looked that way to see if the police were out searching the tracks, looking for body parts. That would be the obvious aftermath of the scream.

But another part of him wanted something to have happened on the line because it would mean he *had* heard something. Or perhaps that someone else had heard something and he wasn't going out of his mind.

But the line was clear.

Two kids on bikes crossed the tracks, their fenders rattling as they bumped over the rails.

Forget about it, he told himself.

Life goes on.

The interview with the falconer had gone better than expected. The man's talk had been animated and he had countless fascinating anecdotes to relate. Each one was usable and the article had practically written itself.

Gardner found himself in the newsroom at three in the afternoon with time on his hands. Normally he would have gone home early, but the company was currently undergoing contract talks with the union and wanted everyone to put in seven-and-a-half hour days, with accumulated overtime given as days off with pay. That suited him just fine. He'd been accumulating overtime for weeks and planned to take the time off when the baby came. Quality time with the family, part of being a dad.

Then, as he rifled through one of his desk drawers in a feeble attempt to look busy, he was struck by a thought. Maybe there was something to the railway line... and the screams. Maybe there was a story behind it, some spooky kind of mystery. Hell, October was less than two weeks away, maybe he could write something up about it for Halloween.

He got up from his desk and headed downstairs.

He'd worked at five different dailies and he'd yet to find a newspaper morgue that wasn't something out of a Stephen King novel. Dark, dirty, and smelling of furnace oil, newspaper morgues were places where old newspapers were kept for reference. Dead stories of long-dead people. But did that mean the place had to *look* like a crypt too?

He descended the last few steps and switched on the light, fully expecting to see a rat's tail curl around the corner of the desk at the far end of the room.

To his surprise, the place wasn't as bad as he'd expected. He'd heard that the paper had hired a summer student to put the morgue in order, and judging by the looks of it, she'd done a pretty good job. Old newspapers were stacked on floor-to-ceiling shelves on the left side of the room, while a row of filing cabinets lined the wall on the right.

He checked the index cards under "T" for train stories, and "M" for Mill Street North. He found nothing under the latter and only a few features on new trains, and retiring engineers under the former. He decided to check "R" for railroad and found what he was looking for. There were six index cards listing railroad-related stories, one of which listed stories concerning accidental deaths, suicides and murders connected with the rail line that ran like an artery through the heart of the city.

A quick scan of the card and he'd found it, a brief reference to a story about a murder committed on the line.

At the Mill Street North crossing.

He jotted down the date of the story on a scrap of paper and noticed for the first time that his hand was shaking. He slapped his right hand over top of it and found his palms were sweating as well.

He took a deep breath and went over to the wall of newspapers. All of this should have been on microfiche, but *The Brampton Times* was a little behind on some of the most basic technological advances. The managing editor had told him that microfilming the morgue was in next year's budget, but a couple of newsroom veterans had told him not to hold his breath.

After a brief search he found the edition he needed. The headline immediately caught his eye.

PREGNANT WOMAN PUSHED ONTO TRACKS

He remained still, reading the article where he stood.

A 19-year-old Brampton woman was killed early Sunday morning when she was pushed in front of an oncoming train.

Iris Higson was killed instantly when she was hit by a westbound freight train at the Mill Street North level crossing just behind the Brampton GO Station.

Higson had been returning home from a party, walking along the tracks with her boyfriend, 27-year-old Bill Purcell.

According to police, the two were having a heated argument after Higson had told Purcell she was pregnant with his child. Angered by the news, Purcell, who admitted to having had alcohol and illegal substances earlier in the evening, pushed Higson onto the tracks.

Higson's death scream awakened people over a block and a half away.

Purcell turned himself in to police late Sunday morning and confessed to the crime.

Charged with second-degree murder is William Allen Purcell of Bramalea.

Gardner was incensed by the killing. His body was flushed with heat and the edge of the newspaper had crumpled into his angry right fist. Swirling somewhere in the midst of his rage, was a heartfelt sadness for the woman and the innocent, unborn child.

He and Susan had been trying to have a child for years and had even booked an appointment with a fertility specialist to find out what the problem was. But then, she'd come home one day with the good news, and a new stage in their life had begun. One of responsibility, commitment, and sacrifice.

Having a child was something they'd had to work for. And here was some punk, probably too drunk or stoned out of his mind to even remember what he'd done.

It just wasn't fair.

But Gardner had been working in newspapers long enough to know that these kinds of things happened all the time. He couldn't let it get to him too much. If he did, he'd be out of the business in a year.

He took the newspaper upstairs to the circulation department and photocopied the article. Susan would want to know about this story. She was a bit of a horror fan, and would be interested in hearing about a local ghost story.

Ghost story?

Was that the scream he was hearing?

He shook his head. "Couldn't be," he said aloud, as if saying it out loud rather than merely thinking it would confirm the notion's impossibility.

"Couldn't be," he said again. "Couldn't be."

He came to an abrupt stop at a light on Main Street and the stuffed Pooh Bear on the seat next to him rolled forward onto the floor. There were plenty of stuffed animals in the crib in the baby's room, but the Pooh Bears were on sale with a fill-up at the Petro-Canada station and he just couldn't resist.

Buying the thing had made him feel good, like a daddy.

When the light turned green he turned left onto Church and drove along the edge of the expansive GO Station parking lot. Each morning it filled to capacity with cars left behind by commuters taking the GO Train into Toronto. By darkfall each night it was empty and barren. A good place to play road hockey with his son... or teach his daughter how to ride a bike.

He was just about to pass the entrance to the lot when he decided to turn in. He had tried to block all thoughts of Iris Higson from his mind, but he hadn't been able to. It was a sad story. A tragedy. Two young lives eliminated in the blink of an eye while another basically useless one was allowed to grow old and gray.

It wasn't fair.

But then life, and death, never were.

He drove to the westernmost corner of the lot and parked the car. According to the story in the newspaper, the murder had occurred just on the other side of the fence.

He got out of the car and walked around the edge of the fence and onto the tracks. He looked south and saw that the light was on in the living room of his house. Susan must be home, he thought. I should hurry this up.

Hurry what up? He wasn't even sure why he'd stopped. Probably his newspaperman's sense of curiosity. He'd often found himself visiting crime scenes, trying to absorb some of their atmosphere, smell some of their smells. It was a little thing, but it was a little thing that had helped him win two Western Ontario Newspaper Awards for his feature writing.

But there was something different about this...

Something...

Was grabbing at his feet.

He looked down and saw nothing there. Just the pale brown suede of his desert boots against the oily wooden ties and dirty black cinders between the rails.

Still there was something there. He could feel it, clawing at him, pulling down on his feet and legs to keep him from moving, from running away.

He tried lifting his feet, but they wouldn't budge.

In the distance, he saw a pin-prick of light. He turned around to look in the other direction and saw the lights over the tracks change.

From red to green.

His efforts intensified. He grabbed at his legs, pulling on them in a vain attempt to lift them off the ground.

The train was nearing, its dot of light growing larger each second.

This is crazy, he thought. This can't be happening.

But it was.

He knelt down and untied his shoes, hoping to leave them behind as he leaped to safety. But his feet were as firmly secured to his shoes as his shoes were to the ground.

The train was even closer, the light grown into a tiny white ball. He could just begin to make out the black silhouette of the hulking mass behind it.

He tried one last time to move. His legs were tired, drained. They would not move.

He raised his arms over his head and began waving them frantically at the train.

Why doesn't the engineer stop?

He could hear the train now, the rumble and clang of it sounding more like some great metal monster than a mode of transportation.

The flashing red lights of the level crossing began blinking on and off. The bell rang *ding, ding, ding.*

And then the light at the front of the train quickly transformed into a big round disk, growing ever larger until it washed out everything in Gardner's world, bathing all of it in a bright, bright white.

Blinding him.

Just before impact, Gardner felt something press against him. It felt like a body. A woman's body. Breasts full and soft against the small of his back.

And something else.

A slight pressure against his right thigh, like a child taking hold of his leg. Holding on tight.

The train was upon him.

He screamed.

And the blinding white light turned black.

Susan sat in the rocking chair in the living room, knitting. The chair had been a gift from Gardner's parents. It was old and worn and a bit uncomfortable, but Susan loved it. What she looked forward to most of all was rocking in it while her child suckled at her breast. A simple pleasure, like knitting booties and sweaters and mittens.

But then, everything had been wonderful so far, not the least of which had been Gardner's attitude. He'd turned out to be more enthusiastic about the baby than she could have ever imagined. He was a good man. Helpful and supportive. She knew, intuitively, that he'd be a good father to her child. It was one less thing to worry about, and it had made the uncertainty about how their lives would change in four short months so much easier to handle.

She glanced at the clock.

It was getting late, but Susan wasn't concerned. She'd been married to a newspaper man far too long to start worrying whenever he didn't call or came home late.

She reached down for another ball of yarn when she heard something.

The scream.

She gave a little laugh.

I've finally heard it, she thought.

I can't wait to tell Gardner when he gets home.

The Pines
TIA TRAVIS

Calgary writer Tia Travis has had stories published in the anthologies Young Blood, Fear Itself, Shock Rock 2 *and the forthcoming DAW book* It Came From the Drive-In.

"I'm a born-and-bred Canadian prairie gal," Tia *informs, "and no stranger to the kind of lonesome winters I wrote about in The Pines. I was compelled to write the story after having to watch a small animal die in the cold. There was nothing I could do about it. On the livelier side of things, I'm, in a band called* Curse of Horseflesh, *which has been called* 'Deliverance *meets* Bikini Beach *hillbilly-surf rock'. We've played everywhere from junkyards to rodeos to a truckbed out behind an outhouse. Our first record has the surface noise scratched right into the vinyl, for that authentic cattle city flavor..."*

Hear the wind blow, love, hear the wind blow
Hang your head over, hear the wind blow
Know I love you, dear, know I love you
Angels in heaven know I love you

"Down in the Valley", Old Folk Song

She takes the 2 north from Calgary, driving her brother's '81 Ford with the broken heater and the staticky radio and the permanently frozen windshield wipers. A two-year old husky sleeps on the seat beside her in an old wool blanket. It is twenty-five below zero in the truck. Colder still in the back, but she doesn't like to think about that. Doesn't like to think at all, because thinking doesn't help a damn bit.

On the floor of the truck sits a half-empty thermos of black coffee, two unopened six-packs of beer, and a battered steel pipe.

The pipe has brain matter on it.

Past Red Deer and Lacombe and Bear Hills Lake and all the small towns between, field after field is covered in a thick counterpane of January snow. The snow is topped with a crust of ice so cold it burns, the kind of ice you see only on the prairies in winter under the blue-white shadow of a Canadian moon.

She has tried to keep them warm, Michele and the husky. But it is cold in the front of the truck, cold in the back. Too cold. Her hands are numb and mechanical in their thin mittens, and the condensation of her breath in the sub-zero temperature has frozen the metal of her parka zipper.

In Edmonton she turns off onto the 32. One hundred miles of cold hard earth. Sakwatamau River with stubble frozen banks. Buckbrush and bristle black current capped with an undisturbed blanket of blue-white snow. After that it is the Northern Woods and Water Route that leads to The Land's End, some call it, a place were there are no towns and no people and the pines stand silently close on the hills. The pines....

She closes her eyes a moment and breathes in deep, and she can almost smell cold hard needles and perfume sap in the arctic air.

"We're almost there, Michele," she says out loud. "Almost there." Her teeth chatter.

By ten o'clock the truck makes it into Peace River Country. She and the husky stay the night in a motel outside Chinook Valley. She almost doesn't stop at this town, but after four hundred and fifty miles on the highway no amount of cold thermos coffee can keep her eyes open. She and the husky are huddled in a ball on the bed. The girl's knees are pulled up to her chest. She has not changed her blood-stained clothes. She has not washed her face or combed her hair, and the blood has dried in it like shiny-stiff paint.

Michele lies on the truckbed under a piece of canvas. Snowflakes have settled on the dark fringe of her lashes. Her eyes are open but they do not see.

The girl has read that when a person dies, the eyes turn green. But Michele's eyes have always been green. So have her own.

She thinks about the pipe on the floor of the truck, and as she thinks her mind travels down the pipe's long, cool lines. She thinks about another line, a railroad line. She thinks about the man she has killed and why she has killed him. She thinks about a girl who wanted to kill, but didn't. And it all adds up in the end.

Outside the little room the snow slopes across the fields in hard-packed drifts. Snow is cut away from them by a bitter-cold wind. The wind takes the snow to The Land's End, some call it, where the sky is black and the earth is white and the moon shines cold and empty on open eyes, and the girl in the room with the two-year old husky has never been more alone.

She is laid out flat on a truckbed.

She does not think.

She does not breathe.

She does not move.

But her eyes are as open as the stars.

She had been told to call him "stepfather", but he hadn't been a stepfather at all. He was just some man her mom had been dumb enough to take up with because they had no money and no place to go. But the girl didn't like to think of her mom as dumb. Maybe her mom was just afraid. Afraid like Michele had been, afraid like the girl herself had been. Finally she'd tired of it all. And when she heard what the other man had done to Michele, she had picked up a steel pipe for the first time in fifteen years.

She could see her stepfather's face clear in her mind, even though she had been ten years old when it happened. She could see him in the cotton workshirts he used to wear. She could see how he sweated in those shirts, could see how the sweat made damp circles under his arms. He was home from work in the middle of the day because he did split-shifts at the gas plant. He had one of his headaches again, and she would have to go into the darkened bedroom and rub his forehead for him. Rub the bridge of his nose where his glasses made dark red indentations. And then when she had dutifully rubbed his head he would take her hand and make her rub another place down lower. She didn't know *why* if his head hurt *why* she had to rub *there*, she didn't know, she really didn't know, but his hand was moving her small one faster and faster, and he wouldn't let her go. She tried to pull away from him but he held her there, and that was how it had started. That was how it started a million times.

Late at night he stood in the hall by her bedroom, a still shadow with eyes that were on her always, always.

But now she had a piece of pipe she had picked up in an empty lot. She laid the pipe under her bed and waited for his shadow to come to her. Then when it came, and it always came, she would bite her lip and think about the pipe, think about it and think about it, and she could not breathe for thinking about it, and she could not move for thinking about it, but she could not pick it up, she did not know *why* but she could not pick it up, and then a heavy hand would cover her mouth, and the shadow would tell her *I'll kill you, I'll kill you if you tell*, and then all that remained of her face were her eyes, her round wide eyes that shone white in the moonlight.

And still she would think about the pipe.

Think about what it would be like to pick it up in her hands. Think, as a ten year old thinks, about what it would would be like to kill.

When she called Michele fifteen years later and Michele had picked up the phone in tears, and she'd heard Michele's boyfriend yelling in the background YOU STUPID PIECE OF SHIT, YOU STUPID PIECE OF SHIT, and the phone had dropped on the floor and Michele had let out a half-scream of terror--

When she heard that, she had come to Michele's welfare-rented townhouse with a pipe.

A different pipe, but a pipe all the same.

The door was unlocked. The air was heavy and still. It smelled like dirty clothes and dirty dishes, like dirty thoughts and dirty lives. Michele's boyfriend stood at the door to the basement, hands at his sides. He was breathing hard, and he was sweaty. A slick sheet of it covered his entire body. It made damp circles under his arms.

He looked at the girl in the doorway, surprised to see her.

"Where is she?" was all she said.

But he didn't have to tell her. She had detected the tiniest, involuntary, sideways movement in his eyes.

"Stand back," she said. "Back there where I can see you."

"I didn't touch her," he said.

"I told you to stand back, Russell." The pitch of her voice had escalated but the pipe was dead level and solid in her hands.

He stood back.

She walked over to the basement door and prodded it open with the toe of her running shoe. She looked down. Michele lay at the bottom of the stairs. One arm was snapped back behind her head like a chicken bone. She wasn't breathing. She would never breathe again.

The girl blinked slowly, and in that blink, that half-second of black and white (black like the sky and white like the snow-blanketed earth), she made up her mind.

She removed her eyes from Michele's red-smeared head on the cement floor, removed them from the long straight strands of Michele's blood-soaked hair, removed them from the pool on the floor that was shiny with the reflection from the basement bulb.

Russell stared at her.

She stared back.

In a room down the hall, she heard the prerecorded voice of a telephone operator. It came from the receiver that lay, where it had fallen, face-up on the floor: *The number you have dialled has been disconnected the number you have dialled has been disconnected the number you have dialled has been disconnected...*

It was like something from a bad made-for-TV movie.

The girl held the pipe in both shaking hands and she did not stop herself, did not *think* of stopping herself, because this time it was Michele's life. Michele's life and Michele's dreams seeping out on that bare cement in a deep maroon pool. And this time, *this time*, she would do something about it.

She held the pipe over her head. Then she hammered it down. Hammered it down on his stupid thick skull with all that she had in her, hammered it down and hammered it down and hammered it down until her hands and her face and her wide staring eyes were slippery red, and the blood splashed from the ends of her shaking white fingers.

After it was done she stepped over his body on the kitchen floor as if it were decomposing meat. In the bedroom she put the receiver back on the phone, and pulled a couple of threadbare sheets from the unmade bed. She stood at the basement door a moment, hands on either side of the frame. Then she walked slowly down the basement stairs and carefully, oh so carefully, she straightened Michele's arms and laid them at her sides. The arms were covered in bruises--blue-black and yellow-green and a tan color that was so faint she could hardly see it at all on Michele's pale skin. Marks of ownership.

But she wouldn't think about that. Wouldn't think at all, because thinking didn't help a damn bit.

Instead she parceled Michele up in the sheets, not caring that her thumbs made dark red prints on the white cotton. She did not look at Michele's face. As long as she didn't look at her face she could do what she had to do. It was five o'clock and already pitch black out. She moved Michele's body into the back of her brother's truck. It was hard work, but it had to be done. There was no one who could help her.

She dumped the pipe on the floor of the truck. It landed with a dull thud. Then she whistled for Michele's husky who had taken refuge in the bedroom, and he jumped up beside her on the seat of her brother's truck.

She left the door to the house wide open.

At home she stopped to pick up some blankets, her parka, and her brother's worn-out hiking boots. Then she drove. Drove to the only place she knew Michele had ever wanted to be.

Drove to The Pines.

At six a.m. the next day the girl fills her gas tank and hits the road, eating stale sandwiches from a truckstop on the 32. In the dark she had not been able to see the landscape transform itself but it had. Before it had been aspen parkland and rolling blue foothills to the west; prairies and open spaces to the east. Empty as far as the eye could see, frozen fields and broken barbed wire fences that had stood for decades and would stand for decades more. Lonely stands of dark fir windbreakers that bent like broken old men in the icy wind.

But now it is trees.

Trees like stripped toothpicks, so close to her, so close, and the northern sun slants through them in pale yellow shafts.

Her breath is a cold white cloud in the unheated truck. But she does not stop driving. It is not because she is transporting a dead body in the back of her truck. It is because she is determined to find the place where the pines are cold and dark and let in no light; the place in the song, that cold dark song that is the song of her soul.

In the pines, in the pines
Where the sun never shines
And I shiver when the cold wind blows.

"Almost there, Michele," she says again, and the husky lifts his head and looks at her with imploring brown eyes. She puts her hand under his chin and feels his warm wet breath on her skin. "Almost there..."

She drives on past Mile Zero of the MacKenzie Highway and takes an unpaved road that stretches 626 miles north to Great Slave Lake in the Northwest Territories. Out here it is all sawmills and bulldozed brush, husky lynx and shaggy wolverines, boreal chickadees and northern hawk owls. The trees by the side of the road have been rubbed smooth of bark by bucks trying to scrape the velvet off their antlers.

By nightfall she makes it to High Level, eighty-five miles short of the Alberta/N.W.T. border. She can hear the plaintive yaps of a pack of coyotes, running and running across the frost-stubbled fields with their bushy black-tipped tails between their legs, running and running but never finding anything because there is nothing to find on that frozen earth that is straight and hard and goes on forever.

She hears a train, far off in the distance, its powerful white light illuminating the black pines that close in on both sides of the track. She sees herself and Michele, ten years old, children of summer, racing past the pale yellow wheat fields beside the train tracks, racing past the Indian Red grain elevators, racing and racing like untamed colts. Their hearts pound with excitement as they barrel through the waist-high fields of shimmering, swaying wheat. Steam billows from their quivering nostrils as they take in the hot prairie air.

Take us with you, take us with you...

But the train never stops in their town. It never stops at all. And because the train is made of iron and steel and ten year old girls are made of

t-shirts and dreams, they have to stop. Panting, shoulders shaking, heads
dropped down to their knees. Thatches of sun-whitened hair falling in their
sweaty faces like manes. And the train goes on and on down the line, the
puffs of white engine smoke making exclamation marks in the still expanse
of the blue sky.

And they watch, she and Michele. Watch as the engineers wave to
them and blow the steam whistle. The cars are loaded with fragrant pines.
They smell the sap, pungent, heady and sweet. They stand there by the
shining tracks and breathe it all in, breathe it all in with their eyes closed
but their hearts open.

Take us with you!

The sound of their voices in that empty land makes them terribly
lonely, but they don't know why.

Take us with you! Take us with you! But the engineers can't hear
them over the whistle.

The girl turns to Michele, who stands beside her on the empty track.
She takes Michele's hand in her own, and Michele smiles, a little sad half-
smile.

"One day," Michele says, her dark green eyes still intent on the red-
painted caboose. "One day we'll catch one."

"How can we do that, Michele?"

Michele shakes her head. She doesn't know. The train disappears
into the distance like a dream, and the whistle echoes back on the wind like
something you can touch, almost, almost... And then the afternoon sky
darkens to deep violet blue and the first glimmer of stars appears high up in
the sky.

"One of these days. One of these days it'll stop."

But the train doesn't stop.

It never stops.

And now here they are, fifteen years later, driving north to the place
where the train-pulled pines had come. Fifteen years later. Fifteen years
too late.

She parks the truck outside a diner in High Level. The temperature has
dropped to -40 and the north wind is up. The wind does not lift the snow
from the sculpted banks but sends it scudding down the ice-dusted high-

way. The cold takes her breath away but she breathes in deeply, because she knows that the cold is not so cold if you are not afraid of it.

She walks slowly and stiffly in her brother's hiking boots. Her head is bowed down low, and her hair lashes at her face like a whip. The husky stays close behind her. The diner is a shapeless shadow in the white wind. When she opens the door everyone turns to look at her. There are four people: two Metis men in fur-trimmed, army green parkas who sit at the counter, a blond woman in a thick wool ski sweater, and a sullen, heavy-set man who sits to the right of the two natives. The girl stands in the door for a moment and stares at them, breathless, as beside her the husky's paws make little clicks on the scuffed white floor.

For the first time in hours she thinks about how she looks. Her eyes are red and her nose has started to run and her hair is frozen stiff with ice. She knows they can't see the dried brown stains on her jeans and her shirt, or the dark red rinds under her broken fingernails. But she does not know why they are looking at her like that, looking and looking but not saying anything. She shakes the snow self-consciously from her boots and sits down at the counter.

"Could I have some coffee, please?" she asks. The blond woman in the ski sweater is the waitress. She has blue eyes and a kind smile.

"Comin' up," she says, reaching for the fresh pot. "Sit down there, now, and warm up a little." Then she tells the girl not to take her parka off because it is cold in here, damn gas lines are frozen, and the girl notices two red-hot space heaters behind the counter. The waitress sets a thick white mug of steaming coffee between the girl's mittened hands. She sips the dark brown liquid and listens to the men talk about work and the cold and the pipelines and the cold, and the waitress fills her cup one more time. "Is there a phone I can use?" she asks.

"Pay phone's over there on the wall, hon," the woman says. "Last we heard the lines were still up, but that was an hour ago and anything could have happened since then."

The girl thanks the woman, puts a dollar in quarters in the phone and makes the long distance call. The phone rings four times before the answering machine picks up. The connection is staticky. *You've reached 337-3462. Russell and I can't come to the phone right now, but leave your name and number and we'll call you back.*

There is a long beep.

She holds the cold receiver close to her mouth, takes a short breath. "Hi," she says. "It's me..." She stops. She does not blink because then the tears will spill down her cheeks like little beads of ice. "I just wanted to tell you..."

Tell her what?

She doesn't know. She hangs up the phone and stands there a minute. Then puts another four quarters into the slot.

You've reached 337-3462. Russell and I can't come to the phone right now, but leave your name and number and we'll call you back.

"Michele?" Her voice is a barely a whisper. "If you're listening, pick up...." She waits. There is silence on the other end. Then: "Call me back," she says.

She goes back to her stool and sits down. She stares at herself in the mirror behind the counter.

"You all right, honey?" the blond woman asks.

But the girl does not hear her. She is staring at her face, at the tired eyes and the tired lines etched below them. She is twenty-six but looks like an old woman.

"Honey--you all right?"

The girl meets the waitress's eyes. She smiles a little. "Do you have anything I can feed my dog? A couple of hamburgers or something?"

"I'll put them on now," the waitress says. "You want anything to eat?"

"No. Thank you," she adds.

"Where you headed?" It is one of the parka men.

"North."

"*North?*"

"That's right."

"There's nothin' up there," the other one objects. She says nothing, but they are waiting for her to reply, so she tells them she is on her way to Indian Cabins at the Alberta/Northwest Territories border.

"Indian *Cabins?*" one of them says, dumbfounded.

"You won't make it." It is the sullen, heavy-set man. "Road's closed up past Steen River," he says. "You'll be lucky to get that far."

"I'll take those to go," she says, as the blond woman starts to set a plate of meat patties on the floor in front of Michele's dog.

"Didn't you hear me, little girl?" the sullen man says. "I said the *road* is *closed.*"

"I heard you," the girl says, staring straight at him. Something in her eyes makes him close his mouth. The girl pays her check and picks up the bag of hamburgers. The diner is silent. "Come on, boy," she says to the husky, and she starts for the door. The dog tags along behind her.

"Wait." It is the blond woman. "Here, you take this, it's Elton's old ski jacket. It's not much but he's not usin' it and you can put it around your knees while you drive, okay? It's cold out there."

The girl takes the faded purple jacket the woman holds out for her. There is something in the woman's tired blue eyes that she has seen before, something desperate and sad, something....

She looks past the woman at the dark and sullen man at the counter, at the still and heavy fists at his sides. "Thank you," she says.

"Lynne," the woman says softly. "My name is Lynne."

The girl smiles for the last time. "Thank you, Lynne. My name is Michele." And she turns and steps out into the swirling white.

It is forty-five below now. The snow has blown itself on to Land's End, and the moon is a pale white circle that shines over the dark outline of trees. The truck has stalled on her twice and will not make it more than a couple of miles. Finally she stops at the side of the highway. The pines are there, black shadows on all sides, black shadows on the blacker still backdrop of northern sky. They have always been there, waiting.

She steps out of the truck and breathes in the arctic air. It is so cold that the sides of her nostrils stick together with each breath.

"We're here," she says to the husky, and he looks at her from under Elton's ski jacket with warm brown eyes. "We're here," she says to Michele. She pops the top off a can of beer. It is a half-frozen slush but she drinks it anyhow. When she has finished it she drinks another, and another after that.

She thinks about what it is like to die from exposure. *It is like falling asleep*, she thinks. *It only hurts if you try to think.*

But it is better to die like this, better to die on a bitter night when the soul is solid ice and breaks off piece by piece, falling and falling down into a black river.

She crunches over the top of the packed snow to the back of the truck and sits down beside Michele. Every part of her is covered in canvas. Every part but her face, which shimmers white in the moonlight. There has been a meteor shower tonight, and the girl wanted them both to see it. She thinks about the silver afterglow trailing across Michele's open eyes like shining train tracks.

The husky jumps up into the back of the truck and comes to sit in her lap. He puts his head on her knee. She rubs her hand in his cold fur and stares out into the black. She can see The Pines, tall and dark, and she can smell The Pines, cold and perfumed, and she can hear The Pines, whisper and whisper:

> In the pines, in the pines
> Where the sun never shines
> And I shiver when the cold wind blows

Far away in the dark she hears the train, and its whistle echoes back on the cold wind like something you can touch, almost, almost, and it is loaded with pines, and it is on its way north, always north.

"It almost stopped this time," she whispers. "It almost stopped...."

The Summer Worms
DAVID NICKLE

David Nickle's fiction has appeared in On Spec, TransVersions, *the British magazine* Valkyrie, *and the anthologies* Christmas Magic *and* Tesseracts 4, *as well as our first two* Northern Frights *volumes. His story "The Sloan Men," which appeared in* Northern Frights 2, *was chosen to be reprinted in* The Year's Best Fantasy and Horror: Eighth Annual Edition.

About The Summer Worms, *Dave writes: "I met them as a kid in the 1970s in Muskoka, Ontario. Every few years the caterpillars show up there in force--the area turns into a veritable Woodstock of horrible green worms. I remember approaching our house just outside of Gravenhurst, and coming to the realization that the large black patches on the shingles and windows and doors were actually armies of caterpillars. In a bad year they could strip trees to the bark and leave a swath across the landscape like nature's own strip-miners. Never mind raging grizzlies, loups-garous, or the Wendigo--for me, tent caterpillars are as terrifying a Northern Fright as anyone needs to know about."*

Sharon's hand came away from the tree-branch covered in them, but she didn't so much as flinch. She brought the hand to her face, studying them minutely as they crawled between her fingers, inched across her palms. Her brow knitted, a little, her mouth opened, a crack, and the tip of her tongue curled over the edge of her teeth, straying only an instant. Sharon watched the caterpillars on her hand, Robert watched Sharon watching the caterpillars.

"They don't seem to bother you," Robert said.

"Should they?" Sharon held her hand forward, and as the caterpillars came to him, he did flinch. The hand withdrew. "I'm sorry, Bob. I'll try and cultivate a phobia too."

She shook her hand, as though she were trying to throw soap-suds off after the supper dishes, and the worms dropped to the forest floor.

Individually, the tent caterpillars were scarcely more than an inch long, and thin as spaghetti. But in numbers, they seemed huge. Several trunks were entirely covered in them, their tiny mottled bodies making a new layer of bark. Silk hung from the dark branches like torn shrouds.

Robert smiled. "No phobia. But no love for them, either." He motioned around them. "By night, the worms will have stripped these trees bare. Turns the bush into a wasteland. Every year they're bad."

"It seems to bounce back," she said mildly. "From where I'm standing, it looks like there's plenty of bush to go around."

He couldn't tell if she was making fun of him. Sharon's eyes had a natural glitter to them, like they were always laughing, at everything they saw.

"The worms don't help it," he maintained, a little too steadfastly.

"Neither does the pesticide," she answered, locking her glittering eyes with Robert's. "Which won't stop you from spraying, will it?"

Robert didn't even answer that. She was laughing -- her eyes betrayed her.

She must have seen something in his eyes, though, because as quickly as it came the mockery passed, her eyes flicked away from his.

"They're caterpillars, not worms, you know." She bent for a moment to study a nest, a tapered lozenge of silk filled with a hard black core. "There's a difference. They're butterflies." She smiled a little, and said in an almost affectionate tone: "Baby butterflies."

"Well these butterflies can make a difference between a good season and a bad one."

She looked away then, and nodded, the way that she did whenever Robert offered up a fact or observation about his land or the business. It was as though she were filing it away, familiarizing herself as intimately as she could with the life that Robert had built here at his campground.

He hoped that was an indication of something... On more than one night back at the cabin, cleaning up after supper or watching her work on her computer or in the afterglow of their nights together, Robert had found himself hoping: this one should stay.

She was younger than most of the women Robert had taken up with over his life. She hadn't said her age exactly, and Robert considered himself too much of a gentleman to ask, but she couldn't have been older than 30.

Robert had met her in Gravenhurst just over a month ago, at the first of the Sheas' summer barbecues. "She's just separated," Pat Shea had told him as she handed him a dripping can of Ex from the cooler. "Allan -- her husband, you remember him?" Robert opened his beer and nodded, although as he thought about it he could not remember Allan Tefield with any clarity at all. "Allan went back to Toronto last week."

Sharon was perched on the edge of the picnic table under the Sheas' ancient maple tree. Her long, blond hair was pulled back in a pony tail to reveal a sculpted jawline and what seemed like an impossibly long throat. Robert had been fascinated -- everything about Sharon Tefield was elongated, a not-unkind caricature of cover-girl good looks. If he couldn't recall Allan Tefield's face, Robert was certain he would have remembered if he'd seen Sharon Tefield before, even once.

"Come on, Bob," Pat had said, noticing him noticing. She took him by the arm and directed him to the picnic table. "We'll do introductions."

A month later, Robert and Sharon stood on the southern ridge of the valley that made up the largest part of the Twin Oaks campground. Peering between the trees, the view was pure Muskoka. A dynasty of beavers had dammed up the stream decades ago and made the bowl of the valley into a small lake that reflected the cloud-filtered sunlight in sharp silver flashes.

In better seasons, the lake would be rimmed with fishermen, and this ridge well-traveled by hikers. But the tent caterpillars had started their crawl in June, and by mid-July the campers were staying at home.

"I have to go back to the cottage," said Sharon. "Just for a day or two."

"Trouble with Allan?"

Sharon shook her head, her lips set into a line. "Allan's finished. He's no trouble at all." She turned to Robert then, and the line of her mouth broke into a reassuring grin. "There are just a couple of things I want to pick up. Clean out."

Robert nodded, taking care to keep the flutter tight inside. Words like those often signaled an end -- *I just have to go back to the city for a week, a few things to take care of... A couple of things I want to pick up.* But until the other shoe fell, there would be nothing to say.

Sharon's arm encircled Robert's waist. "I'm glad," she whispered.

"Glad about what?" he asked. But she didn't answer. They stood still on the ridge-path, while around them the summer worms munched away on leaves and sap and bark, preparing for their long, transforming sleep.

Sharon said she would be back not this night but the following, and Robert answered that was fine with him. He would spend the evening reading, he said, then out to work early in the morning. He had some canisters of EasEnd in the shed, and while he was loathe to use too much of it, he thought he might spray some of the trees up on the south ridge.

"It's a losing battle," said Sharon. They were standing in front of his cabin, beside her old blue Volvo. She had left her tote-bag in the bedroom, and carried her laptop computer under her arm.

"Got to at least put on a brave show for the campers," he replied. There were only three families staying at Twin Oaks that week, but Sharon was kind enough not to point that out.

"I love you," she said instead. "But I don't want to come back to you stinking of bug spray."

"I'll shower," said Robert.

"Promise?"

Robert just laughed.

So they kissed good-bye and Robert watched the car turn around and start down the long driveway to the highway. He waved as it disappeared in the trees, and turned away. The sky that peeked through the maple branches over his cabin was the dull purple of late-August overcast -- any sunset tonight would be lost behind the thickness of the clouds.

Just as well, he thought as he climbed the steps to his cabin. He stopped on the porch, nodded greetings at one of the Torsdale kids who was out playing by the barbecue pit -- unlit, he noted sourly: who wants to barbecue this summer? -- then let himself in.

Robert had built the cabin in 1970. It was cedar log, a bargain-basement kit house that was more suited to his needs then than these days: three rooms, all of them minuscule, with heat coming from an old wood stove in the living room. At the time he'd been inclined to forgo major appliances and a septic system as well, but fortunately had allowed himself to be talked out of it. The flush toilet and electric stove were luxuries that he had since come to appreciate, and as he sank down into the old vinyl recliner, it occurred to him that he -- and Sharon, the two of them -- could well appreciate a few more.

Over the years since he had come to this country, there had been three other women Robert had invited into his home. None had stayed long: the winters were too cold, the rooms too small... It was a man's house, Lynn MacRae had told him as she packed for Toronto in January of 1983. *A bachelor's house.*

Lynn had been on the run from a bad marriage, too. She had been a teacher before she married, and within five months of leaving her husband and taking up with Robert, she determined it was time to go back to work. Thank you, Robert. She held both his hands and looked him levelly in the eye as she spoke, in that grave, affectionate tone that always marked the end. *I've learned so much from you.*

Robert unscrewed the cap off the bottle of Smirnoff's he kept underneath the end-table and poured a finger of vodka into a tumbler. He didn't want to be a lesson for Sharon, any more than he had for Lynn... and Mary, and Laura...

The vodka burned down his throat in a single gulp, and he resisted the urge to pour himself a second. He had been going to spend the evening reading, he remembered.

Robert got up, switched the radio on to CBC, and pulled down the Frederick Forsyth novel he'd been picking at through the summer. He settled down again, and after a moment's consideration poured himself another splash of vodka. The CBC was playing big band music, just getting into a long set of Woody Herman. Robert heaved back and his chair obligingly reclined.

It's Sharon's life, he reminded himself. *Not Lynn's, or Mary's, or anyone else's. She'll decide.*

It was dark; Robert could hear the wind rustling in the maple trees over the house and the jazz show was almost over when the phone rang.

"Hello, Bob." Pat Shea's voice had an uneasy sing-song quality to it at the other end of the line. "How's it going with you two?"

Robert smiled: since Sharon had started talking about moving in, it was clear that Pat was more than a little uncomfortable in her role as matchmaker. It would have been easier on her if they'd just gone out on a few dates, maybe kept up an affectionate correspondence between here and Toronto until the divorce was final; then a proper wedding at the nice old Anglican church the Sheas favored in Gravenhurst. From Pat's point of view, she had created an extra-marital monster by introducing Robert Thacker to Sharon Tefield.

"It's going great," said Robert, then added, to help Pat relax as much as anything, "Sharon's back at the cottage tonight."

"Is she?" There was a measure of change in Pat's voice that Robert couldn't quite place. "That might be just as well. I was actually calling to let you know. Allan phoned here this evening."

Ah, hell. "What did he have to say?" he asked.

"A lot of ugly things. He sounded as though he'd been drinking." Pat paused for a moment -- he could hear her breaths against the mouthpiece as she decided what to say next. "But he told me he knew about you and Sharon. He asked me if she'd moved in with you yet. I'm afraid..."

She'd told him. She was sorry, she didn't know how it slipped out, but there it was. Allan knew that his ex-wife was shacking up with the guy who owned the Twin Oaks Campground.

"I'm sorry, Robert."

"It's all right. He was going to find out anyway." In truth, Robert was surprised Sharon hadn't told Allan already.

"We're just worried about you. The two of you. Allan might be calling there later on tonight. That's why I called."

Robert smiled. "To warn me?"

Pat gave a small laugh. "I know you can take care of yourself, Bob. But you might want to screen your calls for the next few days."

"Well I may just do that." Robert didn't remind Pat that his bachelor's cabin didn't have an answering machine or any other means to screen his calls as she put it. "Thanks for the advance notice."

But Pat went on. "You really don't want to be talking to Allan right now, and when Sharon gets back she won't either. He sounded so..."

Robert held the phone in the crook of his shoulder and uncapped the vodka while Pat searched for the word.

"It was like he was dried out. Like he'd been drinking whisky, straight up, every night. And the things he said... About Sharon, you... Mostly Sharon. Honestly, Bob..."

He set the vodka down, uncapped, on the end table. "I wish he'd called here in the first place," he said. "This shouldn't be your problem."

"Do you want us to go out there? To her cottage?" Pat didn't sound as though she wanted him to take her up on the offer, so he didn't.

"No, no, no. Don't worry; I'll give her a call."

"I just thought I should warn you."

"And you did. Thank you, Pat."

So they said their good-byes and Robert returned the phone to its cradle. He swore softly. If Allan was in as bad a state as Pat seemed to think he was, Robert was more worried about him calling Sharon at the cottage -- or driving there, for that matter -- than he was about him calling here. After a moment's thought, he picked up the phone again and dialed the number of Sharon's cottage. It rang five times before she answered -- she had been sleeping, he could tell.

He would be brief, he said, and told her about the conversation with Pat. "So you might want to, ah, screen your calls," he said.

"Okay," she mumbled through her sleep-haze. "Go to bed, honey."

"Do you want me to come out there?" he asked.

"No."

"If he shows up and you're alone--"

Sharon made a stretching sound. "He won't come," she said.

"What if he does?"

"Bobby, will you please go to bed? Allan can't do anything to me. Believe me -- he's finished."

Finished. That was the second time she'd used that phrase to describe her ex-husband today.

"I'm just --"

But she cut him off again. "I love you, Bobby. But it's late. Go to bed. You've got a long day ahead of you. And I've got things to do around here in the morning. So get some sleep. Love you," she repeated.

"You too," he said, and hung up a second time.

The phone didn't ring again, but Robert sat up waiting for it all the same. At around midnight, he thought again about calling her, driving out there anyway. But her tone hadn't been welcoming. And she was a big girl, he reminded himself.

Finally, Robert decided to give in to sleep, and stood up to go to the bedroom. It was unnaturally quiet -- he couldn't even hear the leaves rustling over the house.

When he opened the window beside his bed, a cool summer breeze teased through his beard. He peered through the screen, out into the dark. A lone caterpillar was curled in an imperfect 'S' shape on the outside of the screen. Robert flicked the wire mesh with his forefinger. The worm went tumbling into the night.

"Summer worms," he muttered and pulled off his shirt and bluejeans. He crawled into bed, pulled up the deep green comforter that Sharon had brought over the week before, and settled onto his side. The night was winter quiet, and through it all Robert slept a fine, dreamless sleep.

The alarm clock jangled Robert awake in darkness, and he fought an inclination to roll over and sleep another hour -- if he did, he knew he wouldn't be out of bed until six. It was so *quiet* in the early morning dark.

With a deliberate groan Robert threw aside the comforter and made his way to the kitchen. The temperature couldn't have dropped too much overnight, but the cabin air was freezing against his bare shoulders and thighs. He measured some instant coffee into a mug and filled the kettle, then went back to the bedroom to get into something warm.

The bedroom was if anything worse than the rest of the house. The window, still open from last night, admitted a north breeze that rustled across the two small curtains like flags. They made a faint flapping noise, and that was the only sound Robert could hear.

The only sound.

He wrapped the housecoat tight around him and shut the window, but he couldn't stop shivering. Some things, he thought, you only notice by their absence. And with a breeze like that, the rustling of the leaves and branches in the maple tree over his cabin should have been steady, all night long.

"Ah, hell." Doing up the belt of the robe as he went, Robert hurried to the front door and slid his bare feet into an old pair of rubber boots. As an afterthought, he grabbed the flashlight from the hook beside the coat rack -- it was still dark outside -- and flipping it on, unlatched the front door and went out onto the stoop. He swung the flashlight beam up, to the branches that dangled over his roof.

"Hell," he said again, slack-jawed at the sight.

The branches were white, wrapped in silk thick as cotton candy. Strands of it hung taut between the limbs of the old maple tree, and as Robert played the flashlight beam across the expanse, he could see that it made nearly a perfect wrap; as though an enormous bag had been dropped over the tree, tied snug at the trunk. The leaves, the branches were all caught tight in the fabric, sheltered by it, and the wind left them still in the night. Robert stepped away from his porch and moved around the nest's perimeter, playing the flashlight up and down it. The morning dew glimmered off the nest like spun sugar.

The nest. That's what it is. Robert was awe-struck by the immensity of it.

The tent caterpillars had come in the night, and before dawn they had woven a nest around a single tree that must have measured more than forty feet across, maybe half again as high. How many caterpillars would that have taken? Millions? A billion?

As he stood wondering, it occurred to Robert that he had been wrong about the silence. The nest wasn't quiet at all. In the darkness there was a drone of tiny jaws, working steadily at the greenery they had locked inside.

Robert started as another sound came up. It was the whistle from his kettle, high and insistent as the water boiled away. When he went inside to quiet it, his hand was trembling.

The morning went badly.

The Torsdales were the first of the campers to rise, at just before seven, and when Jim, their youngest boy, saw the work the worms had done in the night he screamed like a girl. The scream got Don and Jackie Torsdale out of bed -- although their daughter Beth slept until they shook her a moment later -- and before seven fifteen, Robert figured, the other two families that made up his camp clientele this morning were also wide awake.

When he came out of the shed twenty minutes later with the canister of EasEnd over his shoulder and his coveralls, goggles and filter mask on, he noted wryly that those two trailers were in the process of packing up.

"Hey! That stuff's harmful!" shouted Mrs. Poole, setting her fists on her wide hips and glaring across the nearly-empty campground while her husband disassembled the canopy on their trailer behind her. "Don't you go sprayin' it while there's people here!"

No danger of that, he thought, not for much longer. Then he pulled aside his filter mask to answer: "Don't worry, Mrs. Poole. I'm following the instructions."

"They don't mean nothin'!" she snapped before turning to her husband. "Hurry up! I don't wanna stay here no longer than I got to!"

Robert slipped the mask back over his face and walked over to the spot where the branches hung lowest. The weave was thick here, hanging deep over the wood pile and casting a uniform gray shadow over the sandy soil. If Robert reached up, he could touch the silk with his hand, and even through the blur of the goggles he could see the dark mass of the caterpillars. They crawled outside the nest too, and as he stood there they dropped, in twos and threes, landing to die in the sand or insinuate themselves into the crannies of the wood pile. Absently, Robert brushed at his shoulder.

Robert unhooked the hose on the end of the canister. It had a long metal nozzle, and he lifted it to the fabric of the nest. The silk felt rough on the end of the nozzle, and Robert hesitated a moment before pushing it through -- he was struck by an image of the entire nest bursting, the nozzle a sharp pin to the tree's balloon, and he trapped, exposed under the weight of a million summer worms.

But the other option was fire. More than a few landowners in this part of Muskoka used that option readily, and Robert had in the past: just hold a lighter to the silk, watch it catch in gossamer embers and black curls of ash. Nature takes care of itself.

But he wasn't about to burn a nest this big. Any fire that could destroy this nest would take the maple tree, his cabin, maybe even the rest of the campground as well.

The nozzle slid into the nest like a syringe, and Robert squeezed the valve lever. He did it in seven more spots around the tree, until the canister was empty, leaving ragged holes of a size that bullets might make. Finally, he stood back, squinted at his work.

There was nothing he could see, of course -- the silk wrapped it, and even in the harsh morning sunlight the blackness underneath still clung.

Robert pulled the goggles off, wiped the condensation from the inside. He skirted around the tree's perimeter and hurried up the steps into his cabin.

Robert stripped his coveralls off in the living room, leaving them draped over the sofa, and he ran the water in the shower until it steamed before getting in.

Robert drove into Gravenhurst white-knuckled. As he turned onto Bethune Drive from the highway, he had to resist the urge to yank down his collar, pull out the worms. His stop at the Beer Store was quick, and the girl who worked at the counter looked at him oddly -- just for a second, as his 12-pack of Ex rumbled down the rollers from the storeroom -- and once again, he was tempted to brush his shoulders: what had she seen to make her look at him so? He hurried back to his truck, bottles jangling in their case.

He parked on Muskoka Street and walked to the A&P, where he gathered his groceries like an automaton, filling up the little arm basket by rote: extra large eggs, butter, bread, a two-litre carton of two per cent, a package of bacon, a three dollar pepper steak from the meat department. Some days, walking the aisles of the A&P, Robert would actually meet three or four people whom he knew by name. Back in '69, when he came up from Kentucky and started Twin Oaks, he could count on doing so nearly every time he came to town. But Gravenhurst had grown over the past two decades, filled up with too many well-heeled strangers. Retired doctors and lawyers moving up to the brand-new subdivisions by the lakes. Younger families trying to beat the high cost of houses in Toronto. They were transitory, though, just like the summer people.

Just like the women who passed through Roberts' home from time to time: summer women. Robert had to wait until the light changed behind him before he could pull onto the street, and he thought about it.

Was Sharon another summer woman? She had escaped her marriage without the obvious damage that some of the others had brought with them; hell, Mary's husband used to beat her up, and the asshole Lynn had married was cheating with her cousin before she left. They had been on the run, and in retrospect Robert knew he probably should have expected that anyplace they stopped was just a way-station.

But Sharon... Where was the damage, what was it in Allan Tefield that she really had to flee? She had said it herself: He's finished.

Then he remembered Pat, and her warning phone call.

The light at Bay Street turned from yellow to red, and Robert put the truck into gear. He gassed it too hard, though, and it lurched as he swung onto the road.

There was no evidence of the caterpillars in downtown Gravenhurst. But it didn't seem to matter. At the Canadian Tire store, Robert went straight to the men's room, locked himself in a stall and stripped off his shirt. The raw pungency of his sweat hit his nostrils like belly-gas from road kill. With shaking hands, Robert pulled the sleeves of his shirt inside out, and when he found nothing in its lining, he threw it to the floor. He ran his fingers around his belt-line, reached inside -- he was sure he felt something down there, nestling in the warmth -- and snapped the elastic of his briefs hard enough to leave a sting. Then he sat down on the edge of the toilet, pants still up, and exhaled a long, jagged sigh.

The nest was as big as a house. It was bigger than his own house; it would hold a two-storey townhouse and its basement, easy, and still have room for the worms that had spun it.

Jesus.

Finally, Robert reached down beside the toilet and pulled on his shirt.

"Ah, Jesus," he said aloud, fingers fumbling as he did up his buttons.

He stood then, tucked in his shirt-tails and left the stall. At the garden section, he picked up five more canisters of EasEnd -- as many as were left on the barren metal shelf. He paid for them from a roll of Canadian Tire coupons, and when he got them outside he put the canisters in the back of the pickup. He paused for a moment before getting behind the wheel again, to steady himself.

"To hell with it," he said aloud and climbed into the cab. The tent caterpillars had made him twitchy, and it was getting worse the longer he sat and thought about them.

When he got to Bay Street, he made a quick right and started off along the winding lake road in the direction of the Tefield cottage. If Sharon had a couple of things to do there, well she could damn well do them with him hanging around. If she didn't need anything right now, he sure as hell did.

The late-morning sun played across the ripples on Lake Muskoka like cascading jewelry as the road dipped past it. In the distance, a single motorboat hauled a water-skier in wide loops with a noise that from this distance sounded like a model airplane engine, a giant mosquito. Robert barely gave it a glance before the lake and the skier vanished behind a high tongue of bedrock.

If the summer worms had left the Canadian Tire alone, they'd been more conscientious diners along the road in to Parker's Point -- hell, by the time he got to the turnoff to their driveway, it looked as though they'd finished every last pea on their plate.

The trees around here looked as though they were dead. Leaves dangled like tattered doilies, and silk strands drifted across the narrow dirt road to catch on the truck's antenna, flying behind it like spectral pennants.

The driveway was narrower still, barely wide enough for Robert's pickup. It should have been a deep green tunnel this time of year, buried under the overhang of stands of mature maple and oak. But the light that filtered through the branches was grey, only occasionally broken by the shadow of one of the few fir trees. The rest were utterly denuded, not a speck of greenery left.

And the summer worms themselves were nowhere to be seen. Robert couldn't see a single caterpillar through the entire desolate bramble. They had finished the forest, and then they were gone.

Robert pulled the truck up behind the Tefield cottage and got out of the cab.

The packed-earth turnaround behind the cottage was empty, and at first Robert thought that Sharon had parked her Volvo around the far side of the cottage, near the boathouse.

But when he tromped down the steep driveway, what he first took to be her car wasn't hers at all. It was a yellow Porsche. Its driver's window was half down, and it was parked just outside the doors to the boathouse, at the far end of the driveway.

Robert didn't know what kind of car Allan drove -- Sharon didn't talk about him enough for details like that to stick in Robert's mind -- but from what he'd gathered over the past month, the Porsche was completely in character.

Which meant, if Pat Shea were any judge of character, that he had stumbled into what would at best be a very awkward situation.

And at worst...

The damage that Sharon Tefield would finally bring from her marriage was only starting.

Robert turned back to the cottage. It was built high on a ridge so that the lakefront deck stuck out about three feet higher than Robert's head. The branches rustled in a sudden breeze off the lake. The reflection of those dry branches, the electric sky, jiggled as the wind caressed the panes of the cottage's immense picture window. Robert couldn't tell if anyone was up there or not.

"Hello?" he called, cupping his hands around his mouth.

The cottage was silent.

"Everything okay in there?" Robert dropped his hands to his sides and started up the path to the steps onto the deck. "Anyone there?"

When there was still no answer, Robert started to run.

"I'm coming up!" he shouted, taking the steps two at a time. He should have driven out last night, he told himself. No matter what Sharon had said.

He stopped at the top of the stairs, nearly reeling backwards off the deck at the sight before him. He grabbed the railing, righted himself and stepped forward.

"Sharon!"

She wasn't anywhere amid the detritus on the deck, and he couldn't see any movement in the dark beyond the picture windows, but Robert was filled with a sudden dread that she was still here -- maybe in the bathroom, maybe locked up in the bedroom. Left there by her crazy ex-husband to rot and die. After he'd worked her over. And maybe after he'd done this to their deck.

Robert stepped gingerly around the shattered glass that had once been the top of their patio table, through the torn strips of cushion fabric, the thick chunks of foam rubber scattered across the wood.

Allan must have taken a butcher knife to this, Robert thought. *He must have been crazy -- completely goddamn crazy.*

"Who's that?"

Robert looked back at the window in time to see a blur of motion -- a flash of white flesh, quick across the darkness of the living room and blurred by Robert's own reflection. The voice had been a man's, muffled by glass and curtains. It had sounded rough, uncertain.

"Rob Thacker." He stepped over to the screen door, which was ajar. He pulled it open, then lifted his hands, palms-outward, in a belated gesture of truce. The cottage stank, of liquor and spoiled milk, but he resisted the urge to cover his face. "I'm Robert Thacker," he said again, squinting around the dim living room. "No trouble, okay?"

It was a mess in here, too. As Robert's eyes adjusted to the dimness, he could make out more victims of Allan's knife. There was a set of pine furniture -- sofa, love seat and arm-chair -- that had all been overturned. The pillows were sliced to ribbons, and the stuffing was spread across the floor in a way that reminded Robert of the caterpillar nests. There was a large picture on the wall -- Robert recognized it as the work of one of the local artists, a watercolor painting of this very cottage, maybe as seen from the boat-house. The glass fronting it had been smashed and lay on the rug in a glittering jumble. A floor lamp with a stem of lacquered birch lay on its side, bulb smashed, and the ceiling fan had been knocked askew. The floor was also dotted with bottles. He bent to pick up a plastic mickey of Captain Morgan's from a sticky puddle of rum at his feet.

There was a sudden movement in the room's far corner, behind the fireplace -- like an animal, scrambling back into its hole. Cautiously, Robert crossed the floor to the fireplace.

"Is that bitch with you?" The fireplace made a bong, a hiss of flesh on metal, as weight shifted against it.

"I'm alone," said Robert. Now that he was closer, he could see a single foot protruding from behind the fireplace. The tips of its toes were scabbed black where the nails had been chewed down to nubs. As fast as Robert had seen it, the foot withdrew.

"Bullshit."

Robert stopped, shrugged. "Think what you like," he said. "It's just me. Where's Sharon, Allan?"

"How should I know?" Pat had been right about his voice, thought Robert -- it sounded dried-out, whiskey-cured. "I'm not her keeper."

"Did she leave already?" Robert inched forward -- he didn't want to startle Allan, bring on another outburst. "Has she gone?"

No answer.

Robert tensed, kept his eye on the corner.

"Did you do anything to her, Allan?" he asked, struggling to hold the tremor out of his voice.

"Do anything to her?" A dry chuckle. "No."

Robert stepped around the fireplace.

"I'd like to, I have to admit that. But I don't really think I could," he said, reasonably. "Do you?"

Robert couldn't answer.

Nothing in Allan's voice could have prepared Robert for the sight of him. He was completely naked, and his entire body was freckled with black scabs -- including his scalp, which was nearly hairless. From his conversations with Sharon, Robert had placed Allan in his mid-thirties, but the emaciated creature behind the stove might have been in his seventies. His eyes were round and wet under naked brows, and his hollow chest trembled as he breathed. As though he were sobbing.

"Sucks it out of you," said Allan Tefield. "Sucks it right out of you."

Robert crouched down, reached out to Allan, but he scrambled backwards. His hands flashed for an instant, and Robert could see the same thick scabs at their tips as on Allan's toes.

"No! Don't touch!"

"All right, all right," said Robert, raising his hands again. "I'm not moving."

"Everything hurts."

"I know," said Robert, although he knew he could only imagine. What had done this to him?

"I'm sorry things have gone this way for you," he said. "I truly am."

Allan looked up, his round eyes narrowing. "You're sorry that you're shacked up with my wife?"

Robert didn't know what to say to that one -- he wasn't sorry, wasn't sorry at all -- so he didn't even try. "How -- how did this happen?" He gestured to the mess of the house, to Allan's own ruined flesh.

"The worms," said Allan, a narrow, crazy smile growing on his face. "They're crawling this year, aren't they?"

"They are," said Robert. He could feel goose flesh rising on his arms.

"Well. They're almost finished." Allan's peeled lips broke into a full grin, revealing incongruously clean and even teeth. "She's almost finished."

Robert let those words sink in. "She's almost --" he repeated, then: "You finished her?"

Allan's eyes were gimlets over his grin.

The pity dissolved into fear, then reconstituted as anger, and Robert rushed forward. He bent into the space behind the fireplace and took Allan by the shoulders. Allan squealed as Robert's hands closed around his clammy, prickly shoulders, and lifted him from the dirt.

"Where is Sharon? You done anything to her?"

"Nothing!" Now Allan was sobbing, tears streaming down his cheeks, streaking red where they crossed the scabs along his chin. "Nothing, nothing, *nothing*! Let me go! Please, please *please, lemmego*! It hurts!"

Robert let go, and Allan stumbled backwards, nearly falling in the mess at his feet. The scabs had broken where Robert had grabbed him, and had left a sweaty sheen of old blood on Robert's palms. He raised his hand to slap Allan, but stopped as the other man fell to his knees, put up his hands.

"*Don't!*" he whimpered, his eyes pleading as he spoke: "She went back. Back to your place. Half hour ago."

"I'm calling the campground," Robert finally muttered. "She better be there. And she better be okay."

Then he turned and picked his way through the detritus to the kitchen, where the telephone was, miraculously, still intact. As he dialed the number, Allan's sobs turned into a wail.

Waiting for an answer, Robert glanced around the kitchen. It was worse than the living room: a thick steak, going grey in a bed of Styrofoam and cellophane; puddles of liquor and milk, mixing into a pale oil slick on the counter; an overturned pot, spilling burned rice and vegetables into the dish-clogged sink; and everywhere, broken glass, smashed bottles and glasses and plates, jagged metal cans.

Through the doorway to the living room, Robert could see Allan was fidgeting nervously with his hands, rocking from one foot to the other, watching him watching. From a distance, the scabs on his flesh seemed to bundle around where his hair would grow. As though he'd actually ripped his own hair out by the roots. Maybe that's what he'd done.

After the tenth ring, Robert set the phone back in its cradle.

"She's not answering, Allan," he said, in as reasonable a tone as he could manage. "Where's Sharon?"

"I told you. She's gone." Allan smiled.

Robert was trembling again -- worse than at Canadian Tire, worse than he was after the worms.

"I'm going to find her," he muttered, and pushed past Allan into the living room. "If she's here..." He turned and glared back at Allan.

But Allan just shrugged. "Go look," he said. "I'm not going anywhere."

Robert swore, and hurried down the short hallway to the rest of the cottage. There were only three other rooms -- two bedrooms and a washroom -- and it didn't take Robert more than five minutes going through them to confirm Allan's story.

Sharon was gone.

"I know all about you," said Allan as Robert came back into the living room.

"Is that so?" said Robert.

"I called around." Allan had an almost comically smug expression on his face. "I thought about helping you, at first."

I'm not the one who needs help, thought Robert. But he kept quiet.

"People say you were a draft dodger. Didn't want to go to Viet Nam, so picked Muskoka instead." Allan's hands trembled as he brought them up to his chin. "That true?"

"I came up here from the States," said Robert.

"It is true, isn't it?" Blood smeared across his chin, over his lips, as Allan's hands drew circles on his face.

"Where is Sharon, Allan?" Robert felt his fists bunching, and willed them open again.

Allan snorted derisively. "Oh for Christ's sake, Robert, work it out." He gestured around him with his bloody hands. "You saw for yourself that she's not in the house. Did you see her car out there? What, do you think I drove it into the lake? Think about it. She went back to your cabin, like I told you."

Robert didn't answer at first, but he allowed that Allan had a point. The car was gone, and Allan was really in no shape to have disposed of it with any efficiency.

"I'll call again before we leave," said Robert finally. "Look, Allan..." He stepped forward.

But Allan put up his hand. "So you bought a plot of land, put up a sign and cleared the driveway. Built yourself a shack. Then you just stayed on. I guess you put down roots pretty firm here."

Robert stopped. "It's a good place," he said.

"It's a shitty place." Allan leaned against the windows, the skin of his shoulders making a rubber noise on the glass. "Sharon wanted to buy up here. But it's shitty. Mosquitoes every summer, snow up to your ass every winter, two fucking days in the fall when the colors change, and then it rains until November. And this!" He gestured outside to the naked trees, their twisting branches a caricature of Allan's own twig-thin arms. "*The fucking worm!*"

"It's where I am," said Robert reasonably.

"It's where your *roots* are, Thacker." Allan grinned. "These trees have roots too. And from the looks of them, I think they'll have to come down next year." He leaned forward, bare ass squealing obscenely along the pane. "Dead wood."

Robert regarded Allan, and it occurred to him: Sharon was fine. The only person who had come out of this relationship with any damage was Allan Tefield.

"You've really screwed up," he said. "You know that, don't you Allan?"

"Go back to Sharon, you asshole." Allan sneered, showing his white, perfect teeth. "That's what you're here for, isn't it? Go back to Sharon. That's where you belong."

"All right," said Robert. "But before I go -- tell me what happened to you."

"The worms."

"The worms didn't do this. What happened, Allan?"

"Eaten," he said, eyes down. "Eaten by the worm."

At that, Robert made up his mind: Sharon could wait. Right now, it was Allan who needed his help.

"Come on," said Robert. "let's find your clothes."

"No clothes."

He wasn't going to argue -- Allan was beyond reasoning, and Robert wanted them both out of there as fast as possible. "All right. Then I'll get a blanket from the truck to cover you up. We're going to Bracebridge. I'm taking you to a hospital."

"Hospital?"

"I think we'd better," said Robert. "Don't you, Allan?"

The emergency room at South Muskoka Memorial was busy. There had been a pileup on Highway 11 just north of Gravenhurst, and the waiting room and the hallways leading off it were a conduit for paramedics and their patients. The early afternoon heat was filled with the sounds of sirens as more ambulances pulled in.

Robert waited until the latest ambulance had cleared the entrance, then led Allan to the admitting desk. The nurse there was young, barely out of her teens. She looked first at him, and then at Allan. Her eyes betrayed only a little of what she must have felt seeing him.

"I found him like this," explained Robert. "In his cottage. He's in pretty bad shape."

"I can see," she said. Allan was wearing the cotton blanket from the truck's seat, clutched around him like a poncho against the ER ward's air-conditioned cool. His scalp was beginning to bleed again, and it covered his face in a deep pink sheen. "What happened to him?"

"I don't know, exactly." Robert leaned closer to the nurse, and whispered: "I think it may be self-inflicted."

"Like hell." Allan sat down in one of the chairs, glared across the desk at the nurse.

"I didn't think he should be left like that," said Robert.

The nurse looked at Robert suspiciously. She was about to say something when an older nurse came up behind her with a stack of papers. She set the stack down on a bare spot on the desk.

"Is it life-threatening?" she asked Robert, and when he said no, sent the two of them over to a vacant row of chairs, along with a set of forms to fill out.

They didn't wait for as long as Robert feared. Three more stretchers came in from the pileup -- from what Robert could overhear, there had been eight cars involved -- and once the paperwork was out of the way from those, an orderly came with a wheelchair to take Allan away. He was as young as the nurse behind the admissions desk, his blond hair spiked like a hockey player's. He gave Robert an apologetic smile as they helped Allan up and into the chair.

"What happened to you?" he asked as Allan settled.

"The worm," Allan said, staring into his lap.

The orderly looked at Robert, and he shrugged.

"Tent caterpillars," said Robert. "Thinks they did it to him. They're enough to make anyone buggy, I guess."

"It's bad this year," said the orderly, pushing the wheelchair along the corridor. "Did you hear about the pileup?"

Robert made a non-committal noise.

"I hear it's caterpillars that caused it."

"Come again?" Robert slipped behind the orderly as they passed the stretcher of what might have been one of the pileup's victims: a middle-aged man in a blood-stained Blue Jays shirt. He had a compression bandage on his scalp, a plasma bag hooked up on the I.V. tower, and he stared glassily at the ceiling.

"A truck hit a slick of them, crossing the highway." Once past the stretcher, the orderly slowed to let Robert catch up. "Tried to brake, but the tires couldn't get any traction. They were like an oil slick. So the truck jackknifed, and the cars behind couldn't stop." He gave Robert a secretive little smile. "Weird shit."

Robert didn't know whether to laugh. It sounded like another wives' tale -- when the summer worms crossed the highway, they'd pile so thick you couldn't drive. It was ridiculous: almost as ridiculous as...

As a nest of summer worms, the size of a house.

The orderly stopped outside a pair of double-doors. "I'm afraid this is where we get off, sir. You can wait in the lounge, if you like."

"All right." Robert's throat was dry, and he cleared it. "I'll do that."

Before he could leave, Allan's head twisted to face him. "It was just two years!" he snarled. "That's all we were together!"

"Good-bye, Allan."

"Two years!" he called as the orderly wheeled him through the doors.

Robert went back to the waiting room, fumbling in his pockets for a quarter for the pay phone. By the time he finished dialing his number, his hands were shaking.

Sharon answered the phone on the fourth ring, and when she spoke, Robert nearly collapsed with relief.

"Are you all right, Bobby?" Her voice was smooth, the worry in it no more than a vague undercurrent.

"I was at your cottage," he replied. "I'm all right. I don't know about your ex, though."

"He's there?" The worry turned into a rising alarm. "Bobby, you've got to come home."

Robert cupped the mouthpiece close. "He's in pretty bad shape," he said. "I've got him at the hospital in Bracebridge."

"I know," said Sharon quickly. "I was at the cottage today. Look, just come home, okay? Don't make it worse."

"I should stick around," said Robert. "Make sure everything's okay."

Now Sharon's voice grew sharp.

"Don't bother. I've already called his parents in Toronto. I'll call them now, tell them where he is."

"Sharon, will you please tell me what --"

"Just come home!"

Then Sharon said something softly, and when Robert didn't hear, she repeated:

"I need you, Bobby. I need you here."

And she hung up.

Robert nearly missed his turn-off, and when he saw it, he braked so hard he thought he was going to spin out. He wheeled the car around, barely checking the oncoming traffic, and his tires spun on the gravel of the sideroad. He passed the TWIN OAKS CAMPGROUND-1/4 MILE sign at what must have been double the speed limit, and only slowed when he hit the first steep bend in the road.

The caterpillars had caused the pileup. And the maple tree over Robert's house was so enshrouded in caterpillar silk, it looked like rolls of cotton candy. And Allan Tefield had no hair, and when Robert asked him why, he blamed the worm. And Sharon was alone at Twin Oaks.

And she had wanted him back there. She had insisted: *I need you here*, she said.

Robert didn't even look at the trees until he was almost at home.

Robert stopped the truck at the foot of his driveway. He felt his heart racing, his breath raw in his throat.

The sign at the entrance was nearly illegible, the silk had covered it so thick. All the trees facing the road were draped with silk, and the driveway was obstructed by wide, worm-mottled curtains that caught shafts of afternoon sun like columns of dust. Robert could hear the noise of the summer worms' mouths over the pickup's idling engine.

They had sealed the campground off -- nearly as effectively as they had the maple tree this morning.

Robert threw the truck into low gear, and gravel crunched under his tires as he crept up the driveway.

The first curtain of summer worms stretched like nylon hose where the grille pushed against it. Finally, the curtain came unmoored and the silk descended on the front windshield, like a sheet thrown over a fresh bed. Robert had to stop himself from flicking on the windshield wipers: there were too many worms; they would smear. He kept his foot steady on the accelerator, and the truck lumbered forward into the next curtain. His hands trembled on the steering wheel as another layer of silk fell in front of him, and another.

By the fifth curtain, he had to stop. The windshield was completely opaque, and even the back and side windows were so thickly plastered that he couldn't make out anything beyond the vaguest of shapes. He guessed that he was maybe a third of the way up, but it was hard to tell: even in winter he wouldn't have taken the driveway this slowly.

Robert turned off the engine. There were no two ways about it: he'd have to walk it from here. He opened the door and pushed the membranes of silk aside. It made a sound like tearing cotton batten, and maybe a half-dozen worms fell lightly on his arm.

He resisted the urge to draw back, shake them away. If he were going to make the walk, Robert would have to get used to the feeling of worms on his skin. He opened the door the rest of the way and climbed out of the truck.

The worms had made his driveway into a tunnel of white. Every tree was enshrouded with them, and the silk extended through the branches overhead to make a thick ceiling. The bright afternoon seemed overcast in here, under their shadow. Looking back through the tunnel his truck had made, Robert thought he could almost see the clean sunlight on the road. But the shrouds distorted distance, and it was hard to tell for sure.

The truck itself was nearly as well-disguised. The silk draped across it from back to front, and the caterpillars moved across it in thick clusters.

Arm in front of him to ward off the caterpillars that dangled from threads every few feet, Robert walked around to the back of the pickup. The bag containing the canisters of EasEnd were packed back near the cab, barely visible through the mess of worms and silk. Robert reached into it, his hand gathering more worms as he did so, and pulled out the bag.
Robert shut his eyes for a moment, then turned away from the road he imagined he could see and walked towards the next wall of worms.

They gathered on him as he moved. His hands always touched the webbing first, and were sometimes black with the worms up past his wrists. But there were enough worms for all of him. They burrowed into his hair, and he was certain he could feel them under his collar, moving down his back, among the copse of thick hairs that grew on his shoulders. When he looked down, he could see they were all over his jeans, clustering by the hundreds around his knees and thighs, the tops of his boots. He kept his mouth shut and snorted whenever he exhaled to blow away the ones on his lip.

But he didn't brush them off. To do so would be to admit to the spiraling terror in his belly, and such an admission would paralyze him -- or worse, send him crashing into the trees, running blind.

He was nearly blind now. The farther along the driveway he got, the more intricate the weave became. Every few feet he would have to clear another shift of silk, and at times it was only the feeling of gravel under his feet that reassured him he was still on the driveway at all.

He stopped once, to bend over and breathe, shake the sweat from his hair. It was greenhouse hot here, but the air seemed to hold little oxygen. Worms fell to the ground as he straightened and pushed forward.

He knew the campground was getting closer as the silk in front of him began to glow with the yellow of the afternoon sun. At first it was just a dim hue, like the sun through a thinning patch of cloud on an overcast day. As Robert went on, the light grew, making each sheet of silk more luminescent than the last. Finally, with scarcely more than a sheet to go, Robert could see the bright shapes of his campground through the glowing threads of silk.

He ran forward, nearly dropping the EasEnd as he went, and burst from the wall of the nest trailing silk like a bridal train. He shook off his hand, wiped the worms from his lips and opened his mouth to shout:

"Sharon!"

The campground was silent. The silk from the maple over his house now extended over all the trees. The canopy sloped down in places to touch the shrubs and saplings nearer the ground, in the clean parabolas of circus-tent roofs. There was a clearing in the trees maybe 100 feet in diameter, which Robert used mostly as a cul-de-sac and parking lot for the day-trippers. The worms had left it a barren oasis of gravel and scrub grass.

"Sharon!" he shouted again. "You there? You all right?"

His cabin was nearly invisible under the silk, a peaked cube of shadow. No sound came from inside.

Almost absently, Robert peeled the silk from his shoulders and strode across the clearing to the far edge. He tried to imagine how Sharon must feel in there -- cocooned inside his already-too-small cabin, choking on what must be stifling heat. The worms hadn't bothered her the day before, she'd barely given them a second glance in the weeks before. But this...

The cabin was too quiet. *Christ*, he thought, *what's happened to Sharon while I've been gone?*

I need you here.

Robert started towards the cabin. If he'd made it up the driveway on his own, he surely wouldn't have a problem making it through a few layers of silk into his cabin.

But the silk was tougher here. Robert had to use his jackknife to cut through it, and the sound of his passage was like ripping fabric. There were fewer worms on the curtains, but the task was no easier for that: in the worms' place were row upon row of hard cocoons, brittle like plastic and some as large as Robert's thumb. And very soon the silk shadows made his new tunnel into night.

He groped on, cutting and advancing, until he found his cabin -- not by sight, but by touch. He had come through at a point in the middle of the south wall, underneath the kitchen window. His hand glided up to confirm the glass, the rough metal screen. But before he could withdraw, worms tumbled down onto his head, and he shook them away. Dim yellow light shone out from the kitchen, in the spaces where his hand had cleared the screen of caterpillars.

"Sharon!" His voice was weak, gasping.

She didn't answer, but Robert thought he could hear movement inside.

Robert inched along the dry timbers until he reached the stoop to his front door. The overhang kept the space of his vestibule clear of silk, so Robert didn't have to do much more cutting. He stumbled up the stairs and grabbed the door handle.

"I'm here, Sharon," he whispered. The door wasn't locked -- it wasn't even closed properly -- and Robert yanked it open. It banged against the wall with an oddly muffled crunch. "I'm--"

He couldn't finish.

The walls, the floor, the ceiling of the living room were blanketed in them. They crawled over the floor-lamp, tiny bodies making an uneven pattern of curling silhouettes on the shade. They blacked out the three oil paintings on the wall over the Coleman, and they utterly covered his leather recliner, like a new, writhing layer of upholstery. The sofa's stuffing was laid bare, and more worms burrowed into it.

Robert began to tremble. His mouth opened, and he shut it again as quickly: the idea that the worms might get in *there*, too... He shut his mouth and sealed it tight.

Oh Jesus, oh God. Robert felt himself unraveling.

Robert's eyes widened, and the scream that should have come through his mouth forced its way instead through his nostrils. The canisters of EasEnd fell to the floor, and Robert's hands grasped at the lapels of his own shirt, and tore.

The shirt came away in a cascade of buttons. He threw it across the room. He yanked his belt undone next, and stripped off his jeans -- they were filled with worms, as bad as the shirt, and when they hitched over his boots he nearly screamed again, fell into the worms at his feet. But somehow he managed to stay upright, and, jeans at his ankles, kicked the boots free. Then he kicked clear of the jeans as well, and bent to pick up one of the EasEnd canisters from the bag at his feet.

Robert dug his thumb into the nozzle and found the pin. The *Contents* were *Under Pressure* -- that was only the first on the long list of fine-print warnings that ran down the side of the EasEnd canister -- so when Robert pushed the pin in the insecticide came out in a cool, spreading vapor that made Robert's eyes sting. He coughed only once, and turned the spray onto the summer worms.

By degree, the cabin's living room and kitchen filled with billowing, stinking white mist. It settled on the glass of the mirror on the bathroom door like a frost, hung in the air like a stratum of cigarette smoke at an all-night poker game. Robert coughed again, three times. His thumb was getting cold, and he could feel the stinging spread to the quick under his nail. Snot dribbled from his nostrils, running fast over his thin, clamped lips. He kept up the pressure.

The spray got to the ceiling worms first, and they began to fall. Robert felt them land on his shoulders, in his hair, but he resisted the urge to scrape them away. He'd have to let go of the EasEnd for that, and it was still heavy with insecticide.

He moved forward into the living room, spraying as he went. His vision was beginning to blur, but he could hear well enough. And the sound that he heard was the pitter-pat of worms, falling all around him in a solidified rain. Robert wanted to laugh. If only he could open his mouth... He giggled through his nose instead, and thick strings of snot fell onto the backs of his forearms.

This was *his* land. *His* home.

My roots, Robert said to himself, and noted with satisfaction that the worms were coming down from the walls too now.

"Stop it."

The voice was quiet, pained, and it was only after it came three times that Robert remembered Sharon.

He still had to struggle to make himself lift his thumb.

The voice came from the bedroom. Robert was dizzy from the fumes, and his ears had started to ring now as well, but he could tell that much.

"Stop."

Robert had a hard time staying upright -- *I should open a window, that would air the place out*. He coughed some more, tasted salt and copper in the mucous this time. The bedroom door-frame came up under his outstretched hand as the house lurched, and took his weight. He guided himself past it, into the cabin's other room.

"Sharon." The word came like a bark. It hurt in his chest, but he said it again.

"Sharon."

He couldn't see a thing in the bedroom. The light was out, and his eyes felt like they were going to burn out of his head.

Robert stumbled through something on the floor and stopped the spinning house again, this time grabbing the bedside lamp as it passed. He flicked flicked it on with his EasEnd thumb.

Sharon lay curled on the bed, underneath the comforter she'd brought with her. Robert blinked, tried to focus his eyes on her -- it seemed as though she lay in a mist, thicker even than the vapors he'd sprayed in the living room. Christ. How much had he sprayed? Robert felt normalcy returning to him, and with it, a sickening realization of exactly what he'd done. The poison must be everywhere by now. The worms fell here too, landing on him, the comforter. On the mist over Sharon's face, suspended...

"Oh Sharon, honey." He set the EasEnd down on the night-table. As he reached down to touch her, the realization chilled through him:

Sharon was enshrouded in silk. As his fingers pushed through it, Sharon's eyelids fluttered, and she shifted slightly under the comforter.

More deliberately this time, Robert set about pulling away the silk. Sharon blinked her eyes open, and as her lips parted he stopped pulling.

"Bobby." Her voice was gummy, and it had a sleepy drawl to it. "Stinks in here."

Robert yanked the remainder of the threads clear. His vision started to double, but he could make out Sharon's arm as it came up to him. It was so thin, he thought. In his doubling vision, it seemed to undulate, as though it were boneless. Silk wrapped it like the lace sleeve of a bridal gown.

"I'm glad you came back," she said. "I was almost ready to go to sleep without you."

"I'll always come home," said Robert. Her fingertips felt rough as they brushed the back of his neck, and her touch left a sting behind on his sensitized skin.

"You're late, though." Sharon's eyes glittered, and Robert thought: *I'm an idiot with this woman, she makes me slow.*

"I took Allan to hospital," he said. Sharon's hand moved up through his hair, drew him down onto the bed. "I know you wanted me back soon. I'm sorry."

"You should have come," said Sharon. Her hand came over his scalp, leaving it cool where she passed. "Time for bed."

"Honey --"

-- we have to get you out of here, Robert would have said. But at that instant, her hand appeared over his forehead. Clutched in its fist were clumps of brown hair. They were bloody at their roots.

"Jesus!" Robert's scream sounded high, distant in his own head.

He pulled back, but he wasn't quick enough: Sharon's other hand shot out and grabbed his left wrist. She smiled and her lips collapsed inward. As they parted he confirmed it: her mouth was a pink and black pit, toothless. She pushed his bloody hair inside.

Robert yanked at his wrist, but her fingers dug into the flesh there like a tightening noose. He felt his pulse quicken, even as his vision started to grey. The lump of hair and blood traveled down Sharon's elongated throat like a rat through a python.

The worm, Allan had said when Robert asked what had done this to him. Not the worms, not the tent caterpillars, but a singular creature. He said he had been eaten by the worm.

Sharon's free arm lashed at him again, but Robert wheeled back fast enough to avoid it. The arm cracked like a whip in empty air, boneless. His hand was going purple in her grip, but he pulled back anyway. With his free hand, he grabbed the EasEnd from the night-table.

"You drew them here, didn't you?" he asked.

She mumbled something -- butterfly? -- but her mouth had taken on an odd 'o'-shape, and the word mushed.

Robert hoisted the EasEnd canister onto his hip, and pointed the nozzle at the bed. His heartbeat thundered in his ears, and the hand that she still held felt thick, numb. He moved his thumb over the nozzle.

"Allan warned me," Robert said, and pressed the pin.

The mist spread before him. Her fingers unraveled from his wrist, and Robert stumbled backwards under the force of his own weight. She reared out of her bed. She was naked under the covers, although her body was growing indistinct -- her breasts, small to begin with, had shrunk to boyish proportions, and her hips had disappeared in the sinuous curl of her torso.

Robert shook the blood back into his hand then gripped the bottle two-handed. He could feel the chemical as it settled on his bare scalp -- certainly, he could remember that one of the *Cautions* on the packaging was to *Avoid Contact With Open Wounds*. The manufacturers were right -- it stung like battery acid where his scalp bled.

The effect on the thing in the bed was similar. The 'o' of her mouth expanded like an iris, and her eyes glittered black. Her mouth made a sound like *stop*, but Robert kept spraying. She stretched back, her hands touching the wall behind her, and with a quick undulation, she was pressed entirely against the wall. Robert's thumb slipped as he watched her crawl up the sheer surface, toward the ceiling, but he found it again and the spray resumed. He coughed and spat bloody phlegm onto the bedspread.

"You started with Allan," he said softly as the creature mounted the ceiling. "You were going to finish with me. Isn't that right?"

It hung over him, face to the ceiling, and Robert lifted the canister over his head. The chemical rained down on him, and the mist grew, and his hands became numb, and by quick degree the room began to darken.

Sharon's hands slipped from the ceiling then, and for a moment she dangled by her knees alone. At first he thought she was going to fall -- a great worm, dying in the spray.

But she surprised him. Her arms flew forward, and in a single motion knocked the EasEnd from his grasp and wrapped around his chest. She descended, round mouth wide, as the darkness finally overtook him.

Robert woke in blackness. He was on the bed -- he could feel the comforter, the pillow beneath his bare scalp. But the room was utterly dark, more so than he had ever experienced. Hand trembling, he reached for the lamp. He found the switch, but when he pressed it, the darkness remained. He pulled his hand back quickly. The pain of that simple movement was excruciating; his fingernails were gone, and the raw nerves underneath howled. The skin of his arm felt like it had been scraped along asphalt. He opened his mouth, and when he spoke his voice sounded like an old man's.

"Hello?"

The house was silent -- even the sound of the caterpillars was absent. Robert repeated: "Hello? Who's there?" but got no better results.

He was alone.

He started to chuckle at the thought. Lynn, and Mary, and Laura, and now Sharon -- they'd all taken what they needed. The chuckle turned into a snorting guffaw. They'd all stripped him bare, left him in his cabin, on his land. Here where his roots were.

Robert got himself under control and tried to sit up in bed. The effort it took was Herculean, and he had to sit for a minute after that to get his wind back. Lynn had gone back to the city, Mary had gone back to the States, and Laura... she had just gone. Where would Sharon go? Where would she fly?

Gingerly, Robert lowered his feet to the floor. He sat there for some time in his new, silent night, straining to hear the beating of her wings.

PRINTED BY
IMPRIMERIE D'ÉDITION MARQUIS
IN AUGUST 1995
MONTMAGNY (QUÉBEC)